THE OCCULT MAFIA

A Story of Monsters

AUGUST 26, 2019

RYAN GEORGE COLLINS

Acknowledgments

I would, naturally, like to start by thanking God. Faith in Him and His Son Jesus Christ is what has sustained me through many difficult times.

Next, I must thank my parents, Randall and Lehann Collins, without whom I would not be here today. They have supported my endeavors and provided invaluable feedback on my work, including this particular tome.

Also worth thanking is Anna Elisabet Olsen, who provided the cover art for this work. It turned out great. Even though you're not supposed to judge a book by its cover, the cover is still what draws people in, and this one is quite the eye-catcher.

The authors I have met along the way who have provided their moral support over the years also have my gratitude. Let no one ever devalue the idea of having someone to share your ideas with, for that can be very helpful in its own right.

Last, but certainly not least, I would like to thank you for picking up this book. Without an audience to read my work, I am little more than a hobbyist shouting into the wind…or something like that.

God bless.

Dedication

*For Thomas, lifelong friend, collaborator,
filmmaker, fellow creative mind, and lover of monsters.
Thanks for always being there and believing in me.*

I.

Chicago, January 1958

Ben Andante was still shaking off the cold as he rode the elevator up to the fifth floor. This winter season was proving to be especially brutal, even for the Windy City. Frigid air blew over the Great Lakes and into Chicago like a blanket drawn by the Grim Reaper, a blanket designed to trap cold rather than heat. To hear the daytime schlubs talk, the skies had been gray for so long that they had almost forgotten what the sun looked like. Of course, Ben's nocturnal lifestyle meant he rarely saw the sun anyway. It was already eight o'clock at night, and Ben had woken up at seven, as was his custom. He did all of his work at night, even in cold piercing enough to drive Eskimos away.

The real kicker was that he had to be sparing with the heat in his place, to which he was returning after stepping out for breakfast and coffee at the one shop in town that catered to his lifestyle. The coffee had warmed his core just enough to make the trek home a bit more bearable, but it had worn off by the time he had set foot on his street.

Ben had briefly considered borrowing his partner's fur coat on the walk, but they had decided against it. They could not take the risk, and his partner would have just complained about how cold *he* was for the rest of the night. No, better to do that sort of thing in the safety of home, which was but a few floors away.

Do you smell that? Dark blue and pale yellow scents above. I don't recognize either of them. Could mean we have people waiting for us upstairs.

It was Ben's partner speaking to him. Ben nodded in acknowledgment, and allowed partial control of his hands as a precaution. They both had enemies in this town, after all.

The ding of a bell like the kind used in boxing matches announced the elevator's arrival. Ben opened the gate and stepped onto his floor. Once the gate was closed, he quickly shoved his hands into his overcoat pockets, so whoever was waiting would not see anything suspicious.

Sure enough, there were two strangers in the mahogany-lined hallway, and the unfamiliar scents were wafting off of them. They were waiting outside of his office-apartment, the place which Ben Andante called both home and work, as most private detectives on a budget found themselves doing.

They were an odd couple to be sure. A man and a woman. The man was taller than Ben, appeared to be in his mid-forties, and looked strong even with his overcoat obscuring his frame. He had a narrow chin, making his face look somewhat triangular, and a dark goatee framed his mouth. A fine fedora sat atop his head, and loose tufts of black hair stuck out from under the brim. He kept his right hand tucked into his coat pocket, but his left hand was visible. His eyes were large and alert, but also weary. They were the eyes of a man who had seen, and probably done, a lot of terrible things. He was the one from which the dark blue scent emanated. Without obstructions, Ben could now tell that the dark blue held a pattern of red dots which swirled about like drops of blood.

The woman was the source of the pale yellow scent, which contained a mixture of green stripes and dark blue blotches of a similar hue to the man's scent. As he drew closer, Ben realized she was not a woman, but a girl, probably in her early-to-mid-teens. She wore an overcoat with a more feminine cut than the man's, and her curly hair spilled out from beneath a top hat, which Ben thought was an odd fashion choice for a girl. Her facial features closely matched the man's, so Ben surmised that the girl was likely the gentleman's daughter. A pair of earrings shaped like crosses dangled from her ears, and a crucifix charm hung from a bracelet on her left wrist. In contrast with the collected demeanor of the man, she seemed to be on edge. The dark circles under her large eyes indicated that restful sleep was not something she experienced often.

They both noticed Ben immediately, and turned to greet him. "Mr. Ben Andante, I presume?" said the man. His voice carried a mild-yet-noticeable Brooklyn accent.

Ben approached them slowly, trying not to make it obvious that he was bracing himself for trouble. "Who wants to know?" he asked.

The man removed his hat with his left hand and held it over his chest in a polite gesture, though his right hand remained in his pocket. "My name is Donovan Van Sloan, and this is my daughter, Jacqueline."

"Jackie for short," the girl interjected with an accent matching her father's. Her voice had a bit of a rasp to it.

"We've come with a business proposition for you and your partner, assuming you're not otherwise engaged," Donovan continued. "I can promise to make it worth your while, if that's any incentive to hear us out."

Ben relaxed a little. These were clients, then. Even if the stranger had a gun in his pocket, he would have no need for it if Ben played his cards right. He withdrew his human hands from his pockets, and his pace quickened. "Then Ben Andante I am," he said. "I'm afraid my partner is out at the moment, but I'll pass the details along to him when he shows up." He extended his right hand for a handshake. "Pleased to meet you, Mr. Van Sloan."

Donovan stared at the extended hand for a moment, then placed his hat back on his head. "Not to be rude, but would you mind switching hands? I'm what you might call a southpaw." He withdrew his right hand from his pocket, revealing no hand at all, but rather a stump wrapped in bandages.

Ben was taken aback by the sight, but did not let it visibly stir him. He had seen worse in his line of work. Besides, that erased any notion that a concealed weapon was trained on him. "Left it is," he said as he switched hands for the handshake.

With the greeting complete, he took out his keys to open the door, which had "Andante & Garret, Detectives for Hire" etched on the opaque glass. This door led into the main office, a small area with a desk and three chairs, two of which were arranged for clients. Upon the desk was what appeared to be a very large framed picture, but since it was turned away from the door, anyone entering could not see it. A tall liquor cabinet carved in Baroque style sat behind the desk to the left. The space which served as Ben's home lay through a closed door to the right. In true private eye fashion, Ben's policy was that only beautiful women were allowed to meet with him in there.

Ben invited his guests to sit as he approached his liquor cabinet. He was turned away from the duo as he perused the contents. "Either of you care for a drink? Bourbon? Scotch?"

"Nothing for me," said Donovan.

"No thanks, I'm underage," Jackie said timidly, then sharply added, *"but I'll take one anyway."*

This gave Ben pause. Something about the girl's voice had sounded different during his sudden contradiction. It was raspier, heavier, almost distorted. Ben turned, a quizzical look on his face.

Jackie looked frightened as she clutched the right side of her face and dug her fingernails into her skin. "I said no thanks," she said quickly, her voice back to normal. Her father appeared to have tensed and was staring at her warily, but he relaxed as his daughter lowered her hands. Whatever was going to happen, the moment had passed.

Something's not right about these two, Ben's partner said. *Best be ready for anything.*

Ben nodded as he grabbed a tumbler and poured himself some scotch. "So, lay it on me. What's the gig?"

Donovan was seated upright as he spoke, his posture as eagle-sharp as his eyes. "That requires a bit of explaining. What do you know about the Occult Mafia, Mr. Andante?"

Ben stiffened for an instant, though he was fairly certain his clients did not notice. "Same as any shmuck on the street, I suppose," he said in his most convincing tone. He slowly sauntered back to his desk as he continued. "They were near the top of the 'Seditious Criminal Organizations' list Elliot Ness submitted to the FBI back in 1932. It was his last big push toward becoming a bigshot lawman after catching Al Capone. Not that anyone took the list seriously." He sipped his drink as he sat down, exhaled in satisfaction, and placed the glass on his desk. "They're supposed to be an unholy mixture of organized crime and a fanatical religious cult, killing people for some kind of nefarious purpose, right? Then again, there are rumors that they kill monsters, but that's just silly if you ask me."

"My daughter and I don't think it's silly," Donovan answered. "I doubt you think it's silly, either. Moreover, I don't think you're telling me everything you know about us. After all, a smart lycanthrope would want to know his potential enemies."

Ben could not hide his shock this time. This shock quickly turned to anger as his reflexes kicked in. Hints of a transformation became evident. His skin darkened slightly, and hair bristled across his snarling face.

"Calm down," said Donovan. Neither he nor his daughter were the least bit phased by the sight. "We may be with the Occult Mafia, but we ain't here to kill you. I said we have a business proposal, and I meant it. Here." With his left hand, he reached into his coat and produced a revolver, which he then tossed on the desk. It skidded a few inches towards Ben. "My sidearm, loaded with silver bullets, now out of my reach."

"Uh, Pop…?" said Jackie, unsure of her father's actions.

"Consider that an olive branch," he continued in spite of his daughter's attempted protest.

Ben stared at the gun, and allowed himself to calm down slightly. All signs of the transformation faded. "How did you know?" he asked.

"The clues are obvious when you know what to look for." Donovan pointed at Ben's face. "The hint of a unibrow, the stubble on your palms from shaving them, the way your eyes reflect light the way a dog's would…that, and we've been keeping tabs on you for years. It doesn't take much thinking to figure out that Ben Andante's partner, the elusive Louie Garret, is a front to hide the fact that you're a werewolf, the city's infamous Loup Garou, Your secret's safe with us, though. Since there's no point in hiding him anymore, may we speak with your partner as well?"

This feels like a trick, Ben's partner said.

What choice do we have? Ben replied. *He's got us dead to rights. We may as well hear what he has to say.*

All right, Ben's partner conceded, *but I'm ready to jump both of them if they try anything.*

Having reached an agreement, Ben nodded towards the Van Sloans. "Seeing as how you've already got our number…"

He turned the frame on his desk, revealing that it held not a picture, but a mirror. He angled it in a very specific way so his clients could see his reflection. However, it was not his swarthy human face which appeared in the mirror, but rather the face of a wolf. It was a sleek canine cranium covered in fine grayish-brown fur. The snout was long, and the ears sharply pointed. The eyes were the giveaway that this was no normal wolf, for they appeared more human than lupine, and those eyes watched the Van Sloans warily. This was Ben's partner, Loup Garou.

"So," Donovan said, "what do you know about our organization, really?"

"That you're dangerous," answered Loup Garou, his deep voice naturally carrying a hint of a growl. "You're killers, all of you."

Donovan shook his head shrugged. "It seems you have the same misconceptions about us as the world has about you. Allow me to educate you on a few things, if you're willing to hear me out."

When he received no objection from either man or wolf, he began. "What is today called the Occult Mafia began as a collective of young men and women who were either immigrants or the children thereof. They came from different backgrounds, but were united by one commonality: intimate knowledge and experience with the supernatural, or as one of our former members called it, the absurd. In 1920, they decided to officially pool their resources and put that knowledge and experience to good use. We're not so much killers as we are watchmen, dear sirs. We only kill when necessary, and we've disposed of misguided humans just as often as ravenous monsters. We actually didn't even have a name until Ness made that list. He probably thought it would make us sound more dangerous. Over time, though, the name just stuck. One of the founding members was Peter Van Sloan, and I am my father's son, so I've held his seat on the council ever since he retired in Thirty-eight. Wasn't long after that I married one of my fellow hunters, Melissa Hark, and we had Jackie." He drummed his fingers on the arm of the chair, his demeanor adopting a sense of melancholy. "We weren't a traditional American family, since we all continued fighting the good fight, but we were happy."

"Fascinating history lesson," Ben interrupted, "but what has it got to do with the two of us?"

"I was getting to that. Do you know of a warlock named Phillipe Bismuth?"

Loup's hair bristled as he growled at the name. Simultaneously, Ben's expression visibly darkened. "Yeah… Yeah, we've met the bastard," he said. "Long ago."

"I met him last year," Donovan said in an equally dark tone, "and I paid the price for it. Melissa, Jackie, and I all went in to thwart his Pandorum Ritual. He and his followers were in his Arizona compounds, attempting to open the Gates of Hell. That's his ultimate goal, you understand. He's extended his life for decades through black magic, and he intends to control the legions of Hell so he can rule over the world. We were able to stop him, which I suppose is self-evident since the world didn't end, but he got away before we could finish him off, and none of us came out unscathed." He motioned to his mangled right arm. "He cut off my hand with a ceremonial ax, but before he could bury it in my skull, Melissa…" The words caught in his throat, but he forced them out. "She took the hit for me." A tear escaped from Donovan's eye as he remembered the moment in horrific detail. "The next thing I knew, Bismuth had disappeared, and Melissa was…gone."

Donovan lowered his head so the brim of his hat shielded his face, but Ben and Loup had already seem the pain in his expression. Jackie, meanwhile, made no attempt to hide her sadness.

Donovan blinked away his tears and recomposed himself before he continued. "That was just over a year ago. Between then and now, I've thrown myself into research. I studied every scrap of information I could find on Bismuth, every time over the years he's been opposed by man and monster alike. In doing so, I reached the conclusion: the warlock can't be killed by men or monsters…at least, not on their own. If, on the other hand, men and monsters worked together, that just might make all the difference in the world. We've learned that Bismuth is gearing up to perform the Pandorum Ritual again, which means we need to strike before he's ready."

Loup's eyes narrowed. "So you came here to recruit us, is that it?"

"You two have history with Bismuth, and since you help the people of this city with your abilities, that means you have a moral compass. I figure you won't need much convincing. Plus, being a pair of gumshoes, you can help me track down the others I have in mind." Donovan leaned back slightly. "Simple as that, really. If you ain't interested, I'll just find some other werewolf. It ain't like you're the only one in the world."

He rose, reached for his gun, and returned it to his pocket. "If you're in, meet us at the train station tomorrow at midnight. We'll have the area cleared. Bring whatever you need for a long trip, clothes, magnifying glass, dog biscuits, any essentials. If you're not there at midnight on the dot, we're leaving without you. We can't dawdle with so much on the line."

Donovan Van Sloan motioned for his daughter to follow him, and together they left the office.

The door seemed to close slower than usual as father and daughter departed, as though it too could feel the weight of what had just happened. The office was silent as Ben Andante and Loup Garou allowed the tension to naturally flow out of the room.

After a few seconds, Ben turned the mirror back to face him. "What do you think, Loup?" he asked.

"Talk about a loaded question," Loup replied. "I think if he meant to kill us, he would've done it when he drew his gun. Seems unlikely that it's some kind of elaborate trap meant to snare us." He reached up to scratch behind one of his pointed ears. "Still, this is the Occult Mafia we're talking about. Half the gargoyles in Manhattan are permanent stone because of them."

Ben nodded. "Yeah, though remembering the headlines, that half clearly deserved it." He paused to think for a moment, remembering the way their visitors had behaved. "Thinking back, they seemed sincere enough, at least to me."

"Agreed. The part about his wife sure wasn't an act. The old nose told me that much." Similar to regular canines, Loup had a natural ability to sense people's intentions. No matter how good of a performance someone put on, Loup could pick up on subtle hints that Ben might miss. In particular, a person's scent would become stronger from increased sweating if they were nervous about lying. This had helped them on many past cases. Tonight, however, Donovan's dark blue scent had remained constant the whole time. His daughter's pale yellow scent had been strong as well, and she had been behaving oddly, but that seemed unrelated to her father's account. Something much deeper had her on edge, likely connected to the moment her voice became distorted.

"If he was serious about that," Ben continued, "he's probably also serious about going after Bismuth."

Loup once again growled at the name.

"I hear you, brother," Ben said. "It's been almost thirty years, Loup. If this isn't a trap, it's an opportunity. This Van Sloan character really means to kill the warlock, and since he wants to give us a piece of the action…"

Loup leaned forward. "Vengeance or Justice?"

Ben shrugged. "Who says the two are mutually exclusive?"

II.

The follow evening

Donovan Van Sloan checked the large clock which hung above the ticket booth. Eleven forty-five, and Ben and Loup had yet to show. He was confident that they would come, but he had been wrong about things before. Of course, the last time he had been wrong, it had cost him dearly.

As if in response to his silent musing on past failures, a shriek drew his attention to the bench behind him. There sat Jackie, twitching violently, gripping the wooden slats as though she intended to break them. Her head was lowered so the brim of her top hat obscured her face.

Donovan only allowed himself to feel regret for an instant, then he forced back his emotions and went into the routine he was all too familiar with by now. At least there was no one else present to see his daughter's fit.

He knelt down in front of her. "Jackie," he said firmly but calmly. "Jackie, look at me."

Jackie twitched even more, as though she were trying to lift her head, but something was pushing it back down.

Donovan carefully reached up and placed his fingers under Jackie's chin, lifting her head for her.

Jackie's pale face conveyed a mixture of fear and pain as onyx-hued patches swirled around beneath her skin. Wherever the inky blotches moved on her face, her expression changed to one of pure malice.

"Focus on me, kiddo," Donovan said, doing his best not to let his sorrow overwhelm him at this crucial moment.

The darkness moved over Jackie's mouth, twisting her lips into a wicked sneer. From her darkened lips came a raspy, distorted voice that sounded like a mockery of Jackie's own. *"Give up, murderer,"* it said. *"You're just delaying the inevitable."*

Donovan Van Sloan did not give up. He pressed his palm against Jackie's forehead and recited the Lord's Prayer.

The distorted voice hissed in reply as the darkness crawled away from Jackie's mouth. By the time her father finished praying, the discoloration was gone. It had not faded, but rather seeped back into her body.

This done, Donovan rose and stepped back so his daughter to relax and catch her breath. Having averted the crisis, he allowed himself to relax as well, for he knew the immediate danger had passed.

Jackie wiped the sweat from her brow. "Third time today," she said between breaths. "Too many." She looked up at her father with frightened eyes. "She's fighting harder, Pop. She wants out something fierce."

Donovan nodded. "I know, Jackie. I'm with you every time."

"I can't keep doing this," Jackie whimpered as tears welled in her eyes. "She's wearing me down, Pop. She's always finding new ways to chip away at me. I…I don't know how much I got left." She began to sob. "I can't keep it up, Pop. I'm not strong enough. I'm not…"

Donovan sat next to his daughter, placed his arm around her, and drew her close. She turned and cried into his overcoat. "Don't say that, kiddo," he said. "Don't *ever* say that. You've kept that hell spawn trapped inside you for a year now. That's longer than any other possession on record." He gave her a gentle pat on the shoulder. "You, Jacqueline Van Sloan, are the strongest person I know. You believe me, right?"

Jackie slowly sat up again, her face stained with tears and mucus. Donovan offered her a handkerchief, which she took to wipe them away. Sniffling, she nodded in answer to her father's question, though it was only a half-hearted reply.

"I know it won't be easy," Donovan continued, "but you need to be strong for just a little longer. Soon, we'll find Bismuth again, we'll get him to undo this, and then we can both rest for a while. Just a little longer, I promise. You can hold out until we're done, right?"

Jackie nodded again. Her crying finally subsided. "Sorry," she said. "I just can't take it sometimes."

"No need to apologize, Jackie. I know it's hard. I think there's a stash of Rosary beads on the train. You pick another set once we're onboard, okay?"

A cough from behind the bench startled them both. Ben Andante had arrived, and was standing far enough away to be respectful, but close enough that his keen hearing had no doubt heard everything. Jackie blushed. She already felt vulnerable enough without a stranger seeing her so compromised.

Donovan stood, shooting a quick glance to the clock. "I figured you'd come," he said, "and I'm glad you did. With five minutes to spare, no less." His eyes narrowed. "So how long were you standing there watching us?"

"Long enough to form quite a few questions about your girl," Ben answered as he approached, "and being private dicks, we have every intention of asking them, but there's time enough for that once we're on our way."

Donovan noticed that Ben only carried one small suitcase with him. "You travel light, I see."

Ben nodded. "A lesson we learned on our third case. I don't need much to survive, and Loup needs even less. So, where is this late night train we're taking?"

"This way," Donovan said, motioning for Ben to follow him. Jackie trailed behind them, still exhausted from her struggle.

"The Occult Mafia has many resources for our fight against evil," Donovan continued, "including modes of transportation. We have four private trains that run all across the United States, and we'll be taking one of them east. You should feel privileged, Mr. Andante. Few of your kind ever ride on these trains as willing guests."

The train which the trio approached was the only one ready to go at that hour. To Ben, it looked normal enough, which made sense, since the Occult Mafia would likely not want attention drawn to it. The engine was a New York Central Hudson J-3a, its surface dull and streaked with soot from years of service. There were only four cars behind it including the caboose, and though they were sizable for train cars, it made the overall appearance of the train feel small.

"The caboose is for recreation, when there's time for it," Donovan continued. "The foremost car is for storage, then there's the dining car, and the passenger car. Your room is clearly marked. My daughter and I have our own separate rooms, but hers will be locked, and it connects directly to mine, so don't get any ideas."

"Never even occurred to us," Ben said.

"Good." Donovan rapped on the door to the caboose. In response, an attendee opened it from within. "Well, Ben Andante, welcome aboard."

As Ben stepped up, he asked, "Where's our first stop?"

"One of our facilities in Indiana," answered Donovan. "There's some stuff we need to pick up there. After that, the job really begins."

III.

Ben and Loup found the accommodations on the train very nice. Their assigned room was one of six, and though it was small, they found it cozy rather than confining. Then again, neither of them had claustrophobia, and both possessed a natural inclination towards denning. There was one bed that was much softer than others the pair was used to, and a narrow closet to keep his suitcase. There was also a private bathroom so small that it was basically a shower with a toilet inside of it, a feature which was both convenient and a tad disgusting. The other five rooms connected to the narrow hall – two of which the Van Sloans occupied – were closed.

The hall led to the caboose and its spacious drawing room. Being nocturnal, Ben and Loup decided to venture there instead of sleeping. The caboose was set up like a lounge, lined with large cushy chairs. In the middle was a table arranged for various games to be played, including billiards, if the pockets along the edge were any indication. A few smaller tables along the walls reminded Ben and Loup of a coffee shop, and there were newspapers and magazines on these. A radio was built into the wall with speakers embedded in the ceiling, a feature they had not seen before.

It was a nice layout, but with no other passengers to interact with, neither Ben nor Loup saw any point in tarrying there. Realizing he was starting to feel hungry, Ben left and headed for the dining car.

He went past the rooms of his current employers, one of which had a "DO NOT DISTURB" sign hanging on the doorknob. He would have passed by without a second thought had he not heard a sudden loud thud come from within. He stopped at the sound, and listened for anything more.

There was another thud, followed by Jackie's voice. Though it was muffled through the thick wood, he could hear her shouting in two voices, the second being the same raspy sound he had heard twice use by now.

More thuds resounded from within, louder and louder. It sounded as if Jackie were throwing herself against the walls.

Ben considered walking away and minding his own business, but when Jackie's shouting became agonized screaming, he cast the thought aside.

"Be ready, Loup," he told his partner.

Ben tried the doorknob. It was locked, as Donovan said it would be. He braced himself against the opposing wall as Loup Garou took full control of his legs, ready to kick the door right off its hinges.

Just before he could deliver the blow, the door opened for him, revealing Donovan Van Sloan on the other side. Behind him, Ben could see Jackie prone on her bed, her short, sharp breathing gradually slowing down with each exhalation, as though she were recovering from a panic attack. A door on one of the side walls was open, which connected the girl's room to her father's.

Donovan made several observations of his own, specifically how the man outside his daughter's room was canine from the waist down and poised as if ready to charge into a fight. "And just what are *you* doing out here?" he asked in a voice laced with suspicion.

"We were heading to the dining car when we heard a ruckus," Ben answered as his legs became human once more. "Now what were you two doing in there?"

IV.

The rest of the trip passed without incident, and the train arrived at a small private station by midmorning. The station connected directly to an Occult Mafia facility which, on the outside, looked like an unassuming brick factory. It had, in fact, been a textile plant during the Industrial Revolution, but mismanagement had led to the owners closing up shop by 1911. The Occult Mafia had acquired the building immediately thereafter and made various additions, most of them underground so as to maintain the façade of abandonment.

The Van Sloans disembarked, but Ben and Loup remained on the train. Even though they were promised amnesty by Donovan, neither of them felt comfortable entering a place filled with monster hunters. From within, however, they heard Donovan announce to the staff that if any harm befell his guests during their stay, everyone present would be held accountable and punished accordingly.

A threat from Donovan Van Sloan was never made in jest or in vain, so if anyone had been planning something, those plans were abandoned on the spot.

The importance of the gesture did not go unnoticed by Ben and Loup, though it was not enough to completely quell their suspicions.

Every Occult Mafia installation had containment cells for supernatural prisoners. They were no different in overall design from interrogation rooms in police stations, but they incorporated various hidden elements to keep their unusual prisoners from escaping. The concrete mixture contained such things as wolf's bane, lamb's blood, bark from oak, ash, and yew trees, and garlic powder, and the support beams were made of reinforced iron. Even the one-way mirror had a mercury backing. To a regular human being, these elements presented little obstruction, but to a mystical creature, just sitting in the room was uncomfortable. It made these cells effective prisons, not to mention they helped get results during interrogations.

Jackie had made her way to such a containment cell so she could sleep. Being the daughter of a council member, she could have stayed in any bedroom she wanted, but she chose the cell in case the entity within her tried escaping again. It would at least keep her confined until help arrived.

Donovan only allowed himself two hours of sleep before he made his way to the Laboratory. It was, after all, the reason they had stopped at this particular facility.

An entire wing of the facility was devoted to the Laboratory, of which there were three sections. The first part, through which people entered, was the Showcase, a brightly lit, cavernous room where all of the new inventions were housed for inspection and approval. Multiple aisles of shelving units that rose all the way to the ceiling were filled with containers and ammo crates, and a mobile elevator platform allowed access to the higher shelves. There was also an area for demonstrations of new devices, though it was shielded with acrylic glass for safety.

Then there was the Workshop, where the Occult Mafia's scientists constructed and refined their various tools and weapons, from ectoplasm detectors to mercury-infused bullets. It was also where they performed dissections when necessary. This area – which was every bit as expansive as the Showcase – was separated into

slipped away, but I did get a swipe at his back that drew blood. It wasn't much, but I hope it scarred."

"So you actually managed to hurt him? That's more than most people can say. Even we didn't manage that." Donovan smiled. "I knew you two were right for this job."

"Here's hoping," Ben said. "I can promise that if given the chance, we'd give him far worse than just a scratch."

"You'll get your chance." Donovan leaned back. "We all will."

"Outstanding," Ben said. His eyes darted to the utensils that stood embedded in the table like weapons of Arhturian legend. "Sorry about the table, by the way."

Donovan shrugged. "Trust me, Ben, this train has been through much worse."

knuckle grip as he tried to steady his nerves. During the tense few seconds he was like this, fur bristled across his hands and face as though he were fighting back the instinct to transform.

The moment passed, and a mirthless laugh aimed at himself escaped Ben's lips. "Some tough guy I am, right? Thirty years later, and the memory still packs a punch."

A twinge of guilt passed through Jackie for asking. "If you don't want to talk about it-"

"I'm fine." Ben said with a wave of his hand, though he still trembled. "I'm better than your table, at least. Just...give me a second."

He closed his eyes and took one last deep breath, inhaling and exhaling slowly. Donovan and Jackie noted Loup Garou's reflection in the window perfectly matched Ben's movement, which was the only time thus far they had seen the pair in perfect synchronization.

Ben opened his eyes again, calmer, but still troubled. "Okay." After one last breath, he continued his story. "So anyway, he and some of his followers were waiting for us at home, and...and they had already killed both of our parents...or maybe the better word is 'butchered'. We can still see them plain as day." He silently suppressed his emotions as he continued. "If you've ever seen those photos of Jack the Ripper's victims, it was worse than that. I still don't know why they were there, but back then, I didn't care. I only knew that my parents were dead, their killer was right in front me, and I had one way to fight back. That was when I finally came to an understanding with Loup, and the first time he was released."

"What'd you do?" asked Donovan.

"I repaid them in kind," Loup answered. "I tore Bismuth's followers to shreds. Even as a pup, I was dangerous. I would've killed Bismuth too if he hadn't

Donovan hesitated to answer.

Behind him, Jackie sat up, a motion accompanied by a beleaguered groan that drew her father's attention. She massaged her temples. "Let's just tell him," she croaked, her throat sore from screaming. "We don't want him to find out the wrong way."

Donovan sighed, but nodded in agreement. "It's a long story," he said. "Mind if we join you?"

Aside from the chefs, the trio was alone in the dining car. Despite having just had an episode, Jackie insisted on joining the adults, since she was the subject of discussion.

"When we went after Bismuth, he got back at all of us somehow," said Donovan as their food was served. "I lost my hand and Melissa lost her life, but Jackie got it worst of all."

"Worse than death and dismemberment?" asked Loup, who was reflected in the window.

Jackie nodded. "I was the last one standing, so I chased after Bismuth while he made his escape. He got the drop on me, and I blacked out, so I don't know what he did, but when I came to, I felt different. It wasn't until we got back home that the fits started."

"As far as we can tell," Donovan continued, "Bismuth infected Jackie with some kind of evil entity, and it's been trying to take control of her body ever since."

Jackie reached up and gently wrapped her fingers around the new set of rosaries which dangled from her neck. "She doesn't like religious stuff, so I wear things like this to keep her locked up. She keeps finding ways to slip out, though." She sighed. "She *always* finds a way."

Ben, who had been eating a steak while he listened, finished a mouthful before replying. "Sounds like demonic possession to me, which makes me wonder why you haven't handled it yet. I thought you Occult Mafiosos counted exorcism among your specialties."

Jackie shook her head. "I've seen the best exorcists in the world, whether they were ours, the Vatican's, or freelancers. None of 'em can figure out how to get rid of her." Her face turned dark for an instant as she said, *"Bunch of charlatans!"* in the entity's voice. She clutched the rosaries to her face, forcing the entity back inside of her.

"That's why she's coming with us," Donovan said. "Bismuth did this, so he must know how to undo it, and we're going to make him."

"But the plan is still to snuff him when he's done, right?" asked Loup.

Donovan nodded. "As soon as Jackie's back to normal, he's a corpse. That's the goal, and we're sticking to it."

"What about you two?" Jackie asked. "You've run into Bismuth before, so what's the story there?"

Loup Garou growled angrily. It was not directed at Jackie, but simply an automatic response to the memory of when he and Ben had first encountered Bismuth.

Ben was the one who answered. "Bismuth made us orphans. We were ten, and still not comfortable with this whole arrangement." His hand waved back and forth between himself and Loup, clarifying the arrangement he spoke of. "So I'd been resisting letting Loup out. Then one day, I came home from school, and Bismuth was…he was waiting." His hands began to tremble, making it impossible to cut his steak. "He…oh God…"

Ben winced as though the memory brought physical pain with it. A sudden surge of pure terror and anger coursed through his veins, demanding release. He suddenly drove the ends of his utensils into the table with such ferocity that the ends wound up completely buried in the wood. He held onto the handles with a white-

dozens of individual cubicles and packed with special equipment, which made it feel claustrophobic. Only the scientists and council members were allowed to enter the Workshop without an escort.

These two spaces were separated by the Buffer, a room devoted entirely to security. Though it appeared empty and plain, it was similar to the containment cells in that it equipped with all manner of security measures to keep unwanted forces from getting in or out. These measures included sun lamps, nozzles which sprayed holy water, high frequency sound systems, and mummy dust dispensers, among other things.

Donovan was greeted at the door to the Showcase by a tall, lanky, pale man with dirty blond hair, to which he said, "Morning, Neville."

Doctor Neville Rand checked his watch and said, "You're a bit early, Donovan," in a friendly-yet-confused tone. Neville was a council member alongside Donovan, so the pair were on a first name basis with each other.

"Time is of the essence. I'm not *too* early, am I?"

"I suppose not. Follow me."

Neville led Donovan to a glass display case, in which was stored a small yet heavy-looking mechanical device. Neville removed the glass, setting it aside so Donovan could inspect the object unobstructed. "Behold your new right hand, should you find it to your liking."

Donovan examined the device. The majority of its makeup was a thick metal cone about six inches long. Rectangular panels encircled its dull surface. One end of it was open, revealing the cone to be a hollow sleeve. The other end narrowed to a rounded tip, from which jutted a pair of metal pinchers similar to a lobster claw.

"I'm afraid the pinchers are the best we could manage," Neville said. "I would have made you a proper hand if I could, but our technology just isn't there yet. I hope the claw will suffice. You won't be playing any piano solos with it, but you can still pick things up. To compensate, the claw is made of reinforced iron, tipped in diamond, and coated in silver, so it can be used for combat. The panels on the sleeve are for storing useful items. Nothing big, of course. Small things, like garlic cloves or sprigs of wolf's bane, anything you might need in a pinch."

Donovan nodded in approval. "It's just what I need. Let's get this sucker attached."

"Well…" Neville began, then paused as he tried to formulate his next words. "You see, Donovan, I need to warn you about this next part. In order for you to have full control of the appendage, it needs to be attached to your nerve endings."

Donovan detected an air of uncertainty in Neville's voice which he had not expected "You said you make it work by reading those notes we recovered from Auschwitz."

"Yes, and I've had more than a few nightmares after reading them, believe me. Mengele and von Geist were…*very* detailed." Neville shuddered before continuing. "Here's the problem, though. The notes clearly state that the only way to guarantee a working connection between organic tissue and inorganic machinery is for the subject to be alive and fully conscious during the operation. Connecting to dead tissue never worked, and the use of anesthetics on live subjects led to problems down the line. Only by keeping all nerve endings active can we guarantee the wires will receive commands from your brain." He took out the blueprints for the device and spread them on the table. "On top of that, I'll need to bolt this thing to your forearm to make sure it stays in place. Two rods in an x-pattern, passing between the ulna and the radius through the interosseus membrane. That's our best bet."

Neville placed a hand on Donovan's shoulder and looked him square in the eyes. "What I'm saying, Donovan, is that attaching this new hand to your arm will hurt far worse than having the old one severed. I will do it, but you need to be absolutely sure you want me to."

Donovan did not hesitate to reply. "I can't go after Bismuth with one hand and a stump, Neville. Believe me, I'm sure." His thoughts drifted to Jackie. "Besides, compared to what my daughter goes through every day, this'll be nothing."

"Very well." Neville picked up the claw. It was much heavier than it looked due to all the machinery inside. "Off to the Workshop we go, then. We'll be as quick and precise as we can be."

Ben sat alone in the caboose lounge. He had gotten a little sleep during the day, but not very much. The bed was an unfamiliar one, and he always felt uncomfortable on unfamiliar beds in unfamiliar places. So he had come here to bide his time, deciding that perhaps reading some of the magazines he had seen last night would help make him drowsy.

As Ben was perusing an article about a series of mysterious seismic events which had occurred last December, Loup's sharp canine ears heard someone approaching the caboose's rear door. A hint of lime green scent told him that the newcomer was neither Donovan nor Jackie.

A man in nice casual attire with a folder tucked under his arm entered without knocking, and was surprised to see the detective was present. "Oh, you're awake," he said curtly. "I'm Wilkins, and you must be Ben Andante. Mr. Van Sloan asked me to check in on you." His voice carried a bit of tension, and his body was equally stiff, making him lookvery awkward. "First of all, how are you finding your accommodations?"

Ben shrugged as he placed his magazine back on the table. "Still getting used to the whole arrangement. Given how you normally treat lycans, though, I guess we can't complain."

Wilkins nodded. "Good, good. I was also asked to give you this." He placed the folder on the table. It was a manila folder, stuffed thick with papers, with "PLAN M" written on the cover.

Ben flipped it open as he asked, "And what is this?"

"Mr. Van Sloan's compiled notes on the others he wants to recruit," answered Wilkins. There was a noticeable change in the timber of his voice when he spoke, betraying his disapproval of Donovan's plan. "It's everything he was able to learn about them, barring their current whereabouts."

"So why give it to us?"

"Because unlike you, they're good at covering their tracks." The passive-aggressive response stung Ben slightly. Wilkins' desire to not be speaking to the werewolf was becoming more and more evident. "He wants you to figure out where they are, seeing as how you're a detective. Read it and see what you can figure out by the time he's ready to go."

Ben cocked an eyebrow. "What's he doing, anyway?"

Wilkins raised his arms in a manner that made his annoyance with Ben abundantly clear. "Does it matter? You have a job to do, so do it!"

Ben decided that he did not care for this fellow's attitude. "Fine. We work best alone, so scram."

Wilkins left immediately without another word. He slammed the door behind him as he went.

Ben shook his head and glanced at Loup's reflection in the window. "Clearly prejudiced, wouldn't you agree?"

Loup nodded. "That's definitely where the Occult Mafia gets its reputation from."

Ben flipped through the first couple of pages in the binder. "The real question is whether Wilkins or Van Sloan are the majority."

"If the answer is Wilkins, then Jacqueline has bigger problems than being possessed."

Jackie woke up gasping for air. Her throat burned with pain, and as her fight-or-flight responses kicked in, she realized she was being throttled by her own hands.

Except they were not her hands. The skin was unsettlingly dark, like a photographic negative.

The hands of the entity.

Jackie twisted about, hoping that she still had control over the rest of her body. Thankfully, she did. The motion caused her to roll off her cot and onto the floor. She landed face down, which crushed the entity's arms beneath her. The impact jarred them both, and though the entity released her grip for an instant, she did not relinquish control, and she pressed her attack again.

With few options available, Jackie scrambled to a sitting position and rammed her entity-controlled arms into the cot's sharp corner, aiming specifically for the ulnar nerves. She repeated the action until the entity finally gave up and receded.

With the restoration of control came a lingering pain from the impact. It was not as bad as it might have been, since the entity had taken the brunt of the force, but it still hurt.

A doctor and nurse who had been keeping an eye on her through the one-way mirror rushed into the cell. Jackie was so exhausted from the struggle that she was barely aware of their presence as they checked for broken bones and felt her pulse.

So much for resting.

V.

For the past five decades, buildings had been cropping up all over the United States which resembled churches from the outside, but only superficially. They were small square structures with shallowly-sloped rooftops and bell towers at the front, similar to the kind of chapels that were common the Wild West. From the outside, they were not meant to draw much attention. The only peculiar thing about them was how, in place of a recognizable religious icon like a crucifix or a Star of David, there was an infinity symbol emblazoned above the doorway. Apart from that, the exteriors were plain and uninteresting.

Within the structures, however, the layout was quite disturbing. The walls, ceiling, and floor were painted blood red, and the placement of the lighting fixtures combined with the Gothic architecture to form deep shadows in odd places, which made the interiors feel claustrophobic. The pews and pulpit were made of bones, an unholy mixture of human, animal, and monster skeletons as one might find in a mausoleum. Along the walls hung paintings and reliefs blaspheming every religion and philosophy imaginable.

This was a place of worship for those who followed the warlock Phillipe Bismuth. It was his habit to travel the country and speak at these places, but his movements were always random so he could not be tracked. Raids by state law enforcement, the FBI, and the Occult Mafia were known to disrupt his twisted religion's ability to put down roots, but for every one destroyed, another always sprung up. When he was not at these new churches, Bismuth and his closest disciples would take up residence in various ghost towns scattered across the West. These places had been renovated into impregnable compounds, with tight security and expansive facilities underground, though they still appeared abandoned from the outside.

Currently, Bismuth was speaking at one of the newer churches in rural Louisiana. It was located near the marshlands, perfect for disposing of sacrificial bodies. He was there to mark the building's completion, and since there were many new attendees at such events, he chose to go with his most popular sermon as he ascended to the skeletal pulpit. This sermon was the very foundation of his movement.

There had been a dull murmur amongst the congregation which filled the chamber, but this stopped when Bismuth cleared his throat into the microphone, drawing the crowd's attention to him. Bismuth cut a striking figure, standing at six foot four with broad shoulders. His salt-and-pepper hair was slicked back, reflecting the light in a way that made it look metallic, and the features on his olive-toned face were sharp and firm. His eyes were dark and deeply set, and had a wild alertness to them which might have chilled Aleister Crowley. All of these features combined to form a mesmerizing air that instantly commanded people's attention.

"Welcome, my loyal children," he began, "and welcome to those who are new to our philosophy. My message tonight is especially for you." He stepped away from the pulpit, taking the microphone with him, and began pacing about the stage as though he were an actor delivering his grand soliloquy to crowd.

"I ask you this: what is the greatest lie in human history? Is it the existence of benevolent gods? Is it the infallibility of science? Is it the American Dream? Well, all of these are lies, it is true, but none of them are the greatest lie of all. No, the greatest lie is that Man can be redeemed, that he can be greater than what he is. Everything the human race has ever done has been in pursuit of this impossible ideal.

"Man created religions to achieve some form of spiritual perfection. I do not tell you, my friends, that the gods do not exist, for I myself have seen their work with my own eyes, but the religions which surround them are earthly creations. People flock to them in droves, hoping that favor from the gods will bring salvation. The Christian says you will live forever if you follow the words of a carpenter; the Jew says you must be born of a certain heritage; the Buddhist says you must achieve enlightenment to become equal to the gods; the Hindu says good deeds will see you reincarnated into a better life; the Greek of ancient times said you must be a great hero to attain eternal happiness. Yet with all of these religions making all of these promises, the society of Man remains corrupt to its very core.

"When a Man is not satisfied with religion, he turns to science for salvation. In a way, science itself is just another religion. The Scientist promises wondrous discoveries to better our lives. He promises clockwork servants to attend our needs, and automated vehicles to bring us across the globe. He promises to raise long lost creatures from the dead and contact beings from the heavens. He even promises the chance to live on other worlds and travel between the stars. Yet more often than not, the Scientist fails to deliver these promises. Instead, he makes weapons so that his *true* masters, the politicians, may slaughter millions of everyday people, such as yourselves, in some grandiose war for the history books.

"Sometimes a Man does not seek salvation from religion or science, but rather from within. He strives to be the best version of himself that he can be, so he and his loved ones may live long and prosperous lives. In this nation, we call it the American Dream. Yet how often is this dream realized? How often does it fail? How many slave their lives away chasing the glorious horizon, only to die before reaching it?

"The salvation of Man is the greatest lie of all. Man is born a wailing, naked animal driven by instinct and basic desire. It is in his nature to resort to those methods and actions which he has arbitrarily dubbed 'evil' and 'uncivilized'. But if it is our nature, why should we deny it?

"The Man's nature is to be violent, brutal, and murderous. The Woman's nature is to be wicked, duplicitous, and seductive. I say let them be what they are! If you must kill your neighbor to steal his possessions, slaughter him without remorse and stake your claim! If your lust is uncontrollable, take the object of your desires by whatever means you wish! If you crave the taboo, do not fear it, but embrace it! We do not judge animals who murder and devour their own, and what is Man but just another kind of animal?

"Forget your gods, forget your science, and forget your dreams! Only by embracing what you truly are can you attain happiness! This is the only way! This is *my* way! This is the only true path that exists in this wretched world!"

He paused for a moment, soaking in the silence of the crowd. He knew this kind of silence well. It meant he had everyone in the palm of his hand. Bismuth had reached the fiery peak of his sermon, and it was that burning passion, spoken with supreme authority, which won people over, making them accept everything he said without question. Now he just had to deliver the finishing touch.

He lowered his voice to its regular volume, making it seem more inviting as he finished his speech. "I give you the greatest gift of all, my children. I give you true freedom. Go forth and take what is yours."

A few people had left as he spoke, but that was to be expected. Not everyone was ready to accept his radical point of view. Those few did not matter, though. Most of the newcomers had stayed, they had devoured every word he said, and now they were joining his longtime followers as they chanted his name like the citizens of Rome exalting a triumphant Caesar.

In the end, that was all that mattered to him.

The chanting continued as Bismuth left the church and headed to a different structure nearby. It was a barnlike building, its façade as unassuming as the chapel's. Inside were two levels of small rooms. This was where his disciples who ran things in his absence lived, although one room was always kept empty for him.

At the door, Bismuth was met by his most trusted disciple, a younger man whom everyone called Sharpe. This was because he was embarrassed by his given name, Rupert Bubbles. He had given himself the name "Sharpe" when he had joined a street gang in his youth, and it stuck with him into adulthood.

"Master," he said, addressing Bismuth as all of his followers did, "we have received word that Van Sloan is on the move again."

"Really?" Bismuth replied. "I was certain I had broken his resolve."

"Apparently not, Master. He and his daughter seek to challenge us once again. Something is odd, though.

According to our intelligence, they're traveling with a werewolf."

This was so unexpected that even the usually composed Bismuth was surprised. "This werewolf travels with them as an equal, not as a prisoner?"

"From all outward appearances, yes. We're not sure exactly what he's planning at this point. No doubt he knows that you'll soon be performing the Pandorum Ritual again, and wishes to disrupt it. Should we do something?"

Bismuth shook his head. "There's an old bit of wisdom I live by, Sharpe: never interrupt your enemy when he's making a mistake. It's not like the Occult Mafia to ally itself with monsters, so that tells me Van Sloan is desperate, and desperate people often do things they regret. Have our people track him to see what they can learn, but be sure they understand not to interfere unless I say so." He waved his hand as if shooing a fly away, changing the subject. "It doesn't matter now, anyway. Is my room prepared?"

Sharpe nodded. "The bed is turned down, the radio is set to your preferred station, and your brides await."

"You are sure they won't be missed?"

"All waifs and whores who will be mourned by no one. However..." Sharpe wrung his hands, as though nervous about what he was about to say. "I didn't gather them myself, but some of them are a bit darker than you usually prefer. That's to be expected in these southern states, I'm afraid."

Bismuth betrayed no sign of disappointment. "As long as they serve my needs, Sharpe, I don't care how dark they are. They will all wind up the same in the end. Tell the others to be ready for disposal in the morning, and keep an eye out for more in case I stay longer."

With this, he entered.

Sharpe departed. He would not be back until at least three hours had passed. That was how long Bismuth usually took with his brides. Although Sharpe was devoted to the cause, he did not want to be around for what would happen next.

Later that evening, after Phillipe Bismuth had satisfied all of his needs, he used a little bit of the leftover blood to draw a circle on the floor. He whispered a quick incantation, and at his words, the circle rippled and swirled as if disturbed by the wind, which was impossible since the room was as still as death itself.

"Belial," said Bismuth. "Can you hear me?"

There was a brief yet blinding flash of light, and a shadow appeared in the circle. It had no features beyond its humanoid outline, and was faint almost to the point of transparency.

"Yes, Bismuth, I hear you," said the shadow, a fallen angel who responded to the name Belial. "Still using only the weakest of contact spells, I see."

There was a hint of something in Belial's voice that was either condescension or impatience, and Bismuth did not appreciate it. "If you still want me to release you, then I must conserve my energy." He glared threateningly at the shadow. "Unless you'd prefer to stay rotting in Hell, I'd advise you to watch your tone. Never forget that I am the only man in history with the power to release you, though I can decide not to if I am not given the respect I deserve."

"I have not forgotten." Belial shifted his posture in a motion that seemed to be a bow. "Eons in this festering prison breeds impatience. I hope this is to inform me that you'll be opening the gate soon?"

"It will be soon, but there is one last complication to deal with." Bismuth clasped his hands behind his back and slowly paced about the room as he spoke. "The

Occult Mafia intends to interfere once more, only Van Sloan appears to be taking a different approach this time. I don't want him disrupting me again."

Belial assumed a relaxed posture that made it look like he was leaning against a wall. "Do you intend to cut to the chase and kill him this time?"

"You know I've tried that already. Van Sloan lives a charmed life. Even when I have him cornered and wounded, he finds a way to survive." Bismuth shook his head. "No, Donovan Van Sloan is not the kind of opponent you simply kill. He is the kind who must be broken, and the only thing that can break him is utter defeat. He will not give up so long as he believes he can win, so if I can reveal to him that he has already lost, that will be the end of it. I already took his wife from him, and his daughter cannot possibly survive much longer in her condition. One final blow, and I'm sure he will crumble."

"And *then* you can finally release us?"

"Yes, Belial, then I can finally release you." Bismuth stepped towards the blood circle and stared deep into where he presumed Belial's eyes were. "And you, and all the legions of Hell, will serve me as your true master, as we agreed."

"Of course," Belial nodded. "He who holds the prison keys is god of the prisoners. But how long will it take to defeat Van Sloan this time?"

"However long it takes is however long it takes," was Bismuth's blunt reply. "You've already been trapped in Hell for eons, as you put it. What are a few more weeks compared to the eternity of freedom I will give you?"

Belial let out a mirthless chuckle. "I suppose your logic is sound enough. I appreciate that you're keeping me informed, Bismuth. Now stop wasting your energy. We don't want any more delays."

Incensed by the attitude of the fallen angel, Bismuth stepped right to the edge of the blood circle and glared at him. "You do *not* give me orders!"

"Of course not. Please pardon me."

Bismuth stamped his foot on the circle, smearing the blood across the floor. Belial vanished as the circle was broken, ending their conversation.

VI.

Ben must have dozed off, for he found himself suddenly stirring as the caboose door opened again. Donovan and Jacqueline Van Sloan entered, and when Ben saw them, he could not stop himself from saying, "Sheesh, you each look like five miles of bad road."

His assessment was accurate. Though the pair had cleaned up and changed into different clothes, their postures and slow movements spoke to neither of them being rested. Emphasizing this were their haggard expressions, accentuated by dark circles under their eyes. Ben could guess the girl's unusual condition must have kept her awake, but he was not immediately sure why her father seemed so bedraggled. Then he saw that Donovan's right arm was no longer in a sling, but now hung down at his side as though weighted down.

As Donovan removed his long coat, Ben saw that a large, cruel-looking metal claw now resided where his right hand ought to have been. The pinchers twitched slightly as Donovan maneuvered into the chair across from him. Jackie chose a chair away from the adults and collapsed into it with a heavy exhalation.

"So," Ben said, "I see you've got a fancy new pirate hook. Is that what we came here for?"

"Among other things," Donovan nodded. His voice was slightly strained, as the area where the new appendage was attached still hurt quite badly. "Enough with the small talk, though. Did you read through the binder yet, or have you been sleeping since we got here?"

Ben cocked an eyebrow. "I won't take that personally this time. Yes, I read it, and you've got quite the menagerie you want me to find." He flipped through the binder. "A mummy, a vampire, and an ichthoid, whatever that's supposed to be, and you expect them all to work together under your leadership." He shook his head as he smiled wryly. "There's playing with fire, Don, and then there's playing with the A-bomb."

"The A-bomb is what ended the War, which is what I intend to do." Donovan leaned forward, shooting Ben a suspicious look. "If you're not going to cooperate-"

"I didn't say that," Ben interrupted. "I just want to make sure you know what you're getting into. One of our practices as detectives is to make certain our client really wants us to do the job before we commit to it. Just because we make a living at being snoops doesn't mean we're devoid of scruples. Any hint of doubt from our employer means it's probably a bad idea."

Donovan stared directly into Ben's eyes. "I don't have a single shred of doubt in me, Ben Andante." His voice was firm, and his gaze unwavering.

"I believe you," Ben nodded, then turned to look at Jackie. "What about you, kid? You've got more of a personal stake in this than your old man, after all."

With what little energy she had, Jackie propped herself upright to answer. "I can't keep living like this." Even as she spoke, her left eye briefly darkened as the entity within her attempted to manifest, but for some reason, she receded instead. "If Bismuth is the only one who can get this thing out of me, we need the others to give us the edge. I'm with my Pop on this one."

Ben nodded once more, slower this time as he accepted the pair's confidence. "So be it," he said. "In that case, I think our first recruit should be this mummy you lost track of."

"You found her?" asked Donovan.

Ben nodded as he flipped to a page he had marked. "As I was reading through your notes, I realized I'd seen this before." He pointed to a sketch on the page. "This thing, the egg with the pictures inside it."

"It's called a cartouche," Donovan said. "The Ancient Egyptians used them to denote the names of kings."

"If you say so," Ben replied as he reached for a magazine resting beside the binder. "At first, I couldn't figure out where I'd seen it, since I'm obviously no Egyptologist, and then it hit me. Before your delivery boy came along, I was browsing through these magazines, and guess what I found in this month's *National Geographic?*"

He opened to a page in the issue he had read, revealing a picture of a sarcophagus on display at the World Art and History Museum in Boston, Massachusetts. The lid was unusual for a sarcophagus, depicting the body as being enveloped by majestic azure wings, and the face was clearly feminine and lacking the pointed beard and headdress worn by pharaohs. Instead, the upper portion of the face was bright red, as though covered by a mask. Emblazoned in gold on the chest was the cartouche from Donovan's notes.

Donovan was stunned. "Well I'll be darned. How did I miss that?"

Ben shrugged. "Obsessing over details doesn't prevent you from missing a few things. Still, I think she's our safest bet, this, uh…Matt, is it?"

"Ma'at," Donovan corrected. He emphasized the miniscule gap created by the apostrophe. "Her name is Ma'at, Goddess of Justice."

VII.

The trip from Indiana to Massachusetts took a few days, during which Ben Andante and Loup Garou studied Donovan's notes on Ma'at closely and committed the details to memory.

Donovan's sources of information were various scrolls and tablets which had fallen out of the public eye since being recovered. In similar manner to how pharaohs were considered living gods, the mummified Ma'at waiting in the museum was described as an earthbound goddess. Ancient myths told of how the Goddess of Justice, after spending millennia in the ethereal realm of her fellow deities, decided to take a more active role is dispensing justice along the Nile River, and so descended to Earth and became the kingdom's guardian. Though often dismissed as outlandish, Donovan believed there was truth to the myth. Accounts of her actions covered many centuries and always spoke of her actions as an active contemporary force rather than a distant memory. If she were not an immortal goddess, she was still far more than a mere human being.

Ma'at was a heroic figure. Her eternal role in the Ancient Egyptian Empire was to watch over and protect it from foreign powers and subversives, as well as the occasional machinations of Set, God of Chaos. If she had a life outside of her duties, no trace of it could be found in the records. Though records of her exploits were quite thorough, a gap was noted in which no mention of her existed. Donovan noted that this period of silence was also when many scholars believed the Biblical Exodus was meant to have occurred, though he was not certain if that correlation was significant.

Ma'at was said to possess many powers in life, though the ancient texts were inconsistent as to what those powers were. Levitation and control over snakes were mentioned regularly, but other abilities would only be mentioned once. Donovan speculated in his notes that as a reanimated mummy, she would likely possess some new powers, as mummies often did, though he could not predict what those powers might be.

Unfortunately, Ma'at's story did not have a happy ending. When Pharaoh Akhenaten came to power in the 18th Dynasty, he transformed Egypt into a monotheistic culture under the sun god Aten, and worship of all other gods was forbidden. As a result, Ma'at, a goddess of the old pantheon, became an enemy of the empire. After spending a year in hiding, she attempted to kill Akhenaten and his queen Nefertiti, feeling that his complete and utter control of the people's faith was a grave injustice. When she broke into the palace, however, she found herself opposed by the royal guards. Under normal circumstances, she would have had no trouble overcoming mortal soldiers, but to do so at that point would have been an injustice of its own, for the guards were only doing their duty by protecting their king. As the embodiment of Justice, Ma'at could do no injustice herself. She had brandished her weapons, and froze, unable to make any move which might have brought harm to her opponents, none of whom hesitated to cut her down. So it was that Ma'at was slain at the hands of men she once considered allies.

Akhenaten had her lifeless body put on display outside his palace for a week as an example of his supreme authority. It was an all-too-literal proclamation that the old gods were dead. Of course, there were many during Akhenaten's reign who still worshipped the old gods in secret, and it was a collective of underground priests who recovered Ma'at's body and mummified her as they would have done for royalty. No one ever succeeded her as Egypt's protector, nor did the gods ever take physical form on Earth again.

The tomb of Ma'at was hidden deep in the Valley of the Queens to prevent Akhenaten from desecrating it. This meant it was also never looted by grave robbers. It was discovered in pristine condition by Egyptologists in 1932, though the treasures within were not as prolific and lavish as those in Tutankhamen's tomb, since Ma'at had accrued very few earthly possessions in her long life. The most interesting thing about the tomb was the story of Ma'at herself, told in hieroglyphics etched on the walls and scrolled on papyrus. Hers was the only tomb not made for royalty, and the story was so fantastical that archaeologists could only relegate it to the realm of mythology. The tomb was considered a curiosity, and this earned it some fanfare at first, but most people had stopped paying attention by the end of 1933. No implication was ever found of what the "real" story of her life was, so Egyptologists considered researching Ma'at to be a scholastic dead end. Her casket and artifacts made the circuit around various museums for a few years, but no one marveled at them anymore. As a result, the exhibit had been placed in storage in 1939, which is why Donovan Van Sloan had lost track of it.

Not all mummies could be successfully revived without bringing forth some sort of curse, but Donovan's notes expressed his certainty that Ma'at could be without incident. The Occult Mafia had dealt with reanimated mummies in the past, so there was no issue in terms of it being possible, but the revival of mummies was not as easy as simply reading an arcane incantation. More steps were required than that, and reviving Ma'at in particular was a very specific process, since she was no ordinary being. Fortunately, among the various inscriptions in the tomb were directions for how to bring her back to life, a process which required specific ingredients which Donovan had procured for the occasion.

Though they tried, neither Ben nor Loup could make heads or tails of that process. It somehow involved water from the Nile River, scarab amulets, and things called canopic jars. Donovan had also included an extra step to ensure Ma'at could speak and understand English when revived. It was all stuff more complicated than the duo had the patience to understand, though neither doubted it would work.

The doubt only lay in whether or not she would appreciate being brought back.

It was past midnight when the train arrived in Boston. Ben Andante and the Van Sloans went straight from the station to the World Art and History Museum on foot. It was snowing, so the city was relatively quiet. They were, in fact, the only people out on the streets.

Perhaps it was just their imaginations, but Ben and Loup thought Boston seemed like a much nicer city to spend the winter in than Chicago. The lights cast a pleasant warm glow on the streets, the air was not as bitter, and the old world architecture was far more pleasing to the eye than the sleek modern structures of the Midwest. On the other hand, though, the snow cover was much thicker here, and was not likely to melt any time soon.

Progress between locations was steady. Ben was unencumbered, but Donovan and Jackie carried the supplies needed to revive Ma'at in leather bags. Jackie did not have any new episodes on their walk, for she was wearing far more religious paraphernalia than she had before. If one paid attention to the expression on her face, though, it was clear that she was still struggling to keep the entity in check.

The World Art and History Museum was unmistakable in the cityscape. Its Gothic façade carved from pure marble appeared to flow seamlessly into the snow drifts and dangling icicles, making it look like the castle of the Snow Queen straight out of Hans Christian Anderson. A few of the opaque windows were illuminated from within, but most were dark. A pair of bronze griffin statues the size of greyhounds stood sentry at the foot of the stone stairway, their silhouettes distorted by the snow. Behind them, at the top of the stairs, was the entrance.

As they approached the massive wrought iron gate which barred the front doors, Ben asked the obvious question. "So how are we supposed to get in? It's after hours, and the place is sealed up tighter than a drum."

Donovan seemed unconcerned as he checked his pocket watch. "The night watchman owes me a favor. I called ahead to tell him when we'd arrive, so any second now…"

He did not need to finish, for the doors unlocked as his voice trailed off. They only cracked open slightly, however, allowing the night watchman to peer out and see the trio. After a nod from Donovan, the watchman opened the doors wider, unlocked the gate, ushered them inside with haste, and locked the gate once more as soon as everyone was inside.

"Right on time, as usual," said the watchman. "Glad to see you again, Mr. Van Sloan."

"Same, Pete," Donovan replied, addressing the watchman by name. "I'm guessing you haven't had any problems since we last met?"

Pete shook his head. "That creepy old mannequin hasn't moved in months, thanks to you."

"Good to hear. Not to be impersonal, but we've got things to do, so where's the Ancient Egypt exhibit?"

Pete pointed as he spoke. "East wing, just through those doors."

"Okay. Anyone else in the museum? We saw lights from outside."

"A few professors who stayed late, locked up tight in their offices to finish their work. No one from the Egyptology department, though. As long as you don't make a ruckus, they shouldn't notice anything."

"We'll do our best," Donovan replied as he led the way to their quarry.

It was Ben who flicked the light switch to illuminate the east wing, which was originally lit only by a few dim work lights. The Ancient Egypt exhibit was in a long, cavernous section of the museum, and not an inch of it was wasted. Displays were abundant, but the room was not cluttered so as to make observing the items easy. A display case with a bust of Rameses here, a statuette of Osiris there. If not for the glass boxes and signs instructing visitors not to touch anything, the space might have passed for an Egyptian palace in its own right. A wide balcony encircled the room up above, extending the exhibit to the second floor where even more treasures resided. The sarcophagus of Ma'at, however, was on the first floor, resting on a platform towards the center of the hall. It had no glass covering, and a velvet rope encircling the display served to separate it from the public. These ropes were moved aside as the trio began their preparations.

Ben and Jackie had to lift the lid of the sarcophagus. It was a two-handed task that Donovan's prosthetic was not designed for, otherwise he would have been the one assisting Ben. The lid was made of precious metals which were fairly heavy, and the shape make it somewhat awkward to move.

As they went to set the lid on the floor, the entity briefly forced her will into Jackie's hands, making her lose her grip and drop her end before receding. It made a loud crash which froze the trio for an instant.

A few seconds passed as they listened, worried that someone might come to investigate. Thankfully, no one did.

"Sorry," Jackie said as Ben gently set his end down. "She made me drop it." Jackie could feel the entity laughing at her from within. She took comfort in knowing that the wicked thing still could not break out yet, then she lamented the fact that she was becoming so used to those breakouts that she automatically added "yet" to such thoughts.

Inside the sarcophagus was the slender form of Ma'at's mummified body. The deteriorating bandages were bound tightly to her exposed skin, which itself was still well preserved despite the leathery texture. Clutched in one embalmed hand was a gilded kopesh, and in the other was a gold scepter topped by a sculpted cobra's head with rubies for eyes. Resting by her feet was a Deshert, the Red Crown of Upper Egypt, still shimmering a bright crimson after all these millennia. The red spire on the back rose to a sharp, menacing point. Oddly, the front of the crown extended downward and was sculpted in the vague shape of a face, with two holes cut in the front. It was not a typical design for a Deshert, and made it look similar to a mask or a cowl.

Donovan and Jackie began extracting supplies from their bags. Ben, meanwhile, stood silently by the sarcophagus. He looked inside, wondering what Ma'at had looked like in life and if she would look that way again when reanimated. Despite her body looking somewhat like a piece of beef jerky wrapped in gauze, he guessed that she must have been quite a looker in her prime. The images of her from Donovan's notes certainly depicted a woman he would have liked to know.

Having thought this, it occurred to him that he was not being much help at the moment. "So what are Loup and I supposed to do now?" he asked.

Donovan kept his eyes on his work as he answered. "Nothing. No offense, but you'll just be in the way for this next part."

Ben shrugged. "You could've phrased that a bit less offensively, but I catch your drift. We'll just circle around the exhibit, take in the sights and make sure none of those night owl professors catch us."

Ben wandered away from the sarcophagus, heading in no particular direction. He had to admit, though the artifacts surrounding him were impressive in design and quality, he did not entirely understand all of what he was looking at. Neither he nor Loup had ever taken much interest in Egyptology, so the significance of lions with human heads and the designs of obelisks meant little to them. They did see a plaque explaining that the Ancient Egyptians believed the sky goddess was a naked giantess named Nut who arched her body over the Earth, and that was just ridiculous enough to make them snicker. No wonder the Ancient Egyptians had spent so much time outside.

Do you hear that? Loup Garou asked suddenly.

Ben paused and listened. He could hear the low hum of the lights, and he could hear the Van Sloans starting the process of reviving Ma'at, but as he concentrated, he also heard the scuffling of shoes from a separate branch of the Egyptian exhibit.

He followed the sound to a grandiose archway and peered around the Corinthian column. As he did, a series of red-and-yellow striped scents wafted into his nostrils.

These scents belonged to a group of individuals dressed from head to toe in black clothing. Ben counted six, five of which held large burlap bags while the sixth was standing watch. The ones with bags were stuffing them full with artifacts. A cold draft blew in from an open window, one pane of which had a hole cut in it, explaining how they had gotten in.

Burglars, Loup snarled in contempt.

"There could be trouble if they come in here," Ben whispered in reply. "Feel like getting some exercise, pal?"

Always. I've already got eyes on the lookout.

The burglars were only interested in the gold. Nobody cared enough about stone statues and scrolls to buy those on the black market, but gold was universal. Gold could be melted down and fashioned into something else, making it untraceable. Gold coins, gold scepters, gold statues, gold jewelry, any gold that could be carried was stuffed into their sacks.

Centuries later in a different land, and still the pharaohs fell victim to grave robbers.

"Hey guys, look at this," one of the burglars called out to his accomplices. He pointed to a relief which depicted the gods. "Those Egyptians sure worshipped some weird things. These guys look like cartoon characters!"

The other burglars laughed. "That is stupid," a second one agreed. "They thought some guy with a dog's head was a god? Good thing we evolved, right Jack?"

Jack, the one who was standing lookout, did not respond.

The burglars turned. "Where's Jack?" asked one.

From a darkened corner of the hall, Jack's body flew into the light. He sailed through the air limply, like a stuffed doll with loose joints. His body landed hard on the floor and skidded towards his comrades. He was completely unresponsive, but the others could not tell if he was alive or dead, nor did they have time to find out as they beheld his attacker.

Out of the shadows stepped a werewolf.

It had to be a werewolf, for there was no other way to describe the menacing figure stalking towards them. His torso and arms were humanoid, yet his legs appeared more canine, for the way his pants folded as he walked was unnatural for human legs, as though his knees were backwards. He wore no shoes or gloves, allowing him to brandish his long, sharp claws that glinted like metal in the dim light. Every exposed part of his body was covered in grayish-brown fur, including his long tail that swayed in time with each step he took. His head was fully lupine, with lips pulled back in a fierce snarl that bared horrifying fangs dense enough to crush bone. His eyes, however, were eerily human and intelligent, and the sight of them chilled each crook to the bone. In his grip he clutched two sizeable lengths of steel chain with heavy metal hooks at each end. The manner in which he held them was as garrote.

"Who's next?" Loup Garou growled in a fearsome, chilling voice.

The burglars scattered in reply.

Loup Garou whipped his chains forward, aiming for the nearest of the thieves. The hook struck the fleeing burglar in the back of the head, knocking him off balance as it snagged his shirt collar. With a powerful yank, Loup pulled his target backward and caught him by the shoulder, sinking the claws on his hands deep into the flesh. The burglar started to scream, but he was silenced when Loup slammed him into the floor. Just for good measure, the wolf also kicked him in the side.

Another burglar came up from behind and attempted to strike Loup with a wooden marquis, but he spun with his arms raised in a blocking move, and the board shattered against them. With surprising grace for his bulky frame, Loup lunged forward and bit the new attacker's arm, shattering the bone between his teeth. A powerful swipe of his claws across the chest drew blood. Loup spun again and released the burglar, sending him flying awkwardly into the wall. His spine cracked as it connected with a column.

"Three down, three to go" Loup said as he sniffed out the others.

The process was nearly complete. All Donovan Van Sloan had to do now was anoint Ma'at with water from the Nile, and she would live again.

It was just as his daughter was handing him the vial containing this precious liquid when they heard sounds of a fight echoing from an adjacent wing.

"What the-?" Jackie began, only to immediately regret losing focus. The entity forced herself into the hand which held the vial and released it. Jackie's other hand shot out like a bullet to catch the fragile container before it could hit the floor and shatter. Her new grip was so tight that a crack formed in the thin glass. The entity's hand reached for Jackie's wrist, but was stopped when Donovan's mechanical claw lashed out and caught her.

"I'm sorry!" Jackie cried. "I'm sorry! I didn't-"

"I know, kiddo," Donovan said with urgency as he held out his left hand. "Just give me the vial."

Jackie did as she was told, and Donovan released his grip on the entity's hand. Jackie proceeded to bite the entity's fingers until she retreated.

Donovan pulled the cork off the vial with his teeth and poured the life-giving water onto the dried corpse.

The lights flickered.

The room became deathly cold.

Dust swirled around the sarcophagus as Ma'at's bandaged hands shot towards the ceiling.

*****

Loup Garou drove his foot like a jackhammer into the fifth burglar's stomach until he was doubled over in agony. He then delivered one last blow to his opponent's groin out of spite.

Satisfied, he sniffed the air for the scent of the last burglar. The odor had amorphous gray patches in it, which made it hard to see in the dim light, and it was so similar to the other scents – the burglars must have been related somehow – that it mixed with the other and was hard to track.

Loup caught a reflection in a glass case, and saw the thief was behind him, clutching some kind of metal scepter like a club. Loup turned, hand raised to catch the makeshift weapon.

Catch it he did, but the substance burned the padded skin of his palm. Loup recoiled with a pained yelp.

At first, the burglar was stunned that his attack had worked. He looked at the scepter in wonder, then the color of its dully-mirrored surface told him everything he needed to know. "Oh, I get it," he said with a wicked smile as he hefted the object in his hand. "This must be made of silver. I guess the movies were right."

Now certain the advantage was his, the thief swung his new weapon like a baseball bat, and Loup Garou leapt backwards to avoid being struck.

"Hah! Not so tough now, are you?" the burglar taunted, thinking he had the wolf on the ropes. He took a few more swings, backing his opponent into a corner.

Before the burglar could deal another blow, however, he paused when he felt something strange by his feet. It was an odd sensation, one he almost could not describe as he had not felt anything like it before. It was almost as if something was moving down there.

The wolf must have noticed it too, because he was staring in surprise at the burglar's feet.

The burglar looked down, and was horrified to see a cobra slithering up his leg. It hissed loudly at him, bearing its venomous fangs in a menacing display of intimidation.

The burglar dropped his weapon and fell to the floor in a blind panic. He struggled to remove his pants, never once stopping to think how strange it was that the cobra did not bite or spit at him as he flailed about. It just clung to him, threating to do its worst, as if it were toying with him.

He kicked off his pants and scrambled away, only to stop dead in his tracks as he realized the floor was suddenly crawling with hordes of snakes. There were more cobras, as well as pythons, asps, garters, and species he did not know the names of. Some of them sported leathery batlike wings as they reared up to hiss challenges at him.

Standing behind the mass of snakes was a tall feminine figure wrapped in pale tattered gauze that contrasted sharply with her dark brown skin. The shape of her body was like that of a swimmer, slender yet strong. A bright crimson Deshert sat low on her head like a mask, with its red crest rising like the horn of a demon. Her dark eyes were visible through holes in the front, and her straight raven hair spilled out of the top like water from a fountain. Her left hand was extended toward the burglar, clutching a golden, cobra-headed staff with glowing rubies in its eyes. This was Ma'at, the Goddess of Justice restored.

Loup Garou and Ben Andante were instantly taken by the sight of Ma'at, and grateful for her intervention.

Ma'at stepped forward, and the snakes moved ahead of her as one squirming mass. The burglar scurried away from them until he was backed against the wall, cornered and helpless as Loup had been mere moments ago.

With her target trapped, Ma'at raised the scepter so it stood upright, and the snakes halted. As she walked towards the burglar, the serpents parted at her feet to allow her passage among them. Their soulless eyes remained fixed on their original target. None of them threatened to bite Ma'at as she passed through their ranks. With each step, small scraps of bandages fell from her body, disintegrating into dust as they landed. Smooth, flawless skin was revealed beneath the wrappings.

Ma'at stopped inches away from the burglar. She radiated an aura of righteous fury that made him whimper and cower at her feet.

She scowled. "A common thief." She practically spat the words. Her voice was deep, lightly accented, and – at least to Loup's ears – somewhat sultry. "I grow tired of your worthless kind walking the land. Your sins will be weighed heavily against you on the scales before you are devoured by the Ammut, but I think you deserve an earthly punishment first."

Ma'at beckoned one of her snakes to her side. It looked up at her, awaiting her command. She said nothing, but her eyes locked with the serpent's and flashed the same shimmering red as the rubies in her scepter.

Once the glow faded, the snake struck at the burglar, sinking its fangs into his hand. He cried at the sting, and twitched as the burning venom shot through his veins.

"This one's venom will not kill you," Ma'at continued, "but you will be paralyzed henceforth. Let that be your lesson to never steal from the pharaohs." Just to be sure her contempt was clear, she spat upon the burglar, who had gone from twitching to convulsing as his body stiffened.

Ma'at waved her hand to dismiss the snakes, who slithered away and vanished into the shadows. This done, she approached Loup Garou, who had coiled his chains up and hung it on his hip. "Thanks for the save," he said.

"You are welcome," the mummy replied, nodding in the regal manner of a queen. "Tell me, are you a child of Anubis?"

Loup blinked, not understanding the question. "My parents' names were Alfonse and Beatrice."

"He's what we call a lycan," said Donovan Van Sloan as he entered the room. "His name is Loup Garou, and mine is Donovan Van Sloan. I'm the man who just brought you back to life."

"Hmm?" Ma'at seemed confused at first, but then memories of Akhenaten's betrayal flashed through her mind. "Ah yes, now I remember." She shuddered as she recalled the plunging of spears into her body, piercing cold and searing hot all at once, a horrible pain which had slowly faded until she could no longer sense anything. This must have been her death "Tell me, does that wretch Akhenaten still rule?"

Donovan shook his head. "Not for a long time. You've been dead for almost six thousand years, Ma'at. A lot's changed since then, but we still strive for justice in this modern world. Your particular brand is something I need, if you'd be so kind as to hear me out."

Ma'at crossed her arms over her chest, and as she did, another stray bandage fell from her body. "For restoring my life, I shall grant you that favor. I would prefer some new garments first, though. I fear these present coverings will not preserve my modesty for much longer."

"Of course. My daughter has a tunic for you in the other room. She's waiting by your sarcophagus. I'll tell you everything once we're on the train."

"What is a train?"

"You'll see."

Ma'at accepted this answer with a nod before leaving to seek out Jackie.

Loup trailed behind her and stopped at Donovan's side. "I have to say," he mused, "she sure cleans up nicely for a dead broad."

Donovan frowned at him. "You're supposed to be a wolf, not a hound. Stay focused." After making this quip, Donovan took better stock of the room. None of the displays appeared to be damaged, but the burglars' bodies were strewn everywhere, and many of them looked as though they had been savaged by an animal. "You killed these guys, didn't you?"

Loup shrugged. "Probably. There's a chance some of them will make it." His voice betrayed no sign of remorse for his violent actions. "But they're crooks anyway, right? No big loss if a few of them snuffed it."

Donovan shot Loup a judgmental glare. "We can't leave bodies everywhere we go. That would only draw attention from the cops, and we don't need any of that."

"Would you have rather we let them swipe all of this priceless junk?" Loup extended his arms to indicate the contents of the room. "You came to us because you said we have a moral compass. Well, that moral compass told us to step in. That's what we do."

"Fine, you did the right thing. You're a good dog." Donovan's sarcasm gave way to authority as he shoved an accusing finger at Lou's muzzle. "But if something like this happens again, you're to show some restraint. Is that clear?"

Loup growled at the condescension, but he could see Donovan's point. "Sure," he answered flatly. "Restraint it is, *sir.*" The emphasis he put on the last word was full of contempt.

"Don't make me regret hiring you," Donovan said as he marched away from the scene.

By the time the late working professors arrived to investigate the commotion, what they found was the aftermath of something inexplicable. They were understandably stunned to discover the empty sarcophagus, the scattered bags of loot, the bodies of the burglars – some of whom still lived despite their injuries – and a trail of dry bandage scraps leading out the nearest exit. The tracks in the snow outside the door were equally puzzling, consisting of four trails: one made by a man's shoes, one made by a woman's high heels, one made by sandals, and one made by a canine's hind paws which suddenly became another set of men's shoes. The trail had vanished into a bare patch of street, and snow drifts had erased any other tracks that might have been left behind.

Naturally, the police were called to investigate, and the Egyptology exhibit was closed to the public for a few days. Try as they might, though, neither the police nor the staff could prevent the nosier patrons and reporters from peeking in at the crime scene. Thanks to this, the extraordinary accounts of the surviving burglars were leaked and spread like wildfire. Legends of the mummy's curse and strange monsters became the talk of the town.

Pete the night watchman kept mostly silent about the whole affair, as he had promised Donovan Van Sloan. When interrogated by the police, he said he was in a different part of the museum when the crime had happened, and this was indeed true; the night janitor could attest to seeing him in the Renaissance exhibit at the time.

The case would ultimately be filed as unsolved.

VIII.

As promised by Donovan, Ma'at had been provided with a white silk tunic similar to what she had worn in Ancient Egypt. By the time the group had reached the train, most of the tattered bandages in which she had been embalmed had fallen away and disintegrated, but a few small scraps still clung to random patches of her body. After nearly six thousand years, it was only natural that some of the bandages would have permanently grafted themselves to her skin.

She did not give much heed to this marring on her complexion, for she was too fascinated by the world she had woken up in. It was shocking to her how much architecture had changed from the styles she was familiar with. To the surprise of her modern companions, Ma'at was not overwhelmed or horrified by her new environment. When asked why, Ma'at explained that as a warrior, she often found herself in strange lands, and as an immortal, she had witnessed many changes during her long life, so necessity had taught her how to adapt quickly to her surroundings. Ergo, she always accepted her circumstances and made the best of them, whatever they might be.

As soon as they were on the train – which Ma'at found to be an impressive device – Donovan immediately took her to the dining car to explain the reason he had revived her. Ben had gone to the dining car as well, but only to grab a drink which he downed quickly before leaving. He had heard the story already, and did not need to hear it again.

He was heading back to the caboose, but the sounds of struggle drew him to Jackie's room, the door to which was wide open.

He stopped at the threshold and looked inside. Jackie had her right arm pinned to the wall. The entity had full control of it, as indicated by the onyx-hued skin. To Ben's eyes, the arm almost had the texture of snake scales. Jackie pounded on the entity's right arm with her left, driving her fist into the wrist over and over again until the entity dropped the knife she was clutching.

Jackie kicked the knife away just before the entity dove for it, pulling her to the floor as she did. Pounding her fist in anger, the entity released Jackie's hand and pushed her way into the head.

With control established, the entity twisted her head around like an owl to sneer at Ben. *"Pop's going to kill you,"* she snarled. *"Once this whole thing is done, he's going to pump you so full of silver that prospectors will fight for mining rights to your grave."* She cackled with maniacal glee. *"You'll be worth more dead than alive!"*

Jackie's hands – which the entity no longer had control of – reached up, grabbed the entity by the head, and wrenched it around as if breaking her neck. This move restored her control completely, but just to be sure, she lunged for her nightstand, grabbed a vial of holy water, and gulped it down. Immediately, Jackie coughed up oddly-colored blood onto the floor. As she pulled herself back onto her feet, the coughing ceased and she appeared to settle down.

This all happened so quickly that Ben and Loup did not even have time to decide if they should interfere or not.

Jackie took a few deep breaths to steady her nerves before speaking. "She's lying," she said as she wiped a trickle of blood from her chin. "She always lies. Pop's not going to kill you. He gave you his word on that."

Ben did not respond. He simply stood there with his hands in his pockets.

Jackie could see the hint of disbelief in his expression. "You don't believe me, do you?"

"We know that you Occult Mafiosos hunt our kind," Ben answered, "and we know for a fact that you've killed acquaintances of ours in the past. As for what we believe… Well, we believe your 'Pop' will only keep us alive for as long as us needs us. After that, who knows what excuse he'll come up with to justify snuffing us out?"

Jackie took a couple of steps toward Ben. "You wouldn't even be on this train if we meant to kill you. We don't just kill indiscriminately, you know. You're one of the good ones."

Ben crossed his arms, a hint of a scowl on his brow. "Nice backhanded compliment, kid. We both feel so much better knowing we're an exception to the rule."

"That's not…" Jackie began to protest, but found herself unable to say anything to the contrary. She was sure there must be a counter, but she could not for the life of her come up with anything, certainly not after fighting for control, which had left her so exhausted.

All she could muster was a rather pathetic reply of, "I'm sorry you feel that way," as she slowly closed the door.

I don't trust Van Sloan any more than you, Loup said, *but I don't think the kid deserved that.*

Ben felt a slight twinge of guilt pass through him. "Probably not," he sighed. Loup was right. Jackie was just a kid, after all, and one with a lot of baggage. She did not deserve to catch their ire or be saddled with their mistrust towards her father, even if Ben had meant every single word of it.

Neither Ben nor Loup had much time to ruminate on the exchange, for they caught the scents of Donovan and

Ma'at as they approached. Ma'at's scent was a golden hue tinged with rusty streaks, faded and more than a bit musty from centuries of being dead. Still, Ben and Loup found her aroma as pleasant as her appearance. Without her mask, Ma'at's face was quite beautiful. Her features were strong and sharp, though not quite fully aquiline. She was more handsome than cute or pretty, but still feminine, and they had no problem with that.

Donovan shot Ben a suspicious scowl. "And why, pray tell, are you lurking outside my daughter's room?"

Ben rolled his eyes. "Give it a rest, Don. She was having another one of her episodes, and we just wanted to make sure she was all right."

"That's all?"

"I get your overprotective father routine, I really do, but honestly, it's getting old. Loup and I aren't interested in little girls." Ben directed a flirtatious grin at Ma'at. "Truth be told, we prefer the company of older women."

His flirting was not lost on Ma'at, who returned his smile warmly.

The two became lost in each other's eyes.

"Oh, for Heaven's sake," Donovan grumbled. He raised his metal claw and slammed the pinchers together so hard that it sounded like a gunshot, making both Ben and Ma'at jump in surprise. "So help me God," Donovan said sternly to them, "if you two can't stay focused on our mission, not only will I throw you both off this train, I'll do it while we're crossing a bridge. Am I clear?"

"Crystal," Ben said, not appreciative of Donovan's attitude. "So I take it that means the lady is joining your cause?"

"Of course," Ma'at nodded. "I do not know this warlock you hunt, but I exist to serve Justice, and that alone makes him my enemy."

"Even if we aren't in Egypt anymore?"

"Empires fall and pharaohs betray their people, but Justice is eternal. Whatever I can do to bring Justice to this epoch shall be done without hesitation."

"Didn't take much to convince her, really," Donovan said. "But enough chitchat. Who are we getting next, Ben?"

"I'd recommend the icthoid next," answered Ben. "According to your notes, he was last seen in the vicinity of Flathead Lake in Montana. Since you say he's aquatic, and Flathead is the only lake around for miles, I'm guessing he's still there, if he's still alive. Plus, I'm itching to find out what exactly an ichthoid is."

Donovan shook his head. "You may wish you hadn't when you finally meet him."

During the trip to Montana, Ben once again spent his time studying Donovan's notes on the ichthoid, who apparently had a proper if unusual name: Erasmus Webster. Ben also convinced Ma'at to spend time going over the notes with him, partly so she would know who they were up against, but mostly to spend more time with her. She had no objections to either reason.

According to the notes, ichthoids were amphibious creatures, humanoid in build though salamander-like in complexion. They were taller and stronger than the average human, of equal intelligence, and naturally aggressive towards every other species. Their origins were completely unknown. Fossils of them dating back to the age of dinosaurs were known to exist, but no lineage could be traced to any known species. As far as the fossil record showed, they simply appeared at some point, flourished for a few millennia, and then their numbers suddenly dwindled. Only a few hundred still lived in the modern day, mostly in isolated parts of the world where water was abundant. Erasmus specifically hailed from a marsh somewhere in the southern

Appalachian Mountain Range, on the border between Tennessee and Alabama. For some reason, there were no further details given on the region than that.

There were three popular theories as to the origins of the ichthoids. The first suggested that they were an attempt by amphibians to evolve into humanoid beings, though given the gradual nature of evolution, this did not explain their sudden appearance in the fossil record. The second was something called the Aquatic Ape Theory, which said that an offshoot of the primate family adapted to live in the ocean. This was especially popular among those who believed in mermaids. According to Donovan's notes, however, studies of ichthoid specimens did not reveal any relation to primates, or mammals of any kind (besides which, ichthoids bore no resemblance at all to real merbeings). Lastly was the theory that ichthoids might be an extraterrestrial race, either sent as colonizers or perhaps abandoned by another species due to their volatile nature. Yet accounts of ichthoids in myth and legend never overlapped with accounts of star beings, and no alien landings or crashes from prehistory could be linked to them. The ichthoids themselves provided no answers, for it was simply not in their nature to care about their origins.

Erasmus Webster, along with four others of his species, had been captured by the United States government in late 1942. They had been taken to a research facility in Montana for the purpose of experimentation. Apparently, this was part of a program to make enhanced soldiers to fight during World War II. Many names had been redacted from the files which Donovan had acquired, but apparently the ichthoids were predominantly considered guinea pigs. Any debates on whether or not they would be deployed in the field had never been resolved. Of the ichoids experimented on, only Erasmus survived. He had been given several enhancements of a mechanical nature: a pair of wrist gauntlets containing retractable blades, and a set of goggles wired to his eyes that enhanced his vision. He was meant to receive more such enhancements before he escaped.

Erasmus had apparently broken out of the facility in a bloody battle. A side note from Donovan read, "Not surprising. They abduct and torture him, weaponize him, then expected him not to fight back? For being that stupid, they deserved what they got." After fleeing the base, sightings of him had been reported as he made his way toward Flathead Lake. He had survived crossing the desert thanks to a large thermos he had stolen as he fled, and by stealing water from gas stations and bus stops along the way. Without these, he would have dehydrated long before reaching water, for ichthoids needed to stay hydrated. A few sightings of him at Flathead Lake – where he was dubbed as the Flathead Frogman by newspapers –occurred right up to August of 1955, when they suddenly died out. No sightings had been reported since.

There was no evidence that Erasmus was still in Flathead Lake, but there was also no evidence that he had left, either. As such, Ben and Loup thought that at the very worst, Flathead Lake was the beginning of a search that could lead them elsewhere, and at best, Erasmus Webster would still be there waiting for them.

XI.

The train arrived in Frenchtown, which was the closest town to Flathead Lake, being several miles away.

Jackie knocked on Ma'at's door, only to find it slowly sway open at her touch. Inside, she saw Ma'at kneeling beside her bed in prayer, hands clasped and body prostrate on the floor. So focused was she on her praying that she did not notice the door open. Jackie remained silent so as not to interrupt.

As Jackie watched Ma'at, it became clear that something wasn't right. The Egyptian's expression was not one of tranquility, but rather of confusion and concern. Her lips were moving as she whispered her prayer. Jackie leaned further in, listening intently and doing her best to read Ma'at's lips. As she listened, Ma'at's words became clear.

"Where are you? Great Amun Ra, why do you not answer me?"

Jackie cleared her throat, breaking Ma'at's concentration.

"Oh, is it time to disembark?" Ma'at asked as she stood, attempting to play things casually.

"Yeah," Jackie nodded. "Noticed you were praying just now. Everything okay?"

"Yes, yes, there is nothing wrong," Ma'at answered dismissively. She went to the nightstand to gather her weapons and mask.

Jackie noticed modern clothes piled on the floor as though they had been discarded in frustration. "Isn't that the outfit I brought you yesterday?"

"It is," Ma'at replied, "and forgive me, but I refuse to wear it. Those garments are far too heavy and restrictive for my taste." She ran a hand down her tunic. "I much prefer the attire of my people. Tell me, why have mortals abandoned comfortable garments?"

"Search me," Jackie shrugged. "Thing is, though, we need to keep a low profile, and nobody outside of a movie set dresses the way you do anymore." She looked at Ma'at's sandals. "Besides that, it's winter, and you don't want to be trudging through the snow in shoes like that. Frostbite's a real killer. You should at least wear the boots."

"I shall compromise on the footwear, but not the clothes." Ma'at gave her kopesh a few experimental swings, as any good swordsman would do, before sheathing it. "I must be able to move unrestricted should we encounter trouble."

Jackie nodded in resignation. "All right," she said, only for the entity to force her way to surface and add, *"Stubborn ass!"* Jackie clapped her hands over her mouth until the entity receded once more. "S-sorry!" she stammered. "That wasn't me!"

"I understand," Ma'at replied. "And for the sake of maintaining your low profile, I shall don a shroud as your father and Ben wear."

"Shroud?" Jackie asked, and then she understood. "Oh, you mean a trench coat! Yeah, we can get you one of those." She started to leave, but paused when something else occurred to her. "We also need an alias for you. 'Ma'at' ain't exactly a common name these days."

"Nor was it in my day." Ma'at hefted her snake-headed scepter in her hands, checking the balance out of habit. "What name do you suggest?"

Jackie thought for a moment. "How about…Rachel Matthews?"

"What inspires this name?"

"Well, your real name kinda sounds like 'Matt', which is short for Matthew, but that's a boy's name, so adding the S makes it a surname. And I got Rachel from Ra the Sun God, so it's sort of a play on words, I guess."

Ma'at's eyes narrowed as she stared as the girl. "I find that somewhat sacrilegious, child," she said, "but as I have no alternatives to offer, I shall accept it for the time being." She hung her scepter on her belt. "Shall we, then?"

Frenchtown was not especially large for a city, either in terms of acreage or the height of its buildings. The combination of Montana's dry climate and the unusually cold weather that year resulted in the snow being very fine and powdery, not to mention thin, which made traversing the streets easier than it had been in Boston. To Ben, the cold here was even harsher than in Chicago. The air itself felt as though it were comprised of a million needles driving their frigid points into his exposed face.

Being a detective, Ben did all of the talking as the group sought information about the Flathead Frogman. At first, the search was slow going. People only repeated stories they had read in the papers, or wild encounters heard from the friend of a friend. It was only after they had been asking around for an hour that they finally got a proper lead, which sent them to the Flathead Lake Museum at the southern end of town.

The Flathead Lake Museum was something that could only be described as kitschy, clearly a place designed for tourists. Naturally, business was slower in the winter than in the summer, which meant the museum was devoid of patrons that evening. The only other people there were the kindly old man who acted as curator and his eldest son who was being primed to take over for him one day, although he was in the storage area when the quartet entered.

The old curator, who stood at the information desk, gave the newcomers a friendly hello as they entered. He quickly became wary as he watched Donovan and Jackie lock the door, close the blinds, and switch the hanging door sign from "Open" to "Closed".

"Greetings, my good man," Ben said in a friendly tone as he approached the desk. "Are you in charge here?"

The curator nodded, still wary of the suspicious behavior on display.

"Then you're just the man I want to see," Ben continued. "I'd like to inquire about the Flathead Frogman, if you'd be so kind. And none of the folklore you tell the tourists, either; I want the truth, the real skinny on the monster."

"It... It's all folklore," the curator said as he took a step away from Ben. "Folklore and sightings, n-nothing more. It, uh, brings in tourists, but that's it, really. Most rational people know monsters don't exist."

"Never kid a kidder, old man." Ben raised his right hand in front of the curator's face, and it transformed before his eyes, becoming hairy and tipped with claws. "As you can see, I know a thing or two about monsters, and as the curator of this fine establishment, I'm guessing you do too."

The curator was stunned by the transformation. He wanted to run, but the other strangers had him surrounded. Moreover, Ben had him dead to rights. He did know more than he had initially let on, but he was not ready to volunteer anything just yet. "W-why so interested?" he asked, doing his best to sound firm even as his voice stammered and his knees trembled behind the desk.

Loup withdrew from the right hand as Ben continued. "We have our reasons, and a kindly old gent such as yourself is better off not knowing them. We certainly don't mean the Frogman any harm, if that's what you're worried about. We just need to know a few things before heading down to the lake, starting with whether or not he's even still there." He paused, waiting for a response, then prompted, "Well? Is he?"

The curator nodded slowly. "He is. Most of us just don't bother talking about him anymore. He's been here so long he's accepted as part of the lake. He likes to be left alone, and we respect that...even if we do encourage the tourists to go looking for him."

"Looks like we were right to come here after all," Donovan mused.

"Yeah, looks like it," Ben answered. He then asked the curator, "If *we* were to go looking for him, how would we draw him out? Any advice?"

"You'll have a deuce of a time trying," the curator answered. "This winter's been so cold that Flathead is frozen over, though that won't stop the other monsters."

Ben blinked. "*Other* monsters?"

"Other monsters," the curator nodded. "Monsters that were here long before the Frogman showed up. Long serpentine things with antlers and the most ravenous appetites outside of our annual hotdog eating contest. They always hunt, no matter the weather. They'll break right through the ice if they sense prey above it. Sometimes the Frogman stops them, but not always." He shrugged, still feeling on edge in his current predicament. "That might be your best bet. Draw out one of the serpents, and he may not be far behind. You just have to hope you don't get eaten first."

"Thanks for the warning," Ben said, though he and Loup were both less than enthused to learn that other monsters were apparently waiting for them. "Well, keep up the good work," he said as he gave the old man a slightly-too-strong pat on the shoulder.

Before they left, Jackie purchased a commemorative mug from the gift shop as a show of good faith to the curator. Unfortunately, an attempt by the entity to wrest the money back from him only served to further unnerve him, but she was restrained by Donovan and Ma'at before anything serious could happen.

Right as the quartet left, the curator's son returned from storage. "All right, everything's in order back there," he said, blissfully unaware that anything had happened. He then noticed the drawn blinds and sign. "It's a bit early to be closing up, isn't it?"

His father had no response.

"Your notes didn't say anything about lake monsters, Donovan," Ben said as they departed the museum.

"Yes they did," Ma'at corrected. "Was there not an account of the creature we seek doing battle with such a serpentine denizen of the lake?"

Ben pinched the bridge of his nose as if fighting a headache. "I don't know. Maybe. We've flipped through that binder so many times, everything's starting to blend together. Even if it was in there, how are we supposed to deal with ravenous lake monsters?"

"You heard the old timer," Donovan said. "Erasmus will show up to handle them."

"And if he doesn't show up?"

"Relax," Jackie said, unconcerned. "They're usually more lethargic in the winter, and they only get about twenty feet long on average, give or take."

"That doesn't help at all," Ben replied.

Thanks to him offering a large sum of money to the line, Donovan successfully chartered a bus to and from Flathead Lake, no questions asked. Since it was after hours, a driver had to be called in, and his initial grouchiness about the affair subsided when Donovan handed him a large wad of cash. Thanks to that, he was more than happy to drive them wherever they wanted to go.

The group arrived at the lake on the stroke of midnight. The moon was full and bright, and appeared unnaturally large and ominous in the sky, its ashen face as cold and lifeless as the dusting of snow which covered the landscape. Flathead Lake's frozen surface was illuminated by the pale moonlight, but did not reflect it.

Donovan, Jacqueline, Ben, and Ma'at were the only living souls on the shore that night. As they approached the lake, Ben trailed a short distance behind the others. When Ma'at noticed this, she slowed her own pace until they were side by side. "You seem uneasy, Ben," she said. "Is something the matter?"

Ben very nearly responded by saying he was fine, yet he could not bring himself to do so. Lying to Ma'at just felt wrong to him. As such, he chose to tell the truth, but he lowered his voice so the Van Sloans would not hear him. "To be honest," he said, "we're not exactly good around water."

"May I ask why?" Ma'at asked, truly confused. "Where there is water, there is life. Sobek's element is nothing to be afraid of."

Ben nodded. Of course Ma'at would have that perspective. What little he knew about Ancient Egypt told him that the Egyptians held water in high regard, seeing as how their empire had been built along the only major river in an expansive desert. He had no idea what a Sobek was, though. "We don't *hate* water, so long as it's in a glass or a shower. Big bodies of it are what get us. We almost drowned as kids, so… I'd rather not talk about that, actually."

"Very well," Ma'at nodded in understanding. "Then to take your mind away from your fear, explain to me about what you are. I still cannot quite understand the nature of your abilities."

Ben had no qualms with changing the subject. "It's kind of like what you've got going as a goddess, though not exactly. Wolves like Loup are divine beings sent from Heaven who fight the forces of Hell. The problem is that these wolves can't manifest on Earth naturally. They need an anchor, a host they can project themselves into. Only certain people have the ability to be anchors, and I'm one of them." Ben lifted his right hand, and Loup Garou took control in a partial transformation. "It's a symbiotic relationship. The wolf can walk the earth and fulfill its purpose, and the host lives longer than your average person. Loup and I work together, two parts of the same whole, doing what we can in our little corner of the world. We got into the private eye business because law enforcement wasn't for us. Too much red tape." His eyes became distant as he remembered a particular instance that convinced them to quit, but he chose not to delve into it. "So werewolves are naturally good. Unfortunately, since they have free will, some of them turn once they're in the world, and those are the ones who get all of the attention and give the rest of us a bad name. Back before people stopped believing we existed, werewolves were hunted all over Europe, all thanks to the actions of a violent few." He motioned to the Van Sloans. "Their people still hunt our people when it suits them."

"Betrayal from those whom you protect. I can understand the pain that brings." Ma'at wrapped her hand around Loup's. Her bandage-infused fingers gently interlaced with his claws as her dark eyes gazed into Ben's. "For me, that treachery is fresh, as though it happened only yesterday. I can sense that neither of you trust Donovan and Jacqueline, but you have a kindred spirit in me."

A sudden sharp breeze cut through the duo, drawing their attention back to the reason they were in Montana: Flathead Lake. The Van Sloans, shoes already fitted with metal cleats, had not hesitated walking out onto the lake's frozen surface, each one carrying large, heavy-looking duffle bags. They were already about ten feet from shore when Donovan stopped – prompting Jackie to also pause by his side – and turned back to Ben and Ma'at, who were lingering behind. "Are you two coming or not?" he called. His impatience was evident.

"You sure that's safe to walk on?" Ben called back, just barely masking his nerves.

Donovan stamped his foot twice, then raised his metal claw and drove a downward punch into the ice with all of his might. Though a few ice chips were scattered by the impact, and a narrow crack was formed, the frozen surface did not yield to the frigid waters underneath.

"It's fine!" Donovan shouted. "Now get your carcasses out here!"

Guess that means I'm on the clock, Loup said, his nerves as evident as his host's.

Ben rescinded all control to Loup, whose grip on Ma'at's hand tightened as they stepped onto the ice. Both man and wolf tried their best to push all memories of their childhood trauma to the back of their minds. Unfortunately, it is a known fact that actively trying not to think about something only causes one to think about it even more, so the effort only made things worse for them. Loup Garou's breathing became heavy, and his vicelike grip on Ma'at's hand tightened so much that, had he not been fighting the urge to panic, he might have worried that he would break her bones.

Ma'at winced a little as the wolf's claws dug into her skin, but she did not pull away. Loup and Ben were scared, and she was the only one they trusted. She was used to being brave so as to inspire bravery in others, so she remained firm for both of them.

Her boot-clad foot caught on an uneven patch of ice, causing her to stumble and slip. Her free hand struck the jagged crack left behind by Donovan's claw.

She nearly pulled Loup down with her, but he dug the claws of his feet into the ice and remained upright, stooping over only to help her back up. "You okay?" he asked in concern.

Ma'at nodded as she wiped the snow from her hand onto her coat. "I am fine. Ice is not something I have much experience with, but I shall adapt."

As some passing clouds obscured the moon, neither of them immediately noticed that Ma'at had cut her hand when she fell, nor did they notice that the blood and embalming fluid left behind was seeping through the cracked ice and into the water.

Even in frigid depths, there was a scent which any denizen of the lake could recognize: fresh blood.

A being capable of rational thought and reasoning would have been somewhat confused by this blood, for it was not entirely pure, but mixed with something foul and unnatural.

The Flathead Lake Monsters were neither rational nor reasoning creatures.

One such Monster had been hibernating in a shallow cave at the edge of the shore. It had been awoken by a sudden loud impact above the ice, and as soon as it was awake, it felt hungry. Perhaps this was merely a Pavlovian response, associating the act of waking up with the desire to eat, but the Monster did not understand or care about such concepts. It only knew that it was hungry. As it stirred, however, it could sense that it was alone, for everything else in the lake was still asleep.

Then it smelled the blood. It was strange blood, but the Monster did not care. Blood meant food.

It listened, and determined that whatever was bleeding was above the ice, heading away from the shore. It did not care why. This was not the first time the Monster had woken up in the dead of winter to hunt prey above the surface, so it knew that the ice became somewhat thinner – and easier to break through – towards the center of the lake…which was the direction the prey was heading.

Motivated by hunger and filled with adrenaline, the Monster swam in pursuit. The burning cold of the frigid water stung its slippery hide, but this did not deter it from the hunt. The creature was endothermic. It would warm itself as it moved.

The Monster was so focused on the hunt that it did not notice another creature had stirred in the depths, and was pursuing it from a distance.

Donovan raised his left hand, signaling for the group to halt. They were about eighty feet from the shore, and the ice was still thick enough to support them, though it did not require a werewolf's sharp ears to hear tiny cracks forming as the ice strained under their combined weight.

"First things first, we spread out," Donovan ordered as though he were commanding a military operation. "Form a square, ten foot equilateral distance. That'll distribute our weight better and keep us all from becoming popsicles."

The others quickly did as they were told, forming a square. The cracking did lessen, but only slightly, and not enough to put Ben and Loup at ease.

Donovan knelt down to unzip his duffle bag, and withdrew from it the pieces of a large drill, an old-fashioned kind operated by a hand crank. "I need you for this part," he called to Loup as he slid the pieces across the ice to him. "Put that together, then come to the middle of the square and drill until you hit water."

Loup, attempting to mask the quiver in his voice, asked, "Why me?"

"Cause you're the only one of us strong enough to drill through the ice by hand, that's why."

Loup grumbled, but knew better than to argue. If this was a necessary step towards getting revenge, then so be it. He began assembling the drill.

"When the hole is made, then what?" asked Ma'at.

"Then we go fishing," answered Jackie. She opened her duffle bag, and carefully removed a device Ma'at did not recognize. Jackie rested it on the ice as she explained. "This is a little acoustic device our guys whipped up in the Lab. The research says ichthoids respond to sound, so this should be able to lure him to us. It's got enough battery life to last about an hour."

"I do not really understand," Ma'at replied, "but if you say it is so, I shall believe it. What, then, is my role in this?"

"Safety," Donovan replied. "Erasmus probably won't take kindly to us being here, and we got those other Monsters to deal with…"

"Again with those other Monsters," Loup snapped nervously.

"…so if something goes wrong, you help us set it right. Got it?"

Ma'at nodded. She withdrew her bejeweled kopesh from beneath her coat. The blade was grayish-black, having been forged from a meteorite, and it was razor sharp. This kopesh was a favorite weapon of hers, even though it was only good for close-quarters combat.

Loup finished piecing the drill together, gave it a few experimental cranks to make sure it worked, and stepped carefully towards the center of the square, his claws digging into the ice for stability.

He was just about ready to begin drilling when the ice beneath him shook, causing everyone to lose their footing and tumble.

The ice shook again. This time, a portion of it heaved upward slightly between where Ma'at and Loup had fallen.

"Get away from it!" Donovan shouted. "Get out of there now!"

Loup Garou's clawed hands and feet made it easy for him to scramble away on all fours. Ma'at, unfortunately, struggled to get her footing. It was another impact from below that propelled her away, as an irregular chunk of ice rose up to catapult her.

With one final thrust, the ice patch totally gave way, and the Monster emerged.

The Monsters residing in Flathead Lake were not the plesiosaur-type creatures found in other lakes, but were more akin to lungfish, only much larger, with hundreds of needlelike teeth lining their gaping mouths. This particular Monster which erupted from the ice was an impressive specimen at twenty feet long, all of which became visible as it pulled itself out of the water with spine-tipped flippers.

Ma'at finally got back on her feet, her kopesh at the ready. She would have to rely on it, for the frigid Montana weather was too cold to summon snakes, and any dust she might have been able to conjure was covered by snow, thus cutting off her access to it. Even with these disadvantages, she stood firm. She had faced nightmarish opponents with only her blade before, and if things got worse, she had other powers to tap into.

The Monster pulled itself towards her, its slathering jaws snapping hungrily. It was not concerned that its prey was not running. That would just make her easier to catch.

Loup Garou's fear gave way to courage as he leapt onto the Monster's back. Quickly, he whipped his chains forward, allowing the hooks to catch the Monster's upper lip. He pulled with all of his might, causing his serpentine mount to rear up, exposing the pale flesh of its underbelly to Ma'at.

A thin smile formed on the warrior's lips as her confidence grew. Her experience told her that all predators had soft underbellies, a shared weakness to be exploited when the opportunity arose.

With a guttural war cry, she launched herself into the air, kopesh raised to pierce the Monster's flesh and slice its throat open.

Whether the Monster could sense this incoming attack or simply wanted to shake the wolf from its back, nobody knew, but it dodged Ma'at's assault by rolling onto its side. Loup was thrown off, and Ma'at's momentum carried her past the beast's head. She attempted to tuck into a roll, but her landing was hard and rough. She did not have the chance to regain her footing this time, as the Monster's flailing tail smacked her aside as it rolled back onto its stomach.

Having righted itself, the Monster attempted to locate its prey again, only to feel a powerful sting on its thick hide. Turning, it saw Donovan staring it down with a smoking colt .45 in his left hand. He fired again, but the bullets only angered the beast, who picked the human as its new target.

Jackie, who had gotten a safe distance away, saw the Monster lurching towards her father and knew she had to do something. She only took a few running steps towards him before the entity took control of her legs and deliberately rolled her ankle. This made Jackie pitch forward and land hard on her front, knocking the wind from her lungs. Jackie fought to regain control, but the entity refused to let go. She pulled herself forward by her hands, even though she knew she would not reach her father in time.

Donovan dug in his heels and stood his ground as the Monster lunged for him. Just before it could close its mouth around him and satiate its appetite, a massive chunk of ice struck the side of its head, stunning it.

That is what signaled the arrival of the ichthoid named Erasmus Webster.

Erasmus was a quite strange sight to behold as he emerged from the water. He was nearly seven feet tall, and though muscular, the hydrodynamic structure of his sapient body made him appear slender. For all intents and purposes, he appeared to be a bipedal salamander, but with the proportions of a man. His skin was smooth and slick, glossy black broken up by large yellow patches. Four unsettlingly long, claw-tipped digits connected by translucent membranes extended from his hands and feet. His head was a true blend of amphibian and anthropoid, as if the snout of a salamander had been fused to the cranium of a human. A short but thick tail hung behind him.

Yet he was not entirely organic. Upon each of Erasmus' wrists were large gunmetal gauntlets, with what appeared to be raised barrels on the upper portions. Over his eyes sat a visor similar to scuba diving goggles. The lens was tinted, but a pair of bright yellow, menacing eyes glowed behind it.

The Monster rarely committed anything to memory, but it knew Erasmus Webster. He had appeared in Flathead Lake some time ago, and had made a habit of killing its kind whenever he crossed paths with them. Many of the serpentine giants had fallen to his blades.

Of course, they did not know Erasmus Webster by his name. They only knew he was the enemy.

With a ferocious bellowing roar, the Monster charged towards Erasmus. This charge was very awkward, since the thing was not as graceful above water as below, but it was still moving with enough speed and power to be dangerous.

Erasmus clenched his fists, and in response, a pair of long, bright silver blades shot from the barrels of his gauntlets. His whole body tensed at the act, and he grunted in pain, but this passed quickly as he too charged. Unlike the Monsters, ichthoids were just as capable on land as they were underwater.

The Monster snapped its needlelike teeth at Erasmus, but it was not fast enough. The ichthoid leapt into the air and landed on his enemy's head. He moved swiftly, for he knew exactly where to strike. He drove his blades into the nape of the Monster's neck. It was a spot few people could discern, since the Monster's tubular form did not vary until the tapered end of its tail, but Erasmus had years of experience informing him.

He did not simply stab the Monster once. He drove his blades into the spot over and over, destroying the connection between skull and spine. Erasmus moved with the efficiency and speed of a cold, heartless machine as he hacked the Monster's neck to shreds. It did not decapitate the thing, but the damage was still fatal.

The Monster went limp, its breathing strained. Erasmus then drove his blades into the Monster's skull, piercing its brain and finally killing it.

With his foe disposed of, Erasmus slid back onto the ice, where Donovan Van Sloan was waiting for him.

Donovan said, "Thanks," before delivering a powerful right hook to the ichthoid's temple. Donovan was already fairly strong for a regular human, and the added weight and density of his new metal appendage rendered Erasmus unconscious. Erasmus Webster collapsed instantly.

"All right," Donovan called to Loup Garou and Ma'at as he turned away, "take him to the bus!"

When they did not immediately respond to his command, he turned to see them staring at him, expressions of shock and disapproval on their faces. "Something wrong?" he asked impatiently.

"What's wrong with you?" Loup snapped as he and Ma'at approached Donovan. "He just saved us, and you punched his lights out!"

Donovan was not moved, and his response was cold. "I thanked him first. Now load him up."

"This is not right," said Ma'at in a somber voice. "Does he not deserve the same freedom to choose as you offered us?"

Donovan shook his head. "If I gave him a choice, he'd say no. Erasmus hates humans."

"Well, pardon me." Loup replied with intense sarcasm. "I'm sure he'll change his tune after being decked and shanghaied. That always wins people over."

Donovan walked straight up to Loup and glared into his eyes. His voice was sharp when he spoke. "Do you want revenge or not? The only way we'll get our shot at Bismuth is if we have everyone on the list with us, no exceptions. If you have a problem with how I'm handling things, walk away right now, find your own way back to Chicago, and spend whatever time you got left wishing you weren't so determined to keep your paws clean. How's that for a choice?"

Loup snarled, because he had no response. Ben could provide nothing, either. The desire for revenge as just too strong within both of them.

"Fine," he growled as he stooped to lift the ichtoid. He slung one sinewy arm over his shoulder and lifted Erasmus up as though he were a staggering drunkard.

The amphibian was every bit as heavy as he looked, and even with his monstrous strength, Loup was straining to support him. He looked over to Ma'at. "Would you mind getting the other side, please?"

Ma'at's expression was stern and disapproving. "I would mind, and I could not help you even if I didn't. I serve Justice, and I cannot do that which is unjust."

"What's the greater injustice, Ma'at?" asked Donovan. "That we inconvenience one amphibian who's not even supposed to be here, or that Phillipe Bismuth is allowed to keep doing as he pleases while my daughter suffers?"

Ma'at could see Jackie approaching them, having regained control of her legs. She was currently struggling to force the entity from her arms as she collected the duffle bags.

"Scorpions of Set," Ma'at cursed as she relented, undone by Donovan's logic and her own sympathy. She propped herself beneath the ichthoid and aided Loup in carrying him. It was not easy for her, since this morally gray area was still an injustice of its own, but she had enough strength to perform the deed.

As the two conscious monsters dragged the unconscious one away, Jackie – now back in complete control – paused beside her father. "You knocked him out so he wouldn't have a choice?"

"Yup," answered Donovan.

Jackie nodded her approval. "Good. Three down, one to go."

Before following, Donovan slammed his metal claw into the ice beside the Monster, causing cracks which spread across the already weakened surface. As they left, the ice gave way and allowed the carcass to sink to the bottom of the lake, leaving no trace of it behind.

X.

Erasmus awoke on a moving bus, facing the human who had knocked him out. He attempted to rise and return the favor, but found himself bound by heavy chains. As he struggled, he felt something very sharp begin digging into his neck.

"I wouldn't do that if I were you," Donovan said. The layout of the bus allowed him to sit facing Erasmus. "You could probably break those chains if you wanted to, but the way we got them rigged, too much tension will activate the trigger in your collar, which'll send a nice sharp blade to divorce your head from your shoulders. My advice is to relax."

Erasmus stopped struggling, and the pain subsided. "So you caught me," he snarled. His voice was not what anyone on the bus expected it to be. Though it was low and gruff, it sounded fairly human, and carried a hint of a southern drawl to it. "You with the old project, or is Uncle Sam up to something new?"

"We're not with the government, Mr. Webster," Donovan replied. "My name is Donovan Van Sloan, and I'm on the council for the Occult Mafia."

The ichthoid's eyes narrowed in disgust behind his goggles. "So you fellas haven't been wiped out yet. Ain't that a shame?"

The vitriol did not deter Donovan. "I'll just cut right to the chase, Mr. Webster. I need your help against a powerful enemy of mine." He pointed toward Ben and Ma'at, who sat towards the back of the bus. A few seats ahead of them was Jackie, who was once again struggling to keep the entity from interfering. Erasmus could turn his head just far enough to see them. "It's a task that requires me to make unconventional alliances. I already have a werewolf and a mummy, now I have you, and there's one more to track down. Once we're all together, we go after the warlock Phillipe Bismuth, and take him down once and for all."

Erasmus' expression darkened ever-so-slightly when he heard Bismuth's name. Despite this, he averted his eyes towards the window. "I ain't interested."

"Oh, ain't you?" Donovan replied, not believing him. "I know you've got some history with his cult. As I recall, he set up a church on the shores of Flathead Lake a few years back, and you single-handedly destroyed it and ran them out of town."

"They were dumping their refuse into my new home. I stopped them. Simple as that. I'd have done the same to any of you rotten apes."

"And what about the young girl they were going to sacrifice? She says you saved her. Why not just kill her along with the other rotten apes?"

Erasmus did not reply.

"That's right, Erasmus Webster, I've got your number." Donovan leaned against the window, confident that this was going well. "You're not the ravenous beast you want to be seen as. Deep down, you've got a soft spot for humans."

Erasmus hissed, which was how he scoffed. "Any soft spots I may've had were cut into by your kind." He moved his arms as much as he dared to, drawing attention to the gauntlets bolted to his wrists. "These bracelets ain't natural y'know, and neither is what they did to my eyes. You can't possibly imagine how much pain I went through. You can't know how much it still hurts every time I use these blasted things."

"I beg to differ." Donovan raised his right arm, showing the metal claw attached to it. The pinchers twitched slightly, then clanked together twice. "Just had this done, and it's still tender. Not so different from your tech, in fact. The way I see it, we've got more in common than you'd ever care to admit."

Erasmus growled deeply in frustration. Donovan was doing far too good of a job at calmly countering him.

"Listen, Erasmus, this whole thing is a temporary arrangement," Donovan said as he rested his right arm and sat back up. "I don't know which parts of our reputation you're familiar with, but we're not maniacs. We fight evil in whatever form it takes, and you're not currently on our hit list. You kept to yourself all these years, and other than your escape from the lab – which, if I'm being candid, I don't blame you for – you've actually been a help to people. So here's my proposal: you help me kill Bismuth, and you'll be free to scamper off to the nearest koi pond when it's all over."

The skeptical grimace on the ichthoid's face made it clear that he was not convinced. "And I suppose gullible is also written on the ceiling."

"You have my word, Mr. Webster. Join us this once, and you'll be free to live out your days in peace. Listen, what happened to you was horrible, I won't try to convince you otherwise, but what's done is done. You now have the chance to do something more with your life, something far more significant than wasting away in Montana killing oversized mudskippers. Bismuth's the head of a cult that's spreading all over North America, and they aren't singing 'Kumbaya' 'round the campfire. They aim to bring the forces of Hell itself to Earth, and that's just as much your problem as it is mine. So are you just going to stew and wait for that to happen, or are you going to take my offer and be part of the solution?"

Erasmus and Donovan stared at each other in a silent battle of wills, each one waiting for the other to relent first.

It was Erasmus who yielded.

"I have your word that you'll leave me alone when we're done?" he asked.

Donovan nodded. "If we survive, yes. We might even discourage people from going wherever you choose to settle."

"Then we have us an arrangement."

As he spoke, the bus slowed to a halt in front of the train station.

Donovan smiled. "What timing. Now you can't run back anyway. You'd dehydrate before you got halfway to the lake." He opened a panel on his claw, drew a key from it, and undid the collar around the ichthoid's neck. "Please, after you."

As the travelers disembarked from the bus, Ben noticed that Ma'at was staring at the ceiling as she walked to the door. "What's up?" he asked.

"The lizard said that there was writing on the ceiling," Ma'at replied, "but I see no words engraved above us."

Ben could not help but chuckle. "I guess even that joke isn't as old as you. I'll explain it to you once we're back on the train."

The bus driver watched as his charges vanished into the train station. He had a million questions to ask them, even though part of his agreement with them was to mind his own business. He was certain nobody would believe him if he told them about this anyway.

All the driver knew was that this was the strangest night he had ever had in his life.

XI.

As the train departed from Frenchtown, the nearly-completed team went to their separate compartments. They were all exhausted from the ordeal at Flathead Lake, and since it was nearly morning, they all needed sleep. Before turning in, Donovan instructed the conductor to head for Helena, where the Occult Mafia had an outpost. There they would restock the essentials.

The following evening, Ben knocked on Erasmus' door. He and Loup were surprised when they heard the click of the lock followed by the ichthoid inviting him to enter. They had almost expected him to jump ship at some point during the day when everyone was asleep. Then again, they were passing through an area that was mostly desert, and if Erasmus needed water to survive, he did not really have anywhere to go if he made a break for it now.

Erasmus' room was different from Ben's. It did not have a dresser, which was just as well, since Erasmus did not wear clothes. In place of a bed, there was a large tub filled with water, and it was into the tub that Erasmus slid. Judging by the freshness of the paint on the walls, Ben surmised that the tub was a recent addition. It was long and had high sides, so Erasmus could completely submerge himself if he so desired. The rest of the room was empty, save for a solitary chair and a few towels laid out on the floor, already damp from catching the ichthoid's drippings.

Ben and Loup snorted slightly at the smell of the place. Erasmus naturally smelled marshy, and his odor was a putrid swirling mix of brown and orange which was not pleasant.

"So what brings you here?" Erasmus asked.

Ben shrugged. "We just wanted to get a better idea of who you are, seeing as how we'll be working together."

"We?" Erasmus asked. As he did, he noticed Loup Garou reflected in the mirror which hung on the wall beside Ben. "Oh, that's right, you're a werewolf. I suppose that makes us kin after a fashion. So what is it you want to know?"

"Donovan said you're not as surly as you want people to think," Loup said. "I don't know how good he is at judging character, but based on what we've seen, it looks as if he's right. You saved us from that jumbo-sized eel back at the lake – thanks, by the way – and there's that girl you rescued from Bismuth's cult. There had to be a reason you let her go."

Erasmus drummed his long webbed fingers on the edge of the tub. "Maybe I just don't like those eels, and maybe the girl just got away from me."

Ben smirked knowingly. "Yeah, and maybe people only phrase things like that when they want to avoid giving an honest answer. We've been in the private eye business long enough to recognize all the signs, even on a face like yours." He leaned against the mirror, a move reflected by Loup, making it look as though the two were propping each other up. "You can tell us the truth or not, but Donovan's not the only one whose got your number."

"And what about you two?" Erasmus replied. "Why are you on this train? You trust those humans?"

"Not as far as either of us can spit," Ben answered.

"So again, why are you here?"

"Good old fashioned revenge," Loup answered in a grim voice. "We have a score to settle with Bismuth, and Donovan gave us a chance to do it."

"Once that's done, though," Ben continued, "we wouldn't put it past Donovan to make some excuse for killing us."

"And if not him," Loup finished, "maybe his kid, or somebody else in the Mafia. It's what they do, after all. Until then, though, Don needs us alive for his crazy scheme."

Erasmus nodded as he considered this information. "You two have a plan to get away if that happens?"

Loup shrugged. "We were just going to bolt at the first sign of trouble."

"Come to think of it," Ben said with a hint of intrigue in his voice, "you have some experience with elaborate escapes, don't you? Do I, perhaps, detect an unspoken proposal in your query, sir?"

"The prey are strongest together when the predator is on the hunt." Erasmus' words may have been cryptic, but his tone was clear. "I've been hatching a plan since I was loaded onto this rusty heap, but I can include you and your lady friend in it if you want me to."

"That's very neighborly of you," Ben smiled. "Please, good sir, scheme away. We won't tell our most ungracious host a thing."

Perhaps it was thanks to the overwhelming odor of the ichthoid's room, but neither Ben nor Loup were aware that Jackie was on the other side of the door, using a glass from the kitchen to listen to them hatch their plot.

Knowing better than to hang around the hall for too long and raise suspicions – especially since the conversation she was eavesdropping on appeared to be winding down – Jackie darted back to her room to hide.

"I can't believe it," she said to herself while discarding the glass. "They're actually planning to run out on us! I gotta tell Pop."

We don't have to tell him a blasted thing.

Jackie's blood ran cold as the entity's words echoed through her mind. She clutched the crucifix around her neck, gripping it so tightly that her knuckles turned white. "Get thee behind me, Satan," she said in a trembling voice.

No Satan here, sister. Just me. The entity forced more of her will into Jackie's mind. *The way I see it, there's no reason to tell Pop anything the freaks are planning.*

"There are plenty of reasons!" Jackie was trying to keep her voice low, which was not easy in her increasingly frantic state. "If we don't all trust each other, the whole plan is shot!"

Pop deserves to have this blow up in his smug face. It's his fault Mom's dead.

"No it's not! Mom was every bit as good as him! He-"

Jackie suddenly found herself unable to speak, then unable to breathe. Blackened marks appeared around her neck, forming a pattern not unlike choking fingers. Jackie could feel a hand tightening around her throat. Instinctively, she reached up to pull the offending hand away, but this was useless, for there was no hand. The entity was attacking her from within.

You're keeping your trap shut about this, twerp! Is that clear?

Jackie fell to her knees, gasping for air.

I said: Is. That. Clear?

Jackie nodded so hard she nearly gave herself whiplash.

Say it!

Jackie felt the grip on her throat loosen slightly, only enough to let her whisper her strained reply. "I... I won't say a word..."

Good.

The marks vanished from Jackie's neck as the entity released her. Jackie collapsed on the floor, desperately sucking in much-needed oxygen.

The entity had never attacked her from within before. Jackie did not even know she *could* do something like that. Whatever this horrible thing was, she was growing more powerful and more brazen with each passing day. Jackie had no clue why the entity did not want her father to know what was happening, but the reason could only be something terrible. Perhaps she was planning something with Bismuth, serving as his own personal saboteur, doing whatever she could to ruin everything.

Worst of all, Jackie had no idea how to stop her.

XII.

Restocking the train was easy enough, but before it departed from the Helena base, Donovan Van Sloan and Ben Andante sat in the caboose once more, discussing where to begin searching for their last recruit.

"You're sure that New Orleans is where we should start?" Donovan asked. "Iruel hasn't been seen there in years."

"Be that as it may," Ben replied, "that's the last place we know he was for certain, so it's the logical place to look for clues. He must have left something behind. People don't just disappear without leaving any trace."

"Oh yes they do. Ever heard of Ambrose Bierce?"

"Well, not to brag, Don, but if Loup and I had been hired to find Ambrose Bierce, there'd be no mystery. You, however, hired us to find the people on your list, which we've done so far, and we say that New Orleans should be our starting point. I doubt he's still there, but we might find a lead all the same. Besides, I checked with your guys here at the station, and they said the Tracker is currently in that area. It would behoove us to ask her for directions."

"Good point," Donovan nodded. "All right, if that's your call, then New Orleans it is. I'll inform the conductor."

As Donovan left the caboose, he passed by Ma'at, who had been standing in the doorway listening to the pair discuss their next move. He only acknowledged her with a tip of his hat as he passed, which she returned with a slight nod of her head. Once he was gone, she entered and sat next to Ben. "So we now seek this…vampire, you call it?" she asked.

"That's right," Ben nodded. "Did they not have those back in your day?"

"There were blood drinkers who stalked the Nile, but not as you describe this fellow to be." She glanced at Donovan's notes, which lay open on the table. "Iruel… That name sounds Jewish to me." Her tone noticeably darkened as she made this observation. "Is this Iruel of David's lineage?"

"Half, according to the notes," Ben answered. "Why do you ask?"

Ma'at hesitated for just a moment before dismissively saying, "It is nothing." She leaned against Ben, her tone changing to something a bit more alluring. "Put aside these notes for a time, Ben. I feel the two of us should focus on…other things." She ran her bandaged fingers down his arm. "According to the maps I have seen, it is a long journey to this place called New Orleans, and we cannot spend all of that time reading this dry papyrus stack." Her dark eyes gazed into his. "I do not know how courtship proceeds in this age, but I do know when a man is drawn to me." She smiled. "And I know when I am drawn to him."

Ben grinned as he shut Donovan's notebook. Now *this* was territory he was very familiar with. "You know, ever since meeting you in the museum, Loup and I have been curious about scaling the pyramids and exploring the Valley of the Queens." He stood, gallantly offering his arm to the Egyptian goddess. "Would you care to educate us on your ancient customs?"

Ma'at rose and took Ben's arm. "It would be my pleasure."

*****

Naturally, when the pair was not otherwise occupied, they made a point to carefully study Donovan's notes on the vampire named Iruel.

Iruel had been born Dieter Schlegel in the year 1062 AD. His father was a Germanic lord, and his mother the daughter of a Jewish cobbler. Few records survived of their courtship or married life, but what did survive made it clear that their union was a controversial one, and not even his mother's eventual conversion to Christianity was enough to quell rumblings among the people.

Dieter was the first of four children, and was thus heir to the family estate and fortune, but when the Crusades began in 1095, he did not hesitate to go and fight for the Holy City of Jerusalem. Being of both Christian and Jewish descent, he felt it was his duty to go. His noble blood allowed him to be inducted into the Knights Templar, and he rose quickly through their ranks. During this period, he proved to be a surprisingly effective combatant. True, he had learned the ways of the sword in his youth, as most nobles did, but the power and viciousness he displayed on the battlefield was not the sort of thing one could be taught. It was said he could cut through hordes of enemies unaided and stand victorious without a scratch upon him. Those he slew in battle would be left with a Crucifix and a Star of David carved into their bodies, and he left many such bodies in his wake. This made him a legend on the battlefield, a figure who inspired fear even in the bravest of hearts. Though violent, he was not unjust, for he would never kill the innocent, the repentant, or those who laid down their arms. It was during this time that the locals took to calling him Iruel, after the Angel of Fear. It was a fitting title which he wore proudly.

Dieter Schlegel's natural life came to an end in April of 1099. While scouting ahead for a particular raid, he had discovered a chamber beneath a temple which contained several obscure holy relics (many of which, Donovan noted, were now locked away in the Vatican Archives). Knowing these would be invaluable to the Church, he sent his squire back to inform the other Crusaders while he remained behind as a sentry. When the squire returned that night with a full force of Templar Knights, they found Dieter mortally wounded, surrounded by the bodies of raiders with crosses and stars carved into their flesh. In his right hand, he clutched a metal Cross, and in his left, a metal Star of David. Apparently, Dieter had been ambushed in the squire's absence, and though he had successfully beaten and killed his opponents, their surprise attack had still done its job. Dieter Schlegel, the legendary Angel of Fear, was dying.

As the life drained from Dieter's body, the priest who had accompanied his brothers in arms noticed a small clay vessel covered in Hebrew writing among the relics. Two particular word son the vessel stood out to him: "healing" and "drink". When opened, the Templars found within it a liquid that glowed with unearthly light such as they had never seen before. Though no one knew what the substance was, if it could heal their fallen brother, it was worth the chance of using, and so the liquid was poured into Dieter's mouth.

When the contents of the jar were emptied, Dieter's body began to convulse and glow like the sun. It became so bright that the Templars fled the chamber lest they be blinded. The light vanished, and from the entrance burst forth an unkindness of shrieking ravens with feathers of an unnervingly white shade. The birds vanished into the inky desert night, and when the Templars reentered the chamber, Dieter Schlegel was nowhere to be found. The priest declared that what had transpired was one of God's holy mysteries, and the knights could not argue with this conclusion. Rather than tarry longer and risk another attack, they returned to their camp, taking the remaining relics with them.

It was the following night when, much to the shock of his brethren, Dieter reappeared at the camp so he could explain what had happened. It was a tale the knights would have never believed had they not witnessed it themselves. Dieter was no longer dead, nor was he truly alive. He had, for all intents and purposes, become one of the undead, a vampire, but not the typical kind which the people of Medieval Europe knew and feared. Even stranger, his transformation had been the result of the Templars' bid to save him.

There are two methods in which a human being can become a vampire. The most well-known method is to be bitten by another vampire, which transmits the evil of the undead like a disease. The other method is by drinking human blood. It must, of course, be human blood specifically; drinking animal blood does nothing, and eating human flesh turns people into wendigos rather than vampires. The act symbolizes the drinker willingly giving his soul to evil, becoming a creature of darkness.

In Dieter's case, the glowing liquid in the vessel was also blood, but not the blood of a human. As the priest later confirmed by translating the ancient writing, was the blood of an angel, collected during the reign of King David after a battle described in an apocryphal text. By ingesting this blood, Dieter Schlegel was infused with a form of divinity in a way no human being had ever been before. This blood had made Dieter into the immortal undead, but he was able to retain his soul. He became the world's only divine vampire, the true Angel of Fear on Earth.

By his own choice, Dieter left the Knights Templars that night, for he felt his newfound nature would potentially harm their reputation. He made his own way back to Europe, but he did not do so quietly. Stories began cropping up of travelers being accosted by highwaymen, only to be saved by a vampire with a Crucifix burned into one hand, and a Star of David burned into the other. From those symbols would pour pure white light that would burn the evil from men's souls. The especially wicked would be burned away to nothing by this light, for their souls were so evil that nothing would remain afterward. So it was that the legend of Iruel spread beyond the Holy Land.

Word of Dieter's death – spread by the Knights Templars, and not technically a lie – reached the Schlegel family before Dieter did, so control of the estate had fallen to his brother Maxwell, the second eldest. Naturally, Dieter's brother was shocked to see him appear on the doorstep one gloomy night. How Dieter persuaded Maxwell to not raise the alarm and have him disposed of, Donovan's notes did not say. There was only a vague statement from one of Maxwell's journals which read, "After a long and bizarre discussion with my deceased brother, which lasted almost to dawn, I accepted his words as sooth."

Despite his presence, the estate could not be returned to Dieter's control without raising suspicions. Maxwell retained the title, but allowed his brother to reside in the family castle, away from the prying eyes of people who might not believe a holy vampire could exist.

Dieter was not content to simply while away eternity alone and idle. As a man of faith, he was certain his revival must have been part of some divine plan, and so he would spend his nights venturing into the nearby towns, using his supernatural abilities to thwart wrongdoers. As he had done in the Holy Land, he spared the repentant and those who surrendered. If pushed to kill, he would drink their blood to sustain himself, and leave their bodies with crosses and stars to prevent them from rising as the undead themselves. These symbols were now burned rather than carved.

At first, he was feared by all, for no one could comprehend his nature. Several attempts were made to trap and kill him, all of which failed, for he did not have all of the undead's weaknesses; though still vulnerable to garlic, silver, and wolf's bane, religious iconography and holy water had no effect on him at all. Eventually, the people gave up, and slowly came around to accepting that he was not evil. Soon, the warrior called Iruel earned another moniker: God's Vampire.

The years passed. Dieter's younger sisters married into nobility in other regions of Europe, and Maxwell died without an heir. Yet the Schlegel Estate remained active, for this was where Iruel remained. He was mostly left alone, and his legend persisted through the ages. Not even the Renaissance, which attempted to cast doubt on the supernatural by embracing rationality, could dispel people's belief of Iruel's presence.

For reasons known only to him, Iruel moved from Germany to the United States in 1906, making his way south from Manhattan and eventually settling in New Orleans, which had become a hub for the supernatural in America. He spent the next twenty years as the scourge of vampires, witch doctors, cultists, and ghosts who resided there before disappearing in 1927. Where he had gone and why he had vanished were unknown, for he had left no word with his human familiars before departing…or if he had, they had taken his reason to their graves.

As detectives, Ben and Loup knew, as they had said before, that nobody truly just vanished without a trace. Somebody in New Orleans had to know something. It was simply a matter of finding out who that somebody was.

*****

As the train drew nearer to New Orleans, Donovan called Ma'at into the armory, for he wished to speak with her as he gathered his equipment.

"Ben says that if we want information, our best bet is to go where the vampires are," Donovan said as he browsed a selection of pocket-sized crosses displayed in an open drawer. "I know a place in this town crawling with the suckers, but there's no way I'm bringing Jackie there." He selected a cross with spring-loaded arms that folded into the sides, and placed it in his pocket. "She's every bit as good a fighter as I am, but in her condition, she's a wild card. She's staying on the train, and I want you to stay with her."

Ma'at crossed her arms. "Based on my understanding of vampires, they are not creatures to be trifled with. Since I am a warrior, would it not behoove you to have me at your side?"

"Normally yes," Donovan nodded as he placed garlic cloves into a compartment on his prosthetic claw. "I have no doubt in your ability to handle their kind, believe me. Unfortunately, you're the only option I've got. Ben and Loup need to be in the field to do their job, so I can't leave them here. I'm not leaving her with Erasmus, either. He already doesn't like us, so if Jackie had an episode on his watch, I wouldn't trust him to intervene in a helpful manner." He slid the panel door shut and reached for a belt of silver stakes. "And I can't stay, since I need to make sure things go according to plan, and no one else on this train is equipped to deal with her. That leaves you, Ma'at, and I know you'll do right by my daughter because you never do anything unjust."

Ma'at nodded. "I see the wisdom in your reasoning, Donovan. Very well. I shall care for Jacqueline in your absence."

"Thanks." Donovan placed a pistol loaded with silver bullets in his holster. "God willing, nothing'll happen while we're gone, but if it does…"

"I know what to do."

Ben, Donovan, and Erasmus disembarked from the train. Their destination was Bloody Mary's, a pub across town known to be a vampire den. Erasmus wore a trench coat and fedora to somewhat obscure his true nature. It was a paper-thin disguise at best, but since it was night and the streets were poorly lit, it was deemed to be good enough. The natural humidity of the southern air was just enough to keep him hydrated.

"All right," Donovan said as he led the way out of the station. "I don't want either of you getting any ideas about running off, especially you." He pointed an accusatory finger at Erasmus. "There's a lot of water around here, and you ain't going anywhere near it."

Erasmus crossed his arms, his expression defiant. "Suppose I did. What could you do to stop me? Your plan does involve me being out of your sight for a spell."

"Maybe out of *my* sight, but that doesn't mean there ain't eyes on you." Donovan motioned to the cityscape that stretched out before them. There were many low rooftops which, under the dark southern sky, would not have looked out of place in Transylvania, and a damp fog which clung to the ground added a sense of foreboding. "I wired ahead to have my people position themselves all over this town. They're watching us right now, most of them through gunsights, and they're the ones who'll make sure you don't bug out." He glared into Erasmus' goggled eyes. "You so much as take a cautionary step away from me, and you'll only get one warning shot."

"You're bluffing," Erasmus sneered.

"Am I?" Donovan stepped back. "Then please, make a break for it. See how far you get. Just remember that's not a bulletproof coat you're wearing."

Donovan was confident, so much so that Erasmus hesitated. The human either had an excellent poker face, or he was telling the truth.

There was only one way to know for sure. Erasmus started to run.

A bullet ricocheted off the street in front of him, and he recoiled backward.

"There's my bluff, Erasmus," Donovan said. "And don't think you can flip the table, either. Now come on. We've got places to be." He marched out into the street, his focus entirely on his destination.

As they followed, Erasmus shot a discontented look towards Ben.

As they walked, Donovan noticed that Ben seemed a bit on edge. He slowed his pace until they were side by side "What's eating you?" he asked.

"We hate vampire dens," Ben answered as they drew near Bloody Mary's. "The undead don't have scents, and it makes their dens feel…empty, I guess is the best word. Those freaks are creepy enough on their own, but having no scent is just unnerving. Don't get offended if we stick close to you while we're in there. Your dark blue scent will help us stay focused."

Donovan shot Ben a confused look. "Did you just say my scent is dark blue?"

Ben suddenly felt awkward. He and Loup occasionally forgot that nobody else experienced smell the way they did. "Um…yes," he replied hesitantly. "Dark blue with red spots. This may sound strange, but…we can, uh, smell colors. We've always been able to. We experience people's scents as different shades. It helps us track them down." He rubbed the back of his neck. "We know how that sounds, but it's the truth."

Amazingly, Donovan did not respond with confusion, but rather with familiarity. "Oh, so you have synesthesia."

Ben blinked. "There's a name for it?"

"Yeah, synesthesia. It means mixed sensation. It's when the five senses get jumbled, very rare." Donovan's expression was bemused now. "Never met a werewolf who had it before, and with smell, of all things."

Both Ben and Loup felt relieved that Donovan understood. "Most people just think we're crazy when they find out. How do you even know about it?"

"Melissa had a form of it. She could taste sound." Donovan chuckled. "We named our daughter Jacqueline because she said it sounded sweet, and she meant it. It tasted like chocolate chip ice cream to her."

Ben chuckled at this too. In the back of his mind, so did Loup. Ben said, "Maybe once you're out of this racket, you can open an ice cream parlor and name a flavor after her. I bet it would sell."

"Maybe one day." Donovan raised his prosthetic claw. "Then I can replace this with a scoop." This prompted more laughter from the duo.

Though Erasmus could hear their conversation, he did not join in the laughter. Instead, he suppressed the sadness which memories of ice cream brought upon him. He sighed, but did so quietly so his travelling companions would not hear him.

The trio arrived at Bloody Mary's soon after this exchange. The establishment had not had proper signage since the days of Prohibition, and the building's façade was designed to be inconspicuous so as to prevent warm bodies from entering. It was a vampire den, after all.

They paused across the street, and Donovan pointed to the building. "All right, fish stick," he said to Erasmus, "you know where to go from here."

"Yeah, yeah, I know," Erasmus grumbled. "Don't ever call me 'fish stick' again." With these parting words, he darted across the street, ran down the alley beside the den, and climbed up the building's side. This was easy for him to do, since his slick amphibian hide allowed him to cling to most surfaces, so scaling a sheer brick wall was not a challenge. He slung himself onto the roof and crouched, waiting.

Once they were sure he was in position, Donovan and Ben crossed the street, the former placing his artificial appendage back in his coat pocket.

Ben rapped on the door, and a small panel slid open in response. Two red eyes peered out at them. "What's the password?" asked the eyes.

"Lugosi sent us," Ben answered without missing a beat.

The panel slammed shut, then the door creaked open.

Ben and Donovan only entered after the doorkeeper invited them in. Depending on how powerful they were, certain vampires could not enter places without being invited first, so it was customary for doorkeepers at vampire dens to always invite the patrons in, especially if they were newcomers.

The opulence of Bloody Mary's interior contrasted sharply with its unassuming exterior. The overall aesthetic was Victorian, with the main portion of the den resembling a ballroom fused with an opium den. Corinthian columns rose to the ceiling, and the walls were lined with paintings that appeared to be Classical style, but each one depicted a disturbing image of violence and debauchery. The place was swarming with the undead, some of whom levitated up by the ceiling. Goblets of blood were being poured and drained wherever the eye fell, flickering candles cast eerie shadows upon the walls, and wicked laughter filled the slightly hazy air. Certain pockets of the room were sectioned off with red velvet curtains where vampires could privately engage in carnal activities if they wished to. The curtains hid the sights, but did little to muffle the sounds.

As he had predicted, Ben felt uneasy in a room with no scents. So distracted was he that he stopped paying attention to where he was walking, and bumped into a lanky vampire in the garb of a dock worker. "Oh, excuse me," he said.

"It's fine," the dock vampire replied. He examined Ben and Donovan. "I don't believe I've seen you two here before. Name's Steve. You and your friend new?"

"Just got into town," Ben replied. "We heard the Tracker might be here. Is she in tonight?"

Steve jerked his thumb towards a table at the far end of the room. There a female vampire sat alone, an open book in one hand, a goblet of blood in the other. "She's at her usual table. What would you two want to do with her?"

"Oh, you know," Ben said. "We're looking to set ourselves up here, so we need to know the lay of the land, and who better to ask than her?"

"I'd be careful. She's a bit moody tonight." Steve placed a friendly hand on Ben's shoulder. "You want my advice? Come back tomorrow night. She might be in a better mood then, if she's…here…"

The sudden hesitancy in Steve's voice told Ben their ruse was about to drop. Loup took control of his hands and braced for the worst.

"You're awfully warm," said Steve as his grip tightened on Ben shoulder. He examined the detective's face more closely, and noticed the telltale signs of lycanthropy. A glance down at the lupine hands confirmed it.

Steve's expression darkened, figuratively and literally. Shadows from nowhere covered his face, allowing his eyes to glow menacingly bright as he uttered a threat. "You shouldn't be in here, mongrel!"

Donovan cleared his throat loudly, drawing the vampire's attention. The human withdrew his left hand from his pocket, revealing it was closed in a fist. He held it out and opened it, dropping a large handful of sesame seeds onto the floor.

Steve's red eyes twitched as he glared at Donovan, whose own expression was irritatingly smug.

"Damn you!" the vampire snapped before relenting. He released Ben, dropped to the floor, and began counting the seeds, as any vampire would be compelled to do. It was little known weakness of theirs, one which they were embarrassed by. He began counting out loud as he picked up each one.

Ben straightened his jacket with his restored hands. "Thanks," he said to Donovan with a nod.

"Told you it would work," Donovan replied.

"That you did. Guess I owe you five bucks."

"I'll deduct it from your fee."

Donovan dropped another pile of seeds in front of Steve's face before he and Ben proceeded to the Tracker's table. Steve groaned in frustration as he lost count.

The vampire known only as the Tracker was infamous among those who studied the supernatural. She had an uncanny clairvoyance that allowed her to always know where other vampires were, which made her highly desired by just about everyone. The undead paid her for security, and vampire hunters paid her to betray that security. She would serve either side indiscriminately if it suited her to do so. Her loyalty was to herself first and the highest bidder second. She, however, was not so easy to find, always moving randomly and covering her own tracks just enough to present a challenge for the especially determined. Bloody Mary's was one of the few places she was known to frequent, usually if she was looking for business. Naturally, the Occult Mafia kept a sharp watch on her. Though the organization wished to have her at their exclusive disposal, opinions were split on whether she should be employed or captured. Until a resolution could be reached on this subject, they allowed the Tracker to roam free without interference.

Like most vampires, the Tracker's appearance was striking, yet something about her in particular did not look quite right. It was as if she had all the right features to make an attractive woman, yet those features were exaggerated in all the wrong ways. Her skin was too fair, her lips too full, her cheekbones too high, her figure too voluptuous, and her fingernails too long. Her flamboyant attire, like something out of a satirical Shakespeare play, was equally exaggerated in the worst possible ways. It was a wonder that she could go into hiding so easily with an appearance such as hers

The two men approached her table. "Miss Tracker, I presume?" asked Ben.

The Tracker looked up from her book. Even her eyes were slightly too big, but unlike the other vampires in the den, they were not red, but grayish-white orbs with swirling cloudy wisps inside them. She was the only vampire known to have eyes like this. "Who wants to know?" she asked, clearly irritated that her reading was being interrupted. Her voice, much like her body, was an extreme of its own. It might have been deep and sultry, but it was too much of both, almost sounding her sound masculine.

"People who can make it worth your while to put that book down for five minutes." As Ben said this, Donovan placed a small bag on the table, the contents of which clinked as it settled.

The bag slid towards the Tracker as if guided by a magnet, and she reached inside to inspect the contents. Within were gold coins. She checked one with her teeth, and nodded in confirmation of their authenticity. "Then the Tracker I am." She invited them to sit. "How can I help you gentlemen this evening?"

Ben sat, but Donovan remained standing, keeping an eye on their surroundings. "So," Ben started, "is it true that you know the location of every vampire in the world?"

The Tracker motioned dramatically to her crystalline eyes. "Naturally. Are you the hunters or the hunted?"

"A little of both, you might say."

"An enigma? How juicy." The conspiratorial smile that crossed the Tracker's face did little to undo her unsettling appearance. "Well, the amount you're paying is enough for me to be unconcerned which side you're on. So tell me, who do you wish to find?"

Ben lowered his voice slightly so the rest of the den would not hear him. "The one they call Iruel."

The Tracker's eyes narrowed slightly, and her voice carried a slight edge of hostility. "And what do you two want with God's Vampire?"

"I thought you were unconcerned."

"Iruel is every vampire's concern. He's a traitor to our kind."

Ben's voice remained firm. "Well, vampires are traitors to mankind, so don't act like you have the moral high ground, sister. It doesn't suit you. Now can you locate him or not?"

The Tracker looked back and forth at her clients. "You..." she began, but trailed off. She was beginning to feel queasy, so she closed her eyes and shook her head slightly to refocus her senses. "You two definitely aren't vampires."

"And you are definitely avoiding the work we're paying you for," Ben replied. He reached for the purse. "Maybe I'll just take these back."

Ben's hand was stopped by the Tracker's, which shot out like a rattlesnake to grab his wrist. She turned his hand over, examining the rough stubble of his palm. "A ly-" She coughed, shaking her head again. "A lycan? How did you get in?"

"You suckers need better passwords."

Donovan turned to scan the crowd, doing so just in time to see Steve rise, having finished counting the seeds. As he rose, he appeared dizzy. In fact, every vampire was starting to appear dizzy. Some were even visibly nauseous.

A whiff of the air told Donovan the reason why, and he smiled, knowing the amphibian had done his job. Discreetly, he reached back into his pocket, wrapping his hand around his crucifix.

"Both of you need to leave," the Tracker said, sounding as though she had indigestion.

"Something wrong?" Ben asked, though his tone made it clear he already knew the answer. "Feeling a bit sick, and can't figure out why? Well, let me enlighten you." He pointed to the ceiling. "We've got a man on the roof who poured a container of garlic powder into the ventilation, and if he's done that, he must have also made his way back down here. He's not the nicest fellow, and truth be told, neither are we. So if you or anyone else tries something stupid…"

Steve pointed at the interlopers. "Intruders!" he shouted, then coughed again. "Warm bodies! Ge-" he burped, which nearly became vomit. "Get them!"

At his words, all of the vampires turned in the direction of the Tracker's table, but despite their attempts at being menacing, the effect was ruined by their sickliness.

"Stupid it is," Ben said.

In one fluid motion, Ben stood and turned. Loup Garou instantly took control as he did. Loup withdrew a cross from his pocket, extending it towards the encroaching crowd of vampires at nearly the exact time Donovan brandished his. The pair stood shoulder to shoulder against their opponents.

The sight of the crosses not only kept the vampires at bay, but also proved to be the breaking point for their nausea. Within seconds, every vampire had either doubled over or fallen to their hands and knees, vomiting up gallons of blood. Some in the crowd adopted batlike features as they heaved.

Thinking she had the opportunity to escape, the Tracker slipped out of her chair and made a break for the rear exit. She only got halfway there before stopping with a piercing hiss. Her way was barred by Erasmus Webster, who held his extended blades in a cross before him. The blades were dripping with the rear doorman's blood.

Loup's chain lashed out like a whip and wrapped around the Tracker's waist. With a mighty yank, he pulled her back to him, catching her by the throat and holding her at arm's length against the wall. Erasmus took his place beside Donovan to keep the crowd at bay, even though none of them were feeling well enough to attack.

"You didn't cooperate with my partner," Loup snarled at his quarry, "It's only fair to warn you that I'm not nearly as easy going as he is. Tell me where to find Iruel, and you won't learn the difference." He held his cross inches away from her face, moving it from side to side like a cobra preparing to strike. "Do we have a deal?"

The Tracker gagged and choked on the garlic-laced air. "I don't know where he is," she said. "He's protected by the Light. I only know where he used to live when he was here."

"Ah, *now* we're getting somewhere." Loup leaned in close, fangs bared. "Enlighten us."

The former residence of Dieter Schelgel was a lavish estate located out on the bayou. It was surrounded by water on three sides, while the fourth side was barred by an iron gate with various religious symbols atop the spires. Similar symbols rose from the mansion's multiple peaks as weathervanes. The mansion itself had once been a plantation before the days of the Civil War, with a few gothic accents subtly incorporated into the design. There were no telltale signs of it being currently occupied by either the living or the undead. The windows were dark, save for the Moon's reflection. The air around it was warm and muggy, which was appropriate for a swamp, but since the air around vampire lodgings tended to be cold and dry, this confirmed that Iruel was note present. Inside, the mansion was totally barren. There were no furnishings anywhere, making it feel like a crypt.

"I don't know what you expect to find," Donovan said as Loup Garou searched the living room. "There's nothing here. Iruel clearly took everything with him when he left. I don't see anything that'll help us find him."

"I thought you hired us for exactly that reason," Loup replied. He had been on all fours at first, searching for any sort of clue, but he resumed his bipedal posture as he spoke. "Like I said, nobody just disappears. Iruel had to leave something behind."

Erasmus glanced around the room with his glowing goggled eyes. "Doesn't look like he did to me. This place is emptier than the Chicago Cubs Stadium."

"We'll choose to ignore that," growled Loup as he continued to scour the room. "Our experience tells us that vital clues can be easy to miss, no matter what they are. Sometimes they're tiny things that are easily overlooked, and sometimes they're as plain as the nose on your face...present company notwithstanding." He glanced at Erasmus, who had no nose in the traditional sense, when he said this. "Besides, Iruel is a divine being. He wouldn't just disappear. He'd leave something behind so somebody could find him if they really needed his help."

Loup's eyes briefly glanced at a painting above the living room's elaborate stone fireplace. It was the only item which had been left behind, but at first, he did not think much of it, and was about to move into the dining room.

Loup, the painting! Ben told him in sudden realization. *Look at it again!*

At the prompting, Loup gave the painting his full attention. "Hello there," he said in astonishment. "I think we just found our lead."

Donovan and Erasmus approached the fireplace to get a better look. "What, the painting?" Donovan asked.

"Bingo."

"Doesn't look like anything special." Donovan reached up with his left hand and tapped the canvas, then shook his head. "It's not a gateway or a spectral vision, or else it would've rippled. I don't see how this is a clue."

"Ask yourself this, Don: what's a painting of a desert landscape doing in a waterlogged New Orleans mansion? Looks pretty fresh, too, all things considered."

The wolf's words were nothing short of an epiphany. The painting did appear to be fairly new, especially compared to the dull, flaking, cracked frame it was set in. The painting itself – oil on canvas – depicted a freestanding rock formation. If one looked close enough, there was an anomaly at the foot of the centermost rock, something too small to make out clearly from the perspective of the painter, but large enough to distinguish it as an artificial structure.

"Well I'll be," Donovan proclaimed. "Come to think of it, I've seen that formation before, back when I investigated the Order of Quetzalcoatl. It's just outside of El Paso."

"And there's a structure at the base," Loup added. "Of all the things to leave behind, this is simply too specific. Someone just passing by without knowing the building's history would think it's an odd decorative choice, but for us…"

"…it's our clue." Donovan gave Loup a pat on the shoulder. "I knew I could count on you."

Ma'at had just finished eating in the dining car. Adjusting to the modern dishes available on the train was an interesting experience for her. She was used to dining on the rich food of kings in luxurious palaces open to the sky. To find herself consuming such things as hamburgers in a box on wheels was something she never thought she would do. The food was not bad – the flavors were growing on her – but it was certainly different.

After eating, she made her way back to the caboose, which took her past Jacqueline's room. Up until that point, the girl had not gone through any fits as her father had worried she might. The entity's absence meant nothing, though. Ma'at did not pretend to understand anything about the girl's condition, but she knew by now that the entity's manifestations were unpredictable. The only pattern was that she would wrest control from Jackie at times when it would best inconvenience those around her, but even this was not a certainty.

Jackie had gone to her room earlier, and it was always Ma'at's intent to check on her after eating. Just as she was about to knock, a shriek accompanied by a crash told her that there was no time to be polite. She did not bother to see if the door was unlocked, but took the key Donovan had given her and used it.

Jackie was dressed in a nightgown which had probably looked very nice at one point, but was now being torn apart as she struggled against the entity. Her jewelry was absent from her body, instead resting on top of the dresser. Dark patches swirled around her skin like oil spreading through water as she struggled to maintain control.

Ma'at withdrew an ankh from her tunic, grabbed Jackie, pinned her to the wall, and pressed the ankh against her body. At the top of her lungs, she shouted, "By the power of the Amun, I command you to recede!"

Jackie's body convulsed violently as the darkness retreated, and when the attack had passed, she collapsed to the floor, panting heavily to catch her breath.

Ma'at kept her ankh in her hand, ready to act again if the entity returned.

Thankfully, her caution was not needed. Jackie eventually pulled herself back onto her feet, exhausted but otherwise okay. "Thanks," she managed to say between breaths.

"This is the worst I have seen you since we met," Ma'at said. "What happened?"

"I was in the shower," Jackie said as she walked to the dresser, "so I had to take my jewelry off. I tried to be quick so I could get them back on before she tried anything, but…well, you saw how well that worked." She placed her rosary around her neck and sighed. "Guess I need to get waterproof rosaries now. Either that, or give up bathing."

"Well, it is fortunate I passed by when I did," Ma'at said. She kissed her ankh. "The power of my fellow gods has saved you, child."

"Don't be too proud, Ma'at," Jackie said as she put on her crucifix earrings. "The entity hates all kinds of religious symbols. Ankhs, crescent moons, druidic charms, Thor's hammer...heck, she doesn't even like swastikas, as long as their Hindu originals."

"You speak as though to diminish my power," Ma'at said, her displeasure at this thought apparent. "If it does not matter what symbols you wear, then why choose those crosses over something such as an ankh?"

Jackie affixed matching bracelets engraved with John 3:16, King James Version, on her ankles as she replied. "I'm Catholic, like Mom and Pop, so it's a matter of faith."

"Then...you worship the same god as the vampire we seek?"

"Yup."

"The God of Abraham."

There was a slight acidity to the way Ma'at said this phrase which made Jackie pause midway through sliding on her charm bracelets. She turned to face the goddess with a suspicious expression on her face. "Is that a problem?"

Ma'at met Jackie's expression with a stern one of her own. It almost seemed accusatory. "That depends, Jacqueline. Is it a problem that I am the Goddess of Justice?"

Silence followed for a few agonizing moments.

As Jackie tried to think of a response, she remembered how her father's notes had mentioned a lack of activity from Ma'at during the time of the Exodus.

She almost asked about it, but did not. She simply had no energy left to confront that issue after her latest episode. "Well, you helped me keep control, so that's all that matters," she said.

Ma'at was about to say that this response was not an answer to her question, but a sound outside the room signaled the return of the others. Both women stepped out into the hall to meet them. "Welcome back, Mr. Van Sloan," Ma'at said cordially, abandoning any ill feelings which may have been growing.

Donovan noted how the pair had just exited his daughter's room, and his paternal instincts kicked in. "What happened? Jackie, are you all right?"

"I'm fine, Pop," Jackie nodded. "Ma'at took good care of me."

Donovan relaxed. "Good, good. I'll catch up in a moment. Right now, I've got to tell the conductor where we're headed next." With that, he pushed past Ma'at and headed for the front of the train.

Ma'at departed Jackie's room and approached Ben. "So you found the vampire?" she said as she slunk her arms around him.

"I think so," Ben answered as he returned the embrace. "We're going to Texas. I think you'll feel right at home there."

Erasmus retired to his room without speaking a word to anyone.

XIII.

The train arrived in El Paso two days later. This time, the whole team disembarked, including Ma'at and Jacqueline. Donovan led the way from the edge of town towards the rock formation, which was known locally as Widow's Peak. It was so called because of a folk tale about a settler's widow who scaled the rocks in a bid to reach Heaven and find her husband there. That the name was also commonly used to describe a vampire's hairline was a coincidence.

The sun was setting as the group trekked across the desert. Erasmus progressed slowly, feeling sluggish in the dry desert air. He now wore an ammo belt, which held small spray bottles filled with water to spritz himself with rather than bullets. He had already depleted three of them by the time their destination was within sight.

Just as it was in the painting, an unnatural structure sat at the foot of the centermost rock. The style of the building was reminiscent of a small medieval castle, but it was fashioned from sand-colored adobe and red desert stone. Strangest of all was not the structure itself, but the environment in which it resided. From the ground to the sky, everything surrounding the castle looked different from the rest of the desert. The ground was not fine golden sand, but flaking gray ash, and the sky was oddly colored in unnatural dark hues. This change of environment was sudden rather than gradual, with a marked difference as if some invisible barrier enveloped the region.

"Well," Ben said as he observed these strange features, "that's very unsettling. If you'll excuse me." With those words, he vanished, and a startled Loup Garou had taken his place.

"Chicken," the wolf snarled at his partner.

Curious, Ma'at summoned some nearby rattlesnakes and directed them towards the threshold. The snakes went up to the line, but refused to enter. Instead, they hissed and rattled as though frightened by the place, and they retreated the moment Ma'at released control.

"All right," Donovan said to the group as he led the way, "everyone try to stay calm. Don't react, don't talk, don't even breathe unless I tell you to. Iruel isn't evil, but he will defend himself if provoked, and holy relics have no effect on him. Be ready, but don't strike first. Is that clear?"

Donovan made certain that everyone nodded in agreement before they crossed the threshold and of Iruel's estate.

Immediately, a kind of dizziness affected the entire group. It was something like vertigo, making them stagger as they walked through the deathly-cold region.

"Min's phallus!" Ma'at exclaimed as her hands rose to cradle her head. "What arcane force is causing this?"

"Iruel," answered Donovan, who seemed the least affected. "Legend says his dwellings always bend the laws of nature as a form of security. Just keep going forward, and don't touch anything. Stay behind me."

A heavy fog seeped out of the castle and rolled towards the group. It clung to the ground, and came up to their knees. Around them, the cloud swirled and twisted as though unseen creatures were moving within.

Loup's fur bristled when he felt something brush past his foot, but he fought the urge to jump or kick the object, lest it strike back at him.

Erasmus' skin crawled when he saw a scorpion tail as long as he was tall rise out of the fog like a shark fin. It moved a few feet towards them before lowering back into the cloud and vanishing from sight.

Ma'at was stunned when she noticed how the cacti scattered across the property were turning as if watching them, their branches twisting slightly as if preparing to lash out.

Jackie noticed a stark white feather waft down in front of her, which drew her eyes to a trio of what looked like albino ravens circling overhead. When the birds looked down and locked eyes with her, she could feel the entity shudder within her. Jackie felt a hint of relief knowing the entity was not likely to emerge here, but at the same time, the way in which the ravens' eyes scrutinized her was chilling.

Though the threat of danger was all around them, the group stayed behind Donovan, whose focus was entirely on the building ahead.

Fortunately, nothing on Iruel's estate saw fit to attack that night. The group arrived safely at the arched wooden doors, which were tall and wide enough to allow an elephant entrance. Donovan raised his claw to knock, but the doors opened on their own before he had the chance. The loud creaking echoed off the stone walls of the dark antechamber within.

Slowly, the group stepped inside, and the doors closed behind them. Candles and torches flickered to life as they entered, illuminating a grand entryway. Tapestries lined the walls, bearing symbols of a bygone age. Each symbol was either a familial coat of arms or an emblem from a brotherhood of knights. In the middle of the room were two freestanding stairways that arched in opposing curves up to a high balcony. The space behind them remained dark.

A shadow seemingly cast by nothing descended the left stairway, sliding down like water until it met the feet of Iruel, who appeared suddenly at the base of the right stairway.

Iruel's presence alone was enough to stun any onlooker. He radiated quiet dignity in a way no mortal could do, yet his expression and posture were devoid of such things as haughtiness and pride; rather, he conveyed sincere nobility as though this were his most natural state of being. He wore the elegant royal blue attire of an 18th Century nobleman, subtly patterened patterned with lace at the sleeves and an ascot pinned by an iridescent opal. His long black hair was pulled back in a loose ponytail, a look which enhanced his masculinity rather than detract from it. Across his face, running from above his left eye to the bottom of his right jaw, was a faded yet noticeable scar that testified to his life as a knight. Physically, all that betrayed Iruel's nature as one of the undead were his ashen skin, slightly-pointed ears, and glowing eyes, which shimmered like gold medallions instead of the usual unpleasant red.

"So you have finally arrived," the vampire said. Though he spoke softly, his voice – which carried a hint of a Prussian accent – projected with an unearthly power that filled the room. "I was wondering when you would find your way here. You have come to seek my aid against the warlock, have you not?"

One of Donovan's eyebrows arched towards the ceiling in surprise. "You were expecting us?"

"After a fashion," Iruel nodded. "The Lord called me to America for a reason, after all. At first, I thought my task was to undo Satan's grip on New Orleans, but there is more wickedness there than even I can erase on my own. I did what I could there before the Lord called me to El Paso, and here I have waited for you." His sharp gold eyes examined each of his guests. "You are not quite what I was expecting, but I have kept stranger company in my afterlife. And you, sir, have yet to answer my question." He glided to Donovan, floating rather than walking. "Have you sought me out because of the warlock?"

Most men would have recoiled at a vampire's approach. Donovan Van Sloan, however, stood his ground. "We have. I'm looking to end Phillipe Bismuth's reign of terror with the aid of those who stand before you, Loup Garou, Ma'at, and Erasmus Webster. You, Iruel, are the last name on my list."

"And how did you find me?"

Donovan motioned with his thumb to Loup. "The wolf led us here. He's been with me from the start."

Iruel nodded, as if he had derived something important from Donovan's answer. "Everything seems to be in order," he said, and then he was gone. Where he went, nobody knew, for he had simply vanished into the air, leaving his guests alone and confused.

"I don't get it," Jackie said. "What happened? Is he with us or not?"

The front doors were blown open by a sudden cold breeze. Outside, an unkindness of snow white ravens appeared. As they flew about, they slowly formed the shape of an arrow pointing back towards the town. The unkindness maintained this shape just long enough for everyone to understand the intent before it dispersed.

"That's our cue," Donovan said with sudden urgency. "Back to the station, everyone."

"What about the vampire?" asked Ma'at.

"When a vampire tells you to leave his home, you leave his home, no questions asked." Donovan marched for the door. "Everyone out and back to the train. *Now.*"

Their return journey was slow. The arid atmosphere of Texas was sapping Erasmus of his strength, and his breathing was becoming labored. About halfway to the station, the ichthoid had exhausted all of his spray bottles, and he was having difficulty walking as dehydration set in. Even his skin was turning pale and sickly as the moisture left him. Ben and Ma'at had propped themselves under his arms to carry him the rest of the way. Thankfully, the group's journey back did not take them near the more populated areas of town, which meant there were no questions to field from curious passers-by.

Erasmus was embarrassed by his display of weakness, but he did not object to the assistance. Given how ill he felt, there was no way he could have anyway.

As they approached the open-air dock where the train sat waiting, they were surprised to see a stranger appear from behind a pillar. He was a tall, pale fellow dressed in the clothes of a dock worker.

Donovan recognized him instantly. "You've got to be kidding," he said. "You followed us here all the way from New Orleans?"

"That's right," Steve replied with a nasty grin. "We've got a score to settle, after all."

Mist filled the space, slowly forming into an army of vampires from Bloody Mary's. The undead fiends surrounded the group, fangs bared. They hissed and snarled with fury.

Loup Garou took over, dropping Erasmus as he did. Ma'at followed suit, also releasing the ichthoid as she drew her kopesh. Erasmus collapsed, though he still extended his wrist blades as he fell. He still had the will to fight back, if not the strength.

Donovan drew a gun loaded with silver bullets. He pulled Jackie close to him, though this did not accomplish much, since the vampires were everywhere.

"How does it feel, human?" Steve taunted. "Not much fun when *we're* the ones who've gotten the drop on *you*, is it?"

One especially bold vampire drew close behind Jackie, reaching out to grab her and drag her away. He did not see the religious jewelry she wore, which would have likely repelled him anyway, but they never had the chance to work. Just as the vampire's spider-like fingers were about to touch Jackie's shoulder, the girl whipped around with lightning speed, her skin having suddenly become covered in fine black scales. Her hand grabbed the vampire's, crushing his bones with an unholy strength. *"Hands off, freak!"* the entity growled as the vampire recoiled in pain.

Instinctively, Jackie forced herself back into control, but she could still feel the entity trying to claw her way back out to fight the undead hordes.

Let me out! she shrieked. *Let me out!*

For the briefest of moments, Jackie wonder if perhaps that was a good idea, but the risk of letting the entity take full control and never rescind it was too frightening for her to take.

The vampires encroached slowly. Taking their time to attack was just a way to torture their prey and get their blood pumping. There were at least fifty of them, and they had the advantage. With only limited resources and Erasmus down for the count, Donovan's team would not last long before being overwhelmed.

"Relax."

The voice was authoritative, yet calming, and it seemed to come from everywhere. It sounded like Iruel, though he was nowhere to be seen.

A snow white raven landed on a light fixture and stared down at the crowd below.

"Tend to the amphibian. I will handle these interlopers."

Loup's sharp canine ears heard the sound of wings flapping in the distance, drawing closer and closer.

Within seconds, the sound was loud enough for everyone to hear.

The station lights went out, leaving the moon as the only source of illumination.

The white raven swooped down, and a thousand more followed behind it, bursting through the windows and open gaps between the walls and the ceiling.

Someone in the crowd of vampires yelled "WHAT THE-" before he was drowned out by the unkindness sweeping over the horde like an ivory tidal wave.

At least ten of the vampires immediately fled from the station, escaping into the dark Texas night. They had been cowards in life, and nothing had changed in death. Those vampires who remained attempted to fight back. Twenty of them turned into bats and met the ravens in midair combat. Within seconds, the bats were torn to shreds by razor sharp beaks and talons before being devoured.

Steve and a few of his compatriots drew guns in an attempt to shoot Donovan, but their bullets were deflected by a dome which appeared from nowhere. The dome was composed of interlocking crosses and six-pointed stars, all of which shone with the blinding brightness of the sun. The beams seared the vampires' hides, and a chorus of anguished cries rose from their ranks. The light sent more of the surviving vampires running, and stunned those who remained long enough for the ravens to finish them off. Soon, only Steve remained, surrounded by the eviscerated corpses of the army he had led from Louisiana.

Several dozen of the ravens crowded beside Donovan, fusing together until they formed the shape of Iruel, who locked his menacing gaze on Steve. A few ravens remained apart from their master, picking at the fallen bodies of the undead.

"No!" Steve exclaimed in terror. "Not you again! We were rid of you!"

"Silence," Iruel commanded. "It is blasphemy for the dead to speak."

Steve raised his gun again.

"Drop it."

The gun fell from Steve's limp hand. His body trembled as Iruel drew closer.

"Your soul is forfeit," Iruel said, his voice filled with disgust for his opponent. "To Hell with you."

Iruel raised his hands, palms outstretched. On his right hand was burned a Crucifix, and on his left was burned a Star of David. The ancient wounds opened. Blinding light shot out from them and engulfed Steve, who screamed as his body burned. When the light vanished, all that remained of him was a charred husk.

The remaining ravens flew to their master, disappearing into his body as if diving into water.

A sense of unsettling calm returned to the train station.

"By all the gods," Ma'at whispered in terrified awe as she surveyed the carnage. Her feelings were shared by the others.

Donovan holstered his gun as he turned to face Iruel. "Did you know they were going to be here?"

"I did," Iruel replied.

Donovan drew closer to Iruel, glaring into his golden eyes. "Why didn't you warn us?"

Iruel cocked an eyebrow. "Did I not?"

"No!"

"Hmm," Iruel replied, then was silent for a moment as he thought things over. "It worked to our advantage, though. Things are occurring as they should."

Donovan eyed the vampire suspiciously. "Meaning what?"

"Come now, Donovan, you have researched my history, have you not?" Iruel clasped his hands behind his back. "If you have, then you know the way I work."

Donovan's eyes widened as he remembered. "Oh, right, of course," he said. "My mistake."

"No harm done," Iruel answered. "If we understand each other, then I believe we should be on our way. I have already placed my luggage on the train, and my estate will care for itself in my absence." Having said his piece, Iruel drifted towards the train as though the matter was settled.

"He'll be fun to work with," Loup Garou mused.

"All that matters is that we've got him," Donovan replied. "Now we're ready."

Before they left, a call was placed to the Occult Mafia's Texas branch to sweep El Paso for the escaped vampires. Time was of the essence, so Donovan could spare none of it tracking them himself.

XIV.

Once the train was on its way, everyone retired to their cabins to rest.

Everyone, that is, except Jackie. Instead, she made her way to Iruel's room.

She was nervous about approaching the vampire. She was not really afraid of him; thanks to her training, she feared no denizen of the dark (not that Iruel was not such a vile creature). No, her nerves stemmed from what she wanted to ask him, since the stories she had heard filled her mind with thoughts of how things could go terribly wrong.

Still, she determined that she had to at least try.

Tentatively, Jackie raised her hand to knock on Iruel's door. Sensing her intentions, the entity forced her will into the raised hand and held it in place.

Jackie struggled to move her arm, but the entity resisted. It was as though she was gripping an invisible iron shaft and holding on with all of her might.

With a powerful grunt, Jackie pulled on her arm, only to lose her balance and stumbled towards the door.

To her surprise, the door opened on its own before she could collide with it, sending her tumbling head over heels into Iruel's room. She was stopped by Iruel's coffin, on the lid of which landed the entity's hand. This caused the entity to recede in fright, for the lid bore a large Baroque cross upon it.

Though a bit disoriented from her unexpected fall, a simple shake of the head was enough for Jackie to recover her senses. She stood back up slowly.

Iruel's room was as cold as his castle. He had a few belongings there besides the coffin, though it was anyone's guess how they'd gotten there, since she had not seen Iruel with any luggage. On the dresser were a few old fashioned photographs in faded gold frames, no doubt of people who had been important to Iruel in the past. A small plaque baring Iruel's coat of arms was suspended on the wall. Appropriately, the animal it bore was a white raven. Jackie could not help but wonder which had come first: the symbol, or Iruel's ability to become an unkindness.

She did not see Iruel enter, but he suddenly appeared before her eyes. He did not seem at all surprised by her presence as he said, "Welcome, Jacqueline Van Sloan."

"Uh…hi," Jackie nodded in reply. She was slightly embarrassed by her less-than-graceful entrance, and still nervous about what she had come to ask, but she could not let those feelings get the better of her. She tugged a bit at her collar as she worked up her courage. "Sorry to just barge in like this, but…well, I wanted to ask you something…if I may, that is."

Iruel nodded while extending his hand, a gesture inviting her to speak. "Go ahead, child."

"In my Pop's notes, it says you have some…unique powers." A chill shot up Jackie's spine. It was freezing in there. She wrapped her arms around herself to trap as much of her body heat as she could, but her voice still trembled a bit as she shivered. "One of those powers is to burn the evil out of people. The light that comes from your hands can exorcise demons and scorch a soul pure. At least, that's what the legends say. Is it true?"

"It is," Iruel replied.

Jackie nodded, more out of nerves than anything. "Does it…hurt?"

The vampire's voice remained as flat as ever. "It can. There are times when it is fatal."

"Fatal, right." Jackie gritted her teeth. For a moment, she thought of excusing herself and forgetting the whole thing, but she decided to press on. "Well…I got this condition, you see-"

"I am aware of it."

"How…? Never mind. Well, since you know about it, you can probably guess what I came here for." She looked into the vampire's golden eyes. "Can you burn this thing out of me? I know we're supposed to get Bismuth to undo everything, but…well, I don't know if I can wait that long, and if he doesn't for some reason…" She shuddered, but not at the cold. "So, can you?"

"No," Iruel said.

Jackie blinked, astonished by the promptness and flatness of his reply. "But you said -"

"I am capable of it, child, but I will not do what you ask of me."

Jackie's confusion gave way to indignation combined with desperation. "Why not? I'm suffering every day with this! If you can end it-"

"That is not the role I am meant to play in this venture." Iruel folded his arms across his chest and shook his head. "Besides which, you would not want me to intercede in this matter if you knew the truth. Things must occur as they are meant to."

"I don't understand."

"You will in time, if all goes as it should. For now, it is for the best that you return to your room." Iruel stepped aside, opening the path between Jackie and the door. "For what it is worth, child, I am truly sorry that you have suffered so."

At first, Jackie was bewildered by this enigmatic response to her plight. In an instant, her bewilderment turned to anger. "It's not worth much," she spat at Iruel as she stormed out of his room. The door closed on its own behind her.

Iruel did not seem the least bit offended by her retort.

Phillipe Bismuth had travelled from his compound in rural Louisiana to one of his churches in Kansas. He had stopped at several of his other churches along the way, of course, speaking to his congregations and accepting their offerings of local indigent women. He always had to be stealthy about entering and leaving towns, never setting a pattern that his enemies could follow. He looked forward to the day when that would end, when "His Way" became "The Way" across the world. He just had to rejuvenate his powers to the point where he could finish the work Donovan Van Sloan had interrupted.

Bismuth was deep in thought while he sat in a sauna, bathing in a tub of warm blood. He envisioned the day when the term "Hell on Earth" would no longer be a figurative expression, but glorious reality, over which he would be conqueror and king, for he would find a way to dethrone even the Devil himself.

Contrary to what many outsiders thought, Bismuth was not a Satanist. He could channel the Devil's black magic because they were convenient and easily manipulated, but he believed the Devil himself was pathetic and weak. With the right strategy, the Devil could be overpowered without the need for divine intervention. Of that, Bismuth was certain, and Belial had assured him that he was right to think so. According to the fallen angel, the legions of Hell were growing restless waiting for Judgment Day, and would swear allegiance to anyone who would push the schedule forward, which Bismuth alone could do. As such, he knew he would succeed where Lucifer had failed.

The thought thrilled him.

His machinations were interrupted by a knock at the door. "Enter," he commanded. Though the interruption irritated him, he did not want to dismiss any vital news, especially if it concerned Van Sloan.

The door opened only enough for Sharpe to step through without allowing the warm humid air to escape. He gagged at the stench of blood, and drew a handkerchief to his face. "Sorry to disturb you, Master, but there is new word of Van Sloan's activity."

Bismuth had been leaning back to relax in his bath, but now he sat upright to pay attention. "I am sure this disturbance is important if it concerns him. State your report, Sharpe."

"We received a call from a vampire just now, Master, one who said he used to be a follower of yours before he was turned. He said that nearly fifty of his cronies were slaughtered by Van Sloan and his comrades."

"The Occult Mafia kills vampires all the time. Why does this concern me?"

"Well, Master, Van Sloan's comrades weren't agents. You recall how he was travelling with a werewolf?"

"Yes."

"He now has a revived mummy, an ichthoid, and a vampire at his side as well. What's more, the vampire is Iruel himself."

Bismuth stood suddenly when he heard the name, the nakedness of his blood soaked body forgotten in light of the news he had just learned. "God's Vampire has cast his lot with Van Sloan?"

"It would seem so," Sharpe nodded, doing his best to keep his eyes averted from Bismuth's exposed body. "That was all the vampire told us before..." He hesitated for an instant, as what he was about to describe was just so absurd. "Well, his call ended suddenly when he screamed, and then I heard a sound like oil sizzling. The call was made at dawn, so in his panic, he must have lost track of time and dissolved in the sunlight."

"So the hunter really has cast his lot with the hunted." Bismuth stroked his chin as he considered this news. "How interesting."

"And concerning," Sharpe interjected. "Should we be worried, Master?"

Bismuth smiled. "We should be *prepared*, Sharpe, but worry does not suit us." As if to emphasize his point, he sat back down to resume his bath. "I can read Donovan Van Sloan as easily as I might read a child's picture book. After our last encounter, he knows better than to charge at me by himself, so he no doubt plans to make me come to him instead, and use these monsters against me."

As he contemplated this, a flash of brilliance struck him. "Perhaps we should play along for a time." He rose again and exited the tub, extending his hand towards the towels which hung by the door. One crimson-stained cloth leapt from the wall to his hand, and he wiped the blood from his body while he spoke. "How soon can you send a telegram to our compound in Grand Junction, Colorado?"

"I can be at the town offices in half an hour," Sharpe answered. "Why?"

"Send word to Thorne," Bismuth answered, naming the disciple who oversaw the Grand Junction compound. "Tell him we are ahead of schedule, and I have chosen Grand Junction as the new location for the Pandorum Ritual. A massive blood sacrifice will be required, of course, so the town must be destroyed."

Sharpe was confused. "But we're not *actually* ready, are we?"

Bismuth wrapped the towel around his waist. "Of course we're not, but I want you to tell Thorne that we are. I also want this information leaked to Van Sloan so he and his menagerie can arrive in time to do something about it."

Sharpe was stunned by what his master was saying. "But no one at the Grand Junction compound is equipped to handle such those kind of opponents, not even your apprentices. The monsters will slaughter them all!"

"I'm aware of that," Bismuth replied flatly as he opened the door.

"And you *want* them slaughtered, Master?"

Bismuth looked directly at Sharpe. There was no sign of sympathy in his eyes as he answered. "They are just another sacrifice to ensure victory. It is better we gain the world than lose a few dozen souls."

Though his master's logic made his blood run cold, Sharpe nodded in understanding. "As you wish, Master. A sacrifice they shall be."

XV.

Grand Junction, two days later

After searching for many agonizing minutes, Susan Walker had finally found temporary shelter inside a dumpster bin behind Lenny's, a local burger joint. It was not where she wanted to be, even if it was relatively empty after trash pickup, but it was the only place she could find to hide in a hurry. She had no idea what was happening around her, which made her already harrowing situation even more terrifying.

The day had been just like any other day in Grand Junction. The sun had risen, Susan had woken up, seen her husband and children off to work and school respectively, and had gone about her routine of cleaning, grocery shopping, and preparing for dinner.

When dusk fell, the chaos began. Over two hundred crazed men and women armed with makeshift weapons and torches had descended on the town and began tearing it to pieces. They were led by five individuals. These five were dressed in fine attire, commanded authority over the otherwise unruly mob, and had the ability to summon fire in their hands which they could hurl like baseballs. It was these five who had thwarted police intervention. Despite a valiant effort, the small town cops simply were not prepared for such opponents.

Within an hour, the town was nearly overrun. In the back of her mind, Susan knew that these deranged attackers were the cultists who taken up residence in the town's abandoned coal mine, but that did not really matter now. At first, her only thoughts were of finding her family, but these changed quickly to a more primal instinct of self-preservation as Grand Junction succumbed to the devastation.

For a relatively small mob, the cultists had been effective in their unrelenting attack. They raided every building, business and home alike, and set them ablaze. They killed indiscriminately, and those who were not killed suffered fates worse than death.

It was only by an incredible stroke of luck that Susan had come this far untouched, but she knew her luck would eventually run out. Her only hope of survival was to flee the town completely, but that hope was slowly dwindling. The rampaging cultists spread faster than she could run, and now she was surrounded. Panicked and desperate, she had taken shelter in the dumpster because there was nowhere else to go.

In all of her life, she had never felt so alone, or so uncertain. Was her husband still alive? Were her children safe? Would she ever see any of them again? If, by some miracle, she was the only survivor, how would she ever go on?

How long it had been since she ducked inside the dumpster, she did not know. Suddenly, the lid flew open, and a calloused hand reached in and pulled her out by the hair before throwing her onto the pavement. Sharp pain shot through her entire body as she landed flat on her back.

Susan tried rolling onto her front to scramble away, but was thwarted by a heavy boot upon her chest. She tried to struggle, but stopped when she felt the tines of a pitchfork at her throat. She could not move and was strained to breathe.

Her attackers illuminated by the sickening pale glow of a nearby streetlight. The one who had her pinned was a man, his wild beard matching his wild dark eyes. He had five companions with him, three other men and two women, all of whom looked as deranged as he.

"Hey Marty!" he called out. "Look what I found in the trash."

The one addressed as Marty stepped closer. He was a bit sharper-looking than the others, but this did little to lessen his menace. He glared down at Susan. "What an impressive find, Gilbert," he said. "Who in this wretched town would throw something like this away? She still looks to be in good condition to me."

Gilbert smiled a toothy grin that sent chills down Susan's spine. "I don't know. Maybe we ought to test her out and make sure she ain't broken."

A bit of drool dripped from Gilbert's mouth onto Susan's cheek. She attempted to escape once more, but to no avail. The other cultists inched closer to their prey.

Without warning, the sickening sound of metal piercing through flesh and bone signaled the death of Gilbert. He fell to the pavement with a loud thud, his pitchfork clattering beside him.

Susan could breathe again, but she did not flee. She was as stunned as her attackers by Gilbert's sudden demise.

Marty looked at his fallen comrade. A strange-looking bladed object was embedded between Gilbert's eyes. "What kind of crazy knife is that?" he asked, not quite believing what he was seeing.

Over the deafening sounds of torture and pillaging from the rest of the town, there arose a piercing hiss. In an instant, the cultists were suddenly surrounded by more snakes than any of them had ever seen before. The ground was crawling with serpents of all kinds moving as one towards them. Some were rattlesnakes native to the area, but mixed into their ranks were pythons, asps, winged cobras, and still others they did not recognize, but which had devilish horns atop their heads.

Toward the edge of the horde, some of the snakes began to cluster, piling one on top of the other until they formed a writhing, scaly tower almost six feet tall. The snakes squirmed about for a few seconds before falling away, revealing Ma'at. Strands of bandages that still clung to her body billowed around her as if they too were serpents. Through her mask, her eyes burned with righteous fury.

She stretched her arms out to each side. Beneath them, lights of every color imaginable appeared and took shape, forming the feathers on two knifelike wings.

Her eyes narrowed as she spoke one word that filled the air around them.

"Guilty."

Ma'at's wings arced forward, and bolts of rainbow-hued light shot through the cultists like bullets. Each bolt burned with the fury of the sun.

The cultists fell, but they were still alive and conscious as the hordes of snakes slithered forth. At Ma'at's command, the snakes devoured the cultists alive. Their screams were silenced in seconds, and when the snakes receded, only their discarded weapons remained.

Remarkably, Susan was untouched. She remained where she lay, too terrified to move, and watched as Ma'at yanked her kopesh from Gilbert's skull with a sickening shucking sound.

The goddess pointed with her blade towards a street where the flames had ceased. "Go westward, and you will be safe. Keep a straight path; do not turn, and do not hesitate." This was all she said before marching back into the blaze of the cultists' rampage. The army of snakes followed behind her.

Susan Walker did as she was told. She staggered back to her feet and ran as fast as she could. She hoped against hope that this second chance meant she would see her family when this nightmare was over.

*****

Elsewhere in Grand Junction, Ned Walker was also running for his life, but in a different environment that presented its own hurdles.

Ned worked in marketing on the eighth floor of an office building, and had been brainstorming a new ad campaign with his team when the cultists began their assault on the town. Because his office was on the western side of the building, and the cultists had come from the east, he and his team had not realized what was going on until it was too late. Twenty of the fiends had entered his building and spread throughout each floor, taking anything of value and killing anyone trapped inside with them.

Driven by thoughts of his wife and children, Ned immediately thought of escape. He was not a fighter by nature, and even if he had been, he would still not have wished to engage the cultists in battle. Whatever madness drove them made each one a thousand times more dangerous than any prize fighter.

He and a group of coworkers had descended cautiously, for they had no clue where the cultists might be lurking at any given point. Though the group had hoped to remain in the stairwell, they had abandoned that plan several times as the ascending cultists turned up in their path. By this point, Ned was on the fourth floor, weaving through cubicles, and he was totally alone. He did not know what had become of the others, whether they were dead or alive. It was terrible to consider that they might have been caught, given the carnage he had found on his descent. While snaking across the various floors, he had seen the mangled bodies of other coworkers strewn about. He did not even want to think of what had been done to them.

Glancing through the windows on this floor, he could see the city burning, and for a moment, he forgot himself and stood transfixed by the sight. He never imagined this sort of thing could happen here. These kinds of disasters happened in places like Europe or Asia, not in Grand Junction, Colorado. This happened to other people, not to him and his family.

His family...

Where were they? Had they found a way out? He dared not even consider the alternative. He had to survive and find them.

Through the window, something in the distance caught his eye. There was a swirling white mass in the air. At first, Ned thought it was a cloud of smoke, but the longer he watched it, the less he believed it. It was lighter in color than the billowing black haze of the inferno below, and it seemed to move with a will of its own. It also appeared to be drawing nearer, moving against the wind.

The opening of the stairwell door snapped him back to the here and now, and he clumsily ducked for shelter under the nearest desk.

He did not see what happened next, but he heard it with terrible clarity. The collision of the door as it slammed against the wall; the frantic footsteps of someone running; the singing of metal flying through the air punctuated by the piercing of flesh; the halt of the footsteps as the runner fell, the momentum carrying him forward before he was stopped something in his path.

Then came the sounds of other footsteps, accompanied by wicked voices he had never heard before, and hoped he would never hear again.

"Nice shot!"

"Practice makes perfect, you know."

"You've got to teach the rest of us how to do that one of these days."

"After the Master brings on the New Age, you'll have plenty of time to learn!"

Laughter. Awful, gut-churning laughter.

There were at least four of the maniacs on the floor now, though there might have been more. Ned did not dare to risk looking to find out.

He shifted in an attempt to squeeze further under the desk, but his hand slipped, driving his knuckles into the desk's leg. He stifled a cry of pain, and hoped to God that he had not been heard.

"What's that?"

This was it. They must have heard him, and now they were coming for him. Should he run now, or would it be better to just accept his fate? Perhaps, just this once, he should fight back?

He realized that it made no difference what he did now. He was dead either way, and he would never see his wife and children again.

"Looks like a cloud of smoke to me."

What?

"Can't be a cloud! It's moving against the wind, you idiot!"

The cultists had not seen him! They had seen the same strange phenomenon he had seen earlier.

"I don't think it is a cloud. Looks more like…birds."

Ned was at an angle which still allowed him a limited view outside of the window, and he glanced up just in time to see it shatter as countless white ravens forced their way through the glass. Ned curled himself into as tight a ball as he could to protect himself from the falling shards.

The screeching and flapping of the birds lasted for a few cacophonous seconds before subsiding. In their place came a new voice which, when it spoke, carried a mild Prussian accent and an unearthly quality that Ned could not place. "You have many sins to answer for," the new voice said.

Ned's curiosity overcame his fear. He dared to peer over the desk and see what was happening.

A pale skinned newcomer in old fashioned attire stood before the cultists. His complexion reminded Ned of a vampire, like the sort in the movies. He had no idea, of course, that this was no mere vampire, but Iruel.

"It is only fair to offer you a chance at redemption," Iruel said. "You can lay down your arms, renounce your allegiance to Phillipe Bismuth, repent, and leave this city. You will not incur my wrath if you do."

The cultist laughed mockingly in reply, and the one with the knife threw it at the vampire. As quickly as the knife had been released, Iruel raised his hand, and the point became embedded in a glowing dome of crosses and stars that surrounded him.

"So be it," Iruel said, his voice maintaining its even cadence. "If you will not renounce evil of your own free will, then it shall be purged from you."

Then Iruel looked over to Ned. "I suggest you take cover again, sir."

The unsettling golden glow in Iruel's eyes was all the convincing Ned needed. He ducked back down, closing his eyes and covering his ears.

It did little good. He could still hear it all as the cultists attacked the vampire. Sounds of blades slicing, bullets firing, wings flapping, and birds shrieking. Suddenly, he felt an impossibly bright, intensely hot light fill the room. The light was accompanied by screams of agony.

Then the light faded, and there was silence.

Ned opened his eyes slowly, and nearly leapt out of his skin when he saw Iruel crouched in front of him, examining him with those piercing gold eyes. He was wiping a trickle of blood from his chin with an embroidered handkerchief.

"You appear to be unharmed," Iruel said as he held out his hand. "Here, let me help you."

Though hesitant at first, Ned accepted the vampire's help. Iruel's hand was mostly ice cold, yet the center of his palm was surprisingly warm.

As he rose, he beheld what remained of the cultists' charred bodies. The sight made him nauseous.

"It is a shame," Iruel said, regarding the corpses. "They had given so much of their souls to evil that nothing was left to save. I have encountered many this night who are similarly lost. Such is the way of things sometimes." He withdrew a brass pocket watch, glanced at it, and nodded as he replaced it. "Wait here for five minutes while I clear the rest of the building. After that, leave and go west. Do not go east, or north, or south. Go west, and you will live."

With that said, Iruel faded into mist that dispersed from the room.

Ned was not entirely sure what to make of this strange intervention. It was so surreal, so contrary to everything he thought should be possible, that for a brief moment, he wondered if he had been hallucinating. The bodies strewn around him, however, were no illusion.

Though he was squeamish about staying in the room with the burnt husks that had once been people, he forced himself to remain exactly where he was for the next five minutes, at the end of which he fled the building without opposition and ran to the west.

On the one hand, it was fortunate that the elementary, middle, and high schools of Grand Junction were all connected by a cafeteria, because that meant the Walker children – fifteen year old Mike, thirteen year old Jenny, and ten year old twins Kyle and Kayla – were able to find each other quickly when the attack began. They each had something that kept them late after school: Mike had football practice, Jenny had rehearsals for the school play, and Kyle and Kayla had science club.

On the other hand, the connection of the schools was also unfortunate in this circumstance, as it allowed the cultists to easily round up all the children and force them into the cafeteria. They were all lined up along the southern wall and held at gunpoint by three of their captors. Two other cultists stood by the windows, discussing whether it was better to bring the children to the compound for labor and eventual indoctrination, or to just kill them all and be done with it.

The Walker children were huddled together at the edge of the lineup. The siblings did not usually get along very well, either at school or at home, but in the face of danger such as this, they were all determined to stick together, their differences forgotten during this harrowing ordeal.

Though none of them could clearly hear the cultists' discussion, their tone implied that a decision had been reached. One of the fiends marched forward and grabbed Mike by the collar, intending to drag him away from his siblings. Mike fought back, using his football training to gut check his opponent.

The cultist doubled over, but quickly righted himself. He retaliated by slamming the butt of his gun against Mike's temple, which knocked the teenager to the ground. With his quarry stunned, he grabbed Mike by the arm to continue dragging him away.

Jenny and the twins latched onto Mike's feet and pulled with all of their might, desperate to win the tug-of-war for their brother's life, even if victory meant death for them all.

No victor was ever determined, however, for both sides ceased pulling when the sprinkler system suddenly went off.

The sudden downpour was unexpected by everyone. There were currently no fires within the school, and the flames elsewhere in the city were not close enough to trigger the system. The sprinklers seemed to have activated on their own.

A scraping sound of metal on stone came from the hall leading to the middle school, its piercing noise making everyone cover their ears as their skin crawled.

Into the downpour stepped Erasmus Webster, wrist blades sparking as he drew their serrated edges away from the stone walls he had been dragging them across. He paused for a moment in the doorway, then launched into his attack.

He would never admit this to anyone, but the sight of children in danger enraged Erasmus in ways he could only express through violence, and that is exactly what he did.

There was no question that he would be victorious. The falling water disoriented his human targets, getting into their eyes and lungs, simultaneously blinding and choking them, but it gave the amphibian a distinct advantage. He was guaranteed to remain hydrated and at peak energy, and since he was built for the water, he could see and breathe clearly. What ensued was not so much a fight as it was a massacre, but it was the would-be killers of children who fell to the ichthoid's blades that night.

Blood mixed into the pooling water as Erasmus Webster stood triumphant. He was still for a moment as he absorbed water into his skin, allowing the oxygen to spread through his body. Having thus caught his breath, he turned to face the children.

He was relieved to see them unharmed, save for the boy who had been slugged before he got there, though he seemed to be recovering. Yet the children were still frightened of him. He could see the terror in their eyes as they stared, dreading what he might do next.

It occurred to the ichthoid that he should say something comforting, something that would let them know he would not harm them. He never voiced these thoughts, for doing so simply was not in his nature. The wrist blades retracted into their holsters, which was the only hint he gave of his true intentions.

"Head west," was all Erasmus said, pointing in that direction before taking his leave.

The children ran for the west as soon as he was gone.

"Reload."

Cool and focused, Donovan Van Sloan tossed his empty pistol to Jackie, who tossed him a loaded rifle in exchange.

Father and daughter were both in the bell tower of the Church of Saint John, an ideal location for numerous reasons. First, being hallowed ground, any supernatural attacks the cultists might employ would not touch them. Second, its bell tower was an ideal spot to plant a sniper, which is exactly the role Donovan was playing. The church was in the center of town, and it was one of the taller buildings, so it provided the perfect place for a gunman to fire on a target below.

Donovan had brought a vast assortment of guns with him, from basic six-shooters to Chicago typewriters. His strategy was simple: empty one gun, and another would be immediately ready to go, so he could keep firing as Jackie reloaded the empty ones. This also allowed him to keep his daughter close by.

So far, things appeared to be working in the Occult Mafia's favor. Donovan had received the leak about this attack in just enough time to have the train change course. The team had not arrived in time to prevent the attack, unfortunately, but they could still prevent the cultists from total victory.

Thanks to their intervention, the destruction of Grand Junction had not moved beyond the church, meaning the western half of the town was safe. By midnight, reinforcements would arrive from the Occult Mafia's headquarters in Denver, and this whole bloody affair would become a historical footnote, an urban legend people would debate the veracity of for decades to come. That was how things usually turned out when the Occult Mafia intervened in world history, and that was how precisely they preferred it.

Donovan had shot and killed six cultists on the street below before a loud click informed him that the rifle was empty. "Reload," he said once more as he tossed the rifle to his daughter.

Jackie caught the rifle and passed her father a loaded Colt .45 before she set about reloading. She had placed only one bullet into the chamber when she heard the entity's voice cut through her mind. *Shoot him,* she said.

"Shut up!" was Jackie's sharply whispered reply. She dropped the second bullet as her focus became hazy.

This was bad. If the entity somehow got control when she was surrounded by firearms, the whole plan would be in jeopardy, and her father would be in danger. Jackie squeezed her eyes shut as she tried forcing the entity from her mind. She groped blindly for the dropped bullet.

Let me out! the entity demanded.

Jackie dropped the rifle and grabbed her head, digging her nails into her skin.

It was no use. The entity was anxious to escape, as if she were inexorably drawn to the carnage below. Jackie could feel her defenses slipping. She did not have the strength to maintain control this time.

She rose and staggered toward the steps. If she could not fight the entity, she could at least get her as far from her father as possible.

"Reload," Donovan said once again as he tossed the empty Colt .45 to Jackie.

The clattering of the gun upon the floor, as well as the lack of a new weapon landing in his hand, immediately drew his attention away from the street.

"Jackie?" he asked, but there was no reply. He was alone with his armaments in the bell tower, and a trail of discarded religious trinkets led to the stairs.

All of the blood drained from Donovan's face. "No... Not now!"

Thorne, who led the assault on Grand Junction, used the black magic his Master had taught him to create a fireball in his hand, which he then lobbed at a fleeing citizen. He had killed many in this fashion that night, and the violent act had yet to lose its charm.

By this point, he was aware that somebody was up in the church's bell tower taking pot shots at his fellows like some sniveling coward. Thorne did not know who this sniper was, but soon it would not matter, for he would kill the sniper personally. The gunshots had stopped for the moment, which meant Thorne could get close to the church, possibly close enough to take the sniper down with one fireball. If that failed, he would enter and take a more hands-on approach

He found himself temporarily distracted as another cultists appeared ahead of him. He was running from one of the adjacent streets as though he were being chased. As Thorne watched, the cultist turned and frantically fired a few rounds at his pursuer, who had yet to come into view.

Two lengths of chain reached out like the sinewy tentacles of an octopus and coiled themselves around the cultist, binding his limbs at awkward angles before slamming him onto the pavement and dragging him back from whence they had come.

His original target forgotten, Thorne ran forward, fireball still in hand. Resistance from the townspeople had been expected, but no mere mortal was capable of manipulating chains in such a way. Something else was afoot.

He rounded the corner where his companion had disappeared and was met with a grisly sight. The cultist was splayed on the ground, his throat torn out by a werewolf who stood above him, chains dangling from his clenched fists.

Screaming a wordless battle cry, Thorne hurled his handheld fireball at the beast.

Loup Garou flicked his wrists, and his chains rose up before him, briefly forming an X-shape at just the right time to intercept the fireball and send it flying into a ruined storefront. The move was so subtle that the chains appeared to come alive on their own.

Thorne's body went rigid in a moment of terror, but when Loup began marching towards him, he was shaken into action. He started the spell and accompanying hand gestures to summon another fireball, looking down at his hands as he did so, lest his fear of the approaching monster distract him.

A sound of metal colliding with pavement broke his concentration and drew his eyes back to his opponent. The monster was moving slowly but deliberate, cracking his chains like whips. It was an obvious form of intimidation, and unfortunately for Thorne, it was working.

Thorne started backing away from the encroaching monster as he attempted his spell again. His hands refused to work, and the prospect of running away was becoming more and more appealing, even if it meant falling out of favor with the Master.

Thorne bumped into something behind him, but he was so focused on summoning another fireball while keeping his distance from Loup that he did not bother to see what it was. Had he looked, he might have lived a few seconds longer.

His concentration broke once more, this time interrupted by a searing pain worse than anything he had ever felt shooting up the length of his spine. No shriek was loud or shrill enough to express the extreme agony he felt.

Thorne's body went limp, but he did not fall. Through the pain, he became aware that his descent had been stopped by a pair of hands clutching his head tightly, nails digging into his skin. The hands seemed to be reaching up, as if their owner was shorter than him.

The hands had no intention of sparing Thorne. They pulled him back slightly, then drove him face first into the street. The strength which forced him down would have impressed Thorne had he survived the impact.

Loup Garou froze. He had not killed Thorne as he had intended to do. Someone else had beaten him to it.

It was only after Thorne's head had been smashed into the street that he saw the killer. It was Jackie, but at the same time it was not Jackie. Her skin was covered in fine black scales, her fingernails were replaced by sharp talons, her muscles were slightly more defined, and her eyes were inverted to white pupils set in black orbs. She had shed her overcoat, leaving her in clothes too thin for a cold evening, and yet steam radiated from her body.

The entity had taken full control.

She stood before the werewolf, staring at him with a wicked grin, her right hand dripping with blood from having lacerated Thorne's spine. With her left hand, she tipped her top hat in a manner so polite that it must have been sarcastic.

Loup glanced up at the bell tower. He saw no sign that Donovan was still up there, and neither did Ben.

"Thanks for the assistance," Loup said warily as he turned his attention back to the entity.

"I didn't do it for you, fur ball," the entity replied in her strange voice. *"I did it because it felt good."*

Loup took a few cautious steps closer. "It helped either way. Now what say we get you back inside?"

"No chance," replied the entity before taking off like a shot down the street.

She did not get far, as one of Loup's chains lashed out and ensnared her wrist. With a mighty yank, Loup pulled her back towards him.

The entity must have anticipated the move, for she spun in midair so as to pounce on her newfound opponent like a leopard. She tackled him, which sent them both into a tumbling roll down the street. When they finally came to a halt, the entity was on top. She pounded her fists on Loup's chest, forcing the air from them, then she stood and raised her foot.

Loup could tell she was about to stomp on his groin. Unable to right himself, he rolled away. The entity missed her intended target, but she did crush a section of the werewolf's tail, eliciting a startled yelp.

Now driven by both pain and anger, Loup decided not to hold back as he stood. He whipped around and delivered a low punch to the entity's gut, immediately followed with an uppercut to the chin that sent her reeling backwards. Finally, he whipped a chain around the entity's left leg and pulled, sending her sprawling onto her back.

In a flash, he was above her. Loup placed a foot on the entity's neck, applying just enough pressure to make her gasp for air. "Yield!" he shouted.

"Up yours!" the entity sneered.

Loup shifted more weight onto her neck. "You should know better than to mess with me, kid!" Loup snarled.

"I know plenty about you, freak!" the entity spat back. *"I know things that would make Pop kill you on the spot if I told him!"*

"You're bluffing." Loup Garou applied even more pressure. The entity's throat was nearly crushed.

"LOUP GAROU!!!"

The threatening shout came from the steps of the church. It was Donovan, and he was closing in fast. He closed the distance between them before Loup had any time to explain or react.

Donovan clamped his metal claw onto Loup's hand, and its silver coating burned the wolf's skin. He glared into the wolf's eyes with a fury so intense that it chilled Loup and Ben to their core. "Back off, you cur," Donovan commanded, "or so help me, I will rip out every single one of your claws, and I won't be quick about it!"

Loup released the entity, and Donovan released him an instant later. As Loup retreated and clutched his injured hand, he watched as Donovan took a large metal crucifix – one he had no doubt found somewhere in the church – and placed it on top of the entity. It was heavy enough to pin her, and she struggled and writhed as the icon forced her to recede again.

The moment his daughter was fully restored, Donovan shoved the cross aside and scooped her into his arms. It was an awkward move for him, given the state of his right arm, but he managed to hold her closeas he carried her back to the church.

As he passed by, Donovan shot Loup a condemning glare. It served as a reminder for the pair to be wary of Donovan Van Sloan.

Loup did not dawdle after the Van Sloans had reentered the church. There were still cultists to deal with in Grand Junction, and the night was still young.

XVI.

By the end of the night, Bismuth's followers were defeated and summarily slaughtered. The sun rose that morning on a town scarred by the battle; the fires had consumed roughly half of the buildings, and an estimated four hundred of the original one thousand residents had been lost.

In spite of the damage, Donovan still declared it a victory for the Occult Mafia, and this meant it was time to put his master plan into motion. To do so, he and his recruits headed to where the cultists had dwelt.

The compound was situated in the mountains east of Grand Junction. It had once been a coal mine in the days of the Wild West, but it had been abandoned ages ago when the coal was depleted. The area had been entirely renovated, with new buildings alongside old ones that had been gutted and refurbished. The actual mine remained open, for it was a great place to stockpile supplies and weapons for the promised day when Bismuth conquered the world. A large brick wall encompassed the area, with a wrought-iron gate as its entrance. The gate usually had two guards keeping watch, and five crudely-made sentry towers for one guard each were positioned equilaterally around the wall. All of Bismuth's cultic communes had this setup. It was just enough security to discourage trespassers, but not so much that it drew unwanted attention from the authorities.

Upon their arrival, Donovan had one of his agents send a message to Bismuth. He was speak as a cultists and tell the warlock that Grand Junction was destroyed, and they eagerly awaited his arrival. This done, Donovan and his monstrous entourage took a tour of the compound to familiarize themselves with the terrain.

Following that, the group retired for a much needed day of sleep. Iruel had his coffin placed in the building which served as the compound's town hall. Erasmus went to the swimming pool, around which guards were posted to ensure that he did not try leaving. Donovan and Jackie took adjacent rooms in the lodge, while Ben and Ma'at shared a room in one of the housing complexes.

The next evening, Ben awoke before Ma'at, and decided not to wake her. He left their bed as carefully as he could, threw his clothes on, and headed for the cafeteria building. There he found Donovan in the kitchen, making omelets at the stove. He looked a bit awkward doing this mostly with his left hand. Out in the dining area, Ben saw an exhausted Jackie sitting alone, waiting for her breakfast. She stared out at nothing. It was one of the most pathetic sights either Ben or Loup had ever seen.

At first, Ben said nothing as he grabbed a loaf of bread, nor did Donovan speak. They had not really spoken since Loup's sparring match with the entity, and Ben was not entirely sure if Donovan wanted to even see either of them. He likely would have remained silent the whole while had the toaster not been located so close to the stove, which ultimately forced him next to the monster hunter.

Ben placed his bread slices in the toaster, pushed the lever down slowly, drummed his fingers, and finally decided to just bite the bullet. "Good morning, Don," he said, his voice completely neutral.

"Morning," Donovan replied, not taking his eyes off the omelets. His voice was also neutral, and his expression unreadable. Ben could not tell if he was mad or simply focused on preparing the food before him. Loup could read no signs, either.

"About last night," Ben said. "Loup was being rough, I know that, but he wasn't going to kill Jackie or anything. We were trying to help. That's the God's Honest Truth."

"I know," Donovan replied, still not taking his eyes off the stove. "The entity hasn't taken full control like that in a long time, and when it happened again… Well, I was scared I'd lost my little girl for good last night, and the wolf caught the brunt of it. That's all."

Ben's eyes briefly flicked back to Jackie, who was now sprawled out on the table, possibly asleep again. "How is she?"

"Twice as scared as I am, but she hasn't had any problems since last night." Donovan sighed. "The end of this whole mess can't come soon enough."

Ben nodded. He could understand that. "Well, we're both sorry," he said.

"Me too," Donovan replied as he moved the finished omelets from the pans to the waiting plates. For the first time since the previous night, he looked Ben in the eyes. "Let's just put it behind us and concentrate on finishing the job. Water under the bridge, you know? Jackie ain't holding a grudge, so I won't either."

With that said, Donovan took the omelets and left the kitchen.

Ben' glanced at a large metal spoon hanging on the wall. Loup appeared on its reflective surface, a melancholic expression on his face. "I really want to believe him, Ben," he said.

"Me too, bud," Ben nodded. "Me too."

The toaster popped, and Ben sighed in frustration to find the toast was burnt.

*****

After settling for a banana and untoasted bread for breakfast, Ben left the cafeteria and the Van Sloans behind him. He decided to return to his room and see if Ma'at was awake yet. On his way back, though, Erasmus intercepted him and said he had something to show him.

The ichthoid led the werewolf to the mine-turned-stockpile. "I found some old maps from when this place was an active mine," Erasmus said, keeping his voice low so he would not be overheard by Donovan's guards. "Looks like the humans dug pretty far into these hills. So far, in fact, that they wound up in completely different mines, and that caused quite a few claim disputes back in the day. The point is there's a vast network of tunnels down there which leads all over this part of Colorado."

"You think they might be our ticket out of here?" asked Ben, following suit by lowering his voice as well.

Erasmus nodded. "So many branching paths, they'll have a hard time knowing which one we took, and all the openings lead to civilization in one form or another."

"Sounds like a good plan to me," Ben said. "So once Bismuth is worm chow, we'll meet you here and be home free."

"Actually, I've been thinking about that." Erasmus leaned against a nearby crate. "Suppose we high tail it out of here *during* the showdown rather than after it."

Ben blinked in astonishment. "Run out before we've finished him off? You can't be serious."

"You'll notice I'm not smiling."

Indeed, Erasmus was not smiling, but Ben was still unsure. "Listen, the only reason Loup and I took this job was to get revenge on Bismuth."

"Well, the only reason *I* took this job is because Van Sloan took me prisoner," Erasmus fired back. "Besides, you're the one who said he'd probably kill us when this is all over. You still believe that, don't you?"

"Yes... Maybe... I don't know." Ben ran his fingers though his hair, flustered by his sudden indecision. "If he's playing the long game, then he's the best con we've ever met. Loup and I have been with Donovan longer than you have, and, well, it just doesn't make sense for him to kill us all afterward."

Erasmus' eyes narrowed in suspicion. "Don't tell me you're actually starting to trust him."

Ben threw his hands up, raising his voice as much as he dared in frustration. "Who knows if he's trustworthy? If nothing else, he's sincere about his kid. Even with all that aside, Bismuth is a genuine threat. He wants to unleash the forces of Hell on Earth, remember? If he does that, we're all doomed."

Erasmus shrugged. "He's tried it before, and seeing as how we're both standing here talking about it, he clearly hasn't succeeded yet. Van Sloan will still have the vampire, and he could probably stop Bismuth all by himself."

"Probably, but...well..." Ben wanted to disagree, but he could not. Erasmus' argument was not a very strong one, but he spoke it with such confidence that it sounded airtight. Ben and Loup were already questioning things, and being confronted with this in the throes of doubt made arguing difficult. "I'm just not sure it's the right move."

"Well I am." Erasmus walked towards Ben until their faces were inches apart, the ichthoid's glowing goggled eyes staring into Ben's own. "Van Sloan has watchmen all over this place, which is the only reason I haven't made tracks already. When Bismuth shows up, though, it'll be pandemonium, perfect conditions for us to slip away without anyone noticing until it's too late. That's my plan, and I'm sticking to it whether you join me or not." He coughed dryly. "Excuse me. This blasted desert air's drying me out."

Erasmus left Ben standing at the mouth of the cave. He had made up his mind, and nothing was about to sway him.

Ben and Loup, meanwhile, were more uncertain than before.

Jackie had wanted to return to her room, and she had wanted her father to lock her in and place armed guards at the door and window. He had obliged her with both requests. He had also used some charcoal to draw crosses on the walls. He did not, however, allow her to keep the knife she had snuck out of the cafeteria, with which she had intended to carve a cross into her abdomen. He said it was bad enough that she beat the tar out of herself to keep the entity contained, but he drew the line at intentional scarring.

So she sat alone in her room, with no objects to harm herself with in sight. She had nothing to do but sit on the edge of her bed and watch television. She was not really paying attention to it. After about an hour of staring at some mindless sitcom, the broadcasting day had ended, replaced by the classic profile of the Indian chief. Jackie stared at the screen because it was the only distraction she had.

She barely even noticed when her father entered the room. She just sat on the edge of her bed, as still as a statue.

"How're you holding up?" Donovan asked.

Jackie's only reply was the subtle lowering of her eyes away from the screen, which conveyed her inner turmoil.

"Well, there is some good news," Donovan said as he sat down next to his daughter. "A telegram just came in saying Bismuth is on his way. That means we got him, kiddo. Just a couple more days, and this'll be over. You'll finally be back to normal."

Tears welled up in Jackie's eyes. "What difference will it make?" she sobbed. "I lost it, Pop. She got out. I couldn't control her. I…" Her emotions suddenly flowed out of her in a torrent. She clung to her father's chest and bawled into his suit jacket. "I wanted be like you and Mom, but I'm not! I'm worthless! I'm weak! All I do is get in the way and make everything worse! If I hadn't gone with you last year, you'd still have your hand and Mom would still be alive! It's my fault! Everything that's gone wrong is my fault!"

With his left arm, Donovan hugged his daughter close to him, gently rocking her ever-so-slightly with a calm "Shh," on his lips. Jackie's sobbing lessened slightly as she tried to catch her breath.

"None of this is your fault, Jackie," Donovan said. "It's Bismuth's fault, and no one else's."

Jackie sniffled loudly. "I wish I could be more like you."

"I know," Donovan said as he patted her on the shoulder. "I wanted to be like your grandpa when I was a kid. He had a way of fighting evil that was legendary. He didn't just fight the good fight, he did it with style. There was a theatricality to the way he did things, and I tried emulating him when he was training me. I blew it every time, though, and he'd always scold me for it, calling me worthless, threatening to disown me and kick me out on the street. When I told him I just wanted to be like him, he looked right at me and said, 'You never will be,' and that stung in the worst way."

He paused, allowing the revived memory of how he felt that day to pass through him. During this brief silence, he noticed that Jackie's crying seemed to have subsided somewhat, which meant he had her attention. "Eventually, he pulled a trick on me. One night when I was about your age, he sent a ghoul into my bedroom. I didn't know he was behind it at first, though. I just panicked. I'd never fought a ghoul before, and I'd never seen your grandpa fight one, so I had no training to go on."

"What'd you do?" asked Jackie.

"I improvised. It all happened so fast, I didn't even have time to think. It was instinct that drove me. I remembered the doorknob to my room was made of iron, one of the essential metals for warding off evil, so I ripped it from its socket and bashed the freak's head in." He smiled at the memory of his first solo victory. "Basically, I did what I thought would work, and it did. It was ugly, blunt, not theatrical at all, but it was straightforward, and I won. Once the ghoul was dead, that's when the old man came in, smiling and clapping. He was finally pleased with me, and I was angry at him until he explained himself. He said that as long as I kept trying to imitate him, I'd always fail. To succeed, I had to be my own man, with my own way of doing things. It was a lesson that really stuck with me, and I've been a straight shooter ever since."

"Sounds like a lesson that could've killed you."

"Your grandpa had a different way of showing folks he cared."

As gently as he could manage with his mechanical right hand, Donovan lifted Jackie's chin up so he could look her in the eye. "Your mother and I wanted the same for you, Jackie. You're going through a trial like no one else ever has, and I know it's horrible, but you're still here. You're still alive, and you're just a couple days away from being free. You'll come out of this experience changed, but you can use that change to become your own woman."

The tears returned to Jackie's eyes as she buried her face in Donovan's shirt again.

Donovan sighed. "You're probably not in the right frame of mind to accept that now, but you will be soon."

When she had no tears left to cry, Jackie propped herself back into a sitting position and wiped her running nose on her sleeve. "Pop, there's something I need to tell you."

"Go ahead."

Jackie was going to tell her father what she had overheard Ben, Loup, and Erasmus talking about. She was going to warn him of their intention to betray him in some way. She was going to tell him that he had to act before something went wrong.

Don't you dare, twerp.

The voice of the entity echoed in her mind.

Tell him about the wolf and the frog, and I'll make sure you regret it.

Jackie hesitated.

She had to say something.

"I miss Mom," she eventually said.

Donovan nodded, oblivious to his daughter inner conflict. "I miss her too, Jackie."

After his unexpected meeting with Erasmus, Ben and Loup finally caught up with Ma'at, who had already gotten breakfast in their absence. They spent the next few hours exploring the compound. It was Ma'at who discovered that the chapel had various secret passageways built into its walls, some leading outside, other leading to underground chambers. Bismuth doubtless knew about them, but Ma'at thought they could still prove useful in the final confrontation.

After a time, hunger guided them both back to the cafeteria. Ben was feeling relaxed and a bit playful now that he was in Ma'at's company again, so he went behind the bar and put on the air of a bartender. "Welcome to Bismuth the Bastard's Bar and Grill, my dear," he said with a cheesy grin on his face. "Can I get you anything to drink? Vermuth? Tequila, perhaps?"

Ma'at leaned on the counter, a smile on her face as well. "I would fancy a beer, if there is any."

Ben was a bit surprised. "Beer? That's not a very ladylike drink."

"Beer was a delicacy in the empire" Ma'at explained. "The drink of kings and warriors. It would be a shame if it no longer existed."

Ben began checking the contents of the bar. "Oh, they still make it, doll face. Beer's an industry unto itself these days. Kind of surprised you didn't try it on the train."

"I did not know there was any on the train."

"We asked Donovan to get some after we picked up Erasmus. Guess it slipped our minds to tell you. Would've made some of our evenings more fun. Let's just see... Ah!" Ben produced a bottle from one of the lower cabinets and placed it before the Egyptian, popping the top with an opener as he did. "One room temperature beer for the lovely lady in bandages."

Ma'at examined the bottle. "Are there any straws to filter out the dregs?"

Ben poured himself a glass of bourbon as he answered. "Our modern American beer is one hundred percent dreg free." His voice became even cornier. "That's the Ben Andante guar-an-tee!"

"That is enough for me. To the Glory of the Pharaoh," Ma'at toasted. She raised the bottle to her lips and downed the contents in five big gulps. As she lowered the bottle, a quizzical look crossed her face. "So..." she began, her voice carrying a hint of uncertainty. "This is what you call beer, then?"

Ben shrugged. "The recipe may have changed in the last couple centuries. Do you not like it?"

"I am not sure," Ma'at said. "May I have another to help me decide?"

Ben retrieved the whole case and placed it on the counter. "In case you decide you do like it," he grinned.

A cold cloud of mist passed by the couple, taking the form of Iruel beside Ben. The vampire held a bottle in his hand, and his golden eyes scanned the bar until he found a stemmed glass that was to his liking.

"Good evening, Iruel," Ben said in a friendly voice. "Can I interest you in a drink?"

"Thank you, no," Iruel replied. "I have brought my own." Setting the glass on the counter, he poured the bottle's contents into it, a thick red substance that was definitely not wine.

Ben chuckled. "Let me guess." He adopted a fake Hungarian accent. "You never drink...wine?"

He laughed at his joke, but his laughter faded as he realized no one else had joined him. Ma'at was staring at him blankly, and Iruel's expression was as unreadable as ever. Ben shrugged. "Never mind," he said.

I got it, Ben, Loup consoled.

"Joking aside," said Iruel, "I would very much like to speak with you, Mr. Andante. Please." He glided away from the counter, motioning for Ben to follow him. Ben did so, leaving Ma'at to continue making up her mind about modern beer.

Iruel stopped at the far end of the bar, behind which was a mirror. Loup appeared in place of Ben's reflection. Iruel, being a vampire, cast no reflection. Only a pitch black hole bearing his outline stood in the mirror's surface. He took a sip from his glass, and turned. "Why are you two here, Mr. Andante? With Van Sloan, I mean."

"Revenge, plain and simple," Ben answered.

"Is that all?"

"It's all that matters," said Loup from the window.

"Then why have you not pursued this vengeance before?"

"Because we know better than to face Bismuth on our own. But Donovan's got a plan, and he let us in on it, so we're taking the chance."

Iruel cocked an eyebrow. "Then you trust Van Sloan?"

"Absolutely not," Ben replied.

"You don't trust him, yet you follow him?" asked the vampire as he took another sip.

Ben and Loup glanced at each other, unsure of how to answer. It was somewhat paradoxical. True, neither of them had fully trusted the Van Sloans at first, but they were no longer confident in that mistrust. It was only now occurring to them that they were starting to see Donovan and Jackie in a different light. Their hesitancy to abandon them upon hearing Erasmus' escape plan was evidence of that.

"Well, what about you?" Ben asked, hoping to turn the tables. "You leapt right onboard without much convincing. Do you trust a man who kills vampires for a living?"

Iruel shook his head. "You misunderstand me, good sirs. I trust in the Lord, and I go where His will guides me."

"Bah!"

This loud scoff came from Ma'at, who had, impressively, finished the entire case of beer, and the alcohol was clearly affecting her. She was hunched over the counter as she glared past Ben at Iruel. "And what does the God of Abraham know of Justice?" she slurred.

"Quite a bit," Iruel replied flatly. "He created Justice, after all."

"I *am* Justice," Ma'at snapped. She stood upright, using the counter to steady herself. "Justice gives victory to the righteous and punishment to the wicked. Your God...your God has no Justice, vampire! Your God is a murderer!"

Iruel finished his glass and drifted a few steps in the mummy's direction. "And what, pray tell, has led you to this conclusion?"

"The Plagues!" Ma'at shouted as she stomped closer. "Your God and His wretched mouthpiece, the Pharaoh's half-brother, sent the Plagues upon my kingdom! Parasites, blood, darkness, famine... We suffered by your God's will, and I was powerless to do anything!" She became intensely sad. "I lost so many friends to starvation and disease, so many..." Just as quickly, she was filled with rage again. "And why did your God do it, vampire? For the sake of the slaves? What sort of god favors vermin over kings?"

"The sort who sees both as equal," was Iruel's calm, even reply.

"Slaves equal to kings? Nonsense!" Ma'at drew even closer, her hands clenching into fists. "The Plagues were an injustice of the worst sort!"

"Then why could you do nothing to stop them, Ma'at?" Iruel was still calm even as he presented this challenge. "You are the enemy of injustice, but you are also incapable of being unjust yourself. Why, then, did you do nothing to stop the Ten Plagues?" He did not wait for an answer. "Though you may deny it, I believe that deep down, you know that the true injustice was the persecution of the Jews, and it was your commitment to Justice that stayed your hand."

"How *dare* you!" Ma'at drew her hand back, clearly telegraphing a slap aimed at the vampire's pale face.

Suddenly, her body tensed, joints locking and holding her in place. She twitched in an attempt to move, but it was to no avail.

"What are you waiting for?" asked Iruel. "If I am slandering you unjustly, strike me."

Ma'at struggled, urging her unmoving hand to fly forward, but it refused. She could not strike the vampire. Doing so was...was...

Ma'at screamed in anger as her hand finally moved, but it did not go forward to hit Iruel. Instead, it rose up, balled into a fist, and came crashing back down onto the counter. The wood splintered on impact. She then swept it across the flat surface, a move which sent the empty beer bottles sailing through the air before shattering against the floor.

She turned from the vampire and stormed away. She could not even utter the parting insult she so desperately wanted to scream at him.

Ben ran after her, leaving Iruel alone in the cafeteria. As stoic as ever, he poured himself another glass.

"God's Will be done."

"Ma'at, wait!"

Ben's call stopped Ma'at, and he thought this was a good sign. He would embrace her, calm her down, tell her not to let Iruel's words bother her, and then they would go back to their room so he could continue consoling her.

Before any part of Ben's desired vision could occur, Ma'at turned and asked, "Which God do you serve?" Her voice was low and carried a hint of fear behind it, as though she dreaded the answer.

Ben stopped a few steps away from her. He and Loup both had a sinking feeling about her question. "What do you mean?" he asked, hoping that playing dumb might diffuse the situation.

"You said werewolves are divine beings," Ma'at said as tears began to form in her eyes. "By whose divinity are they made? Is it the God of Abraham?"

Ben said nothing.

"Tell me!" Ma'at demanded.

"…Yes," Ben said. "Loup and I aren't the best at following the rules, but yes."

"I see." Ma'at sounded as though a knife had just been driven into her heart. "And…do you agree with Iruel?"

Of course she had to ask that question. Answering it truthfully was guaranteed to make things worse, but Ben could not bring himself to lie about that subject. "Yes," he finally admitted. "Slavery is…" He sighed. "Well, this country was almost split apart because of it a century ago. They weren't Jewish slaves, but enslaving anyone…well…it's just inhuman."

Ma'at lowered her eyes, as though this answer stung her even more than the last one. "Then you think me inhuman as well." It was not a question. She had already decided it was true.

"That's not what I mean!" Ben said as he hazarded to get closer. "None of this changes how we feel about you."

Ma'at turned away. "I cannot say the same," she said, her voice heavy with sadness.

Now Ben felt stabbed in the heart. "You don't mean that."

"Leave me alone…please." With that, Ma'at walked away, moving as quickly as she could. She still attempted to hold herself regally, but there was no disguising her sadness.

Ben stayed rooted in place. Since he and Loup had woken up, not a single one of their interactions had gone the way they expected. After a night such as this, neither of them knew how to feel about this journey they were on, or how this unrest would affect things when Phillipe Bismuth arrived.

Ma'at locked herself in her room and broke down in tears.

When she had first been revived and brought into this new century, she had accepted quickly that things would be different from what she had known. Yet the longer she was here, the more things she encountered that challenged her.

The memories of the Ten Plagues were still fresh in her mind. The horror of that time was unlike anything she had ever faced, yet she had been unable to intervene. Even when the people – their emaciated bodies covered in boils and sores – crawled to her and clung to her feet begging her for help, all she could do was apologize to them for her inaction. She was the immortal Goddess of Justice, so she had remained alive and healthy as the empire around her suffered, yet she could still do nothing.

That agonizing period was the first time it had ever occurred to her that the world could end one day.

It was all by the God of Abraham's will that her people had suffered, and He did it to rescue those who were subhuman. She could not fathom how a being more powerful than all of the empire's gods combined would show favor for such worthless creatures.

Were Iruel and Ben correct? Was she unable to stand against the God of the slaves because slavery was an injustice? Ma'at's status in the empire had allowed her the right to own slaves, including Jewish ones, but she had never really treated them poorly. Her slaves actually lived better than those of the many pharaohs she had known.

Still, slaves were property, and she had treated them accordingly. She rewarded them for doing well, and punished them for doing poorly. It was just an accepted practice of her culture.

Then again, had her culture really been so perfect? Had it not been a pharaoh who betrayed her? But Akhenaten had been a heretic, a pharaoh who served a false god of his own making, and he had risen to power well after the Plagues.

What to conclude about the Plagues, then? If the Plagues were truly undeserved, she would have had the strength to oppose them, yet she had not.

Ma'at did not know what to believe about her past. She only knew that in the present, the here and now, she had been summoned for a reason. The man she now followed served a deity whom she had long viewed as an enemy, yet he opposed evil in much the same way she did.

She wondered if she could just leave, washing her hands of the whole matter. This was Donovan Van Sloan's private war, one in which she had no personal stake. As such, perhaps she had no reason to stay.

The thought was banished from her mind just as quickly as it had come. Based on everything she had seen and learned, she knew Phillipe Bismuth's life was itself a grave injustice. He advocated violence and chaos to rival Set himself, and she had seen a whole settlement of innocent people razed by his orders.

Ma'at's choice was clear. She could not allow her personal grudges to prevent her from doing what she was born to do. The warlock had to be vanquished, no matter what.

As if in response to her decision, there came a knocking on the door. "Miss Ma'at?" asked a voice from outside. It was one of the Occult Mafia agents who had been sent in as backup. "Mr. Van Sloan requires your presence in the chapel. He wants to go over the plans for when Bismuth arrives tomorrow."

Ma'at opened the door, forcing her emotions to subside for the time being. "Lead the way, Sir. Justice must be served."

XVII.

One night remained before Bismuth's expected arrival, and Donovan had laid out his plan perfectly. He had seen to every detail, accounted for every eventuality he could think of, and now all anyone could do was wait and memorize their roles. That was probably why the others were all keeping to themselves that night.

It was nearly midnight, and Donovan had just gotten Jackie through another strenuous bout with the entity. She was in her room recovering, since this one had been especially draining for her. Or rather, that was what she had told him. In the past, Jackie had recovered quickly from these struggles. She had only become lethargic after the battle at Grand Junction. Not even his encouragement in the wake of it had done anything to ease her feelings of worthlessness.

All Donovan could do for her was respect her desire to be left alone, though he still made sure his agents were watching her, and that she had no access to anything she could harm herself with.

Donovan was currently outside, allowing the cool, dry air of the desert night to fill his lungs and calm his spirits. Memories of the bloody battle still lingered with him, and though he did not regret killing any of the maniacs, doing so was something he never truly adjusted to. This discomfort was the one thing he had to remind him of his own humanity.

He wandered through the compound with no particular destination in mind, but found himself passing by the old mine. He was surprised to see Ben wandering out of it, but not as surprised as Ben acted when Donovan called out to him. He walked very quickly to where Donovan stood, almost too quickly, as if he had just been caught lurking someplace he should not have been.

"You all right?" Donovan asked as Ben drew near.

Ben cleared his throat. "Um… Loup and I are just apprehensive about tomorrow, I guess," he answered.

"Is that all?" Donovan pressed, detecting a hint of something more in his voice.

Ben hesitated, licking his lips as his eyes darted around nervously. "Well…" he began, then sighed and slumped his shoulders slightly. "If you must know, things haven't been going so well with Ma'at since yesterday."

Donovan nodded as the two began walking back towards the heart of the compound together. "I thought something seemed different between you two. Anything you want to talk about?"

"Nah, it's just a rough patch. It'll pass, and if it doesn't, we had fun while it lasted."

"Spoken like a genuine hardboiled detective."

"What can I say? Some clichés are true to life. Speaking of which…" Ben took a flask from his pocket and knocked back a swig of its contents. He then extended the flask to Donovan. "Care for a taste to wet your whistle? Does wonders for nerves, too."

"Why not?" Donovan replied, taking the flask and gulping down a sip before handing it back.

"…Huh…" Ben mused.

"What?"

"Just a little surprised, is all. You drank from the same flask as a monster without giving it a second thought."

Donovan sighed. "Are you really still hung up on that after all this time? What'll it take to convince you I'm not a sadistic killer?"

Ben shrugged. "Old habits die hard. Like I've said, you've killed friends of mine."

"If I did, they probably had it coming. Evil is my enemy, Ben. Think about it, were these so-called friends of your good people?"

Ben thought for a moment. "If I'm being honest, most of them were underworld types, and I guess they did do some pretty nasty things in their time. We only got to know them through the cases we took, and in the private eye business, you don't generally meet good people anyway." He took another swig from his flask. "Still, they were the only friends we had."

"Well, if they really mattered that much to you, then I'm sorry," Donovan said. "I can't take back what I did, and I can't say I regret it, but it wasn't personal. It's just the nature of the job."

"Is that all it is to you? Just a job?" Ben pocketed his flask.

"It's my life, and I would think you'd know a thing or two about that." Donovan paused under a spotlight that was flickering. He slammed his claw against the pole, and the light stabilized. "Like I said when we first met, I've kept tabs on you for a while. You and Loup have spent your whole lives helping people, the way you lycans are supposed to. Why else would you become a private eye? It sure ain't for the glory and the money. That tells me you two feel very strongly about doing the right thing."

"You could say that, I guess," Ben admitted. "We've always done our best to take cases that feel right...you know, morally speaking. Way back when, I think we were trying to break the stereotype, but after a while, that didn't matter. We just want to do the right thing."

Donovan smiled wryly. "And get revenge on Bismuth, of course."

"Of course," Ben said, returning the smile.

"Well, you may not have had many friends in the detective business, but for what it's worth, I've decided you've got a friend in me." Donovan gave Ben a friendly pat on the shoulder. "I've got both of your backs, and I trust that you've got mine too."

Ben's body tensed slightly as he cleared his throat. "Yeah, same here," he lied, and felt terrible for doing so.

Donovan nodded in approval before glancing up at the sky. "It's a shame there won't be a full moon tomorrow. You'd be at peak strength if there were."

"Oh, tomorrow will be interesting no matter what," said Ben.

"You know," Donovan continued, oblivious to the subtext of Ben's reply, "once this is all over, we'll still drop you back off in Chicago, but you can also stay with us, if you want to. I think we make a pretty good team, occasional disagreements aside. If you and Loup wanted to permanently sign up with us, you could."

Ben blinked in shock. "I didn't think the Occult Mafia let guys like us join."

"Normally not, but this whole experience has me thinking some changes are in order. We'd have very discerning criteria, of course, but I think we could do much more for the world working together. Not to mention it would clear up our reputation a bit. Good against Evil, not Man against Monster. So what do you say? You want in?"

Ben and Loup were too stunned to respond for a second. Yet again, this was something neither of them had expected.

Ben finally stammered out a reply. "Um… That's, uh, that's very generous. I… We…Can we think about it?"

"Absolutely," Donovan nodded, "as long as it doesn't distract you tomorrow. We've still got a job to do, after all." He looked at his watch. "Hate to cut and run, but I should go check on Jackie. Thanks for the drink." He broke away and headed back to the lodge.

Ben watched Donovan leave, then redirected his gaze to a nearby window, in which Loup was reflected. They had to be face-to-face for this conversation. "He sounded pretty sincere just then, Loup."

"I heard," Loup said. He felt just as torn as his human host did. "You think it's still a trick? Because I'm not so sure anymore. He hasn't slipped up at all. No con is that good."

"Agreed," Ben conceded. "Maybe it's not a trick, but should we really take the risk?"

"Do you think we should?"

The two fell silent, neither one answering the other's question.

Finally, Loup Garou said, "I guess we'll see what happens tomorrow."

XVIII.

A three-quarter moon rose over Colorado on the night Phillipe Bismuth arrived. He had travelled by private caravan with Sharpe and fifty followers hand-picked for the occasion. Naturally, Bismuth had not told these followers they were likely to die that night, for they did not need to know. They were just another sacrifice to his cause.

His three privately-owned buses arrived at the compound at eleven-thirty. There was no one to greet them, no watchmen at the heavy iron gates, which hung open, creaking slightly in the light desert breeze. There was a stillness in the air, as though the old mine was once again abandoned.

As the last of Bismuth's followers entered, the gate suddenly slammed shut with a startling clank. A murmur went through the group, but Bismuth simply smiled. He could see plainly what was happening.

A breeze blew in, forming ripples in the sand. As the velocity increased, the sand rose up from the ground, forming into a ring that expanded towards the wall. The wind grew stronger and the sand grew thicker until both combined into a swirling sandstorm. It encircled the entire compound, blotting out the rest of the world with a blinding maelstrom. Within the walls of the compound, things remained calm, like the eye of a hurricane.

"Master?" Sharpe asked, unable to mask his uncertainty.

"Fear not," Bismuth said calmly. "Fear is just what Van Sloan wants from us. Soon enough, the fear will be his own." He raised his hand and his voice as he spoke to the rest of followers. "We have been invaded, my children! The Occult Mafia has come to attack us, to enslave us to their dogma of hypocrisy! Donovan Van Sloan has let wild beasts into my house, and this shall not stand! Go forth, and spill the blood of the invaders!"

"YES, MASTER!" his followers shouted in unison, and their devotion brought a smile to Bismuth's thin lips. He did not even need to hypnotize them for such loyalty. Hypnotism was but a parlor trick. What he wielded over his subjects was true power, the kind that did not break easily.

The cultists spread out in search of their prey. Bismuth and Sharpe stayed behind.

Sharpe tugged at his collar, nervously staring at the sandstorm behind them. "Are you really not afraid that we might lose, Master?" he asked.

Bismuth flicked his wrist at the sandstorm, and a hole opened in the swirling wall, revealing the gate which had been obscured by it.

"No, Sharpe, not at all. Van Sloan already lost this battle a year ago, though he seems to have forgotten this fact. I am here to remind him who the real victor is."

"Something is wrong," said Ma'at.

She was the one who summoned the sandstorm. It was meant to trap Bismuth and whomever he brought with him inside, and its dramatic flair was meant to add a psychological component. From there, the other Occult Mafia agents would herd Bismuth towards the chapel, where Donovan's team waited.

"What is it?" asked Donovan.

"The warlock did something to my storm." Ma'at focused her energy as she tried to figure out what had happened. "He opened a gap somewhere in it."

"Can you close it?"

"I am trying, but it does not appear to be working." A chill ran up Ma'at's spine. "Never before have I encountered power such as he wields."

Erasmus leaned in close to Loup Garou. "It's already starting," he whispered, referring back to when he had said Bismuth's arrival would lead to chaos.

The sound of a gunshot in the distance startled everyone in the chapel. The burst was followed by another, and another. The cries of an angry mob rose alongside the gunfire, and the sounds increased until they all blended together into a single cacophonous roar.

The chapel's front door swing open, and an Occult Mafia agent ran in. "Mr. Van Sloan, we have a problem!" the agent said. "Bismuth brought more cultists with him than we anticipated. They're overrunning us out there! It's as if he expected us!"

A look of concern flashed in Donovan's eyes. "Where's Jackie?"

"Still in her room," the agent replied. "We still have two men posted at her door, but we need them in the field."

Donovan pounded his fist on a nearby pew. This was not part of the plan. Normally, he had full faith in his daughter's ability to fend for herself, but in her current emotional state, she was in danger. If she did not lose control to the entity again, she might possibly surrender to the cultists and let them kill her. He could not let that happen.

"Can you bring her to me?" he asked.

The agent shook his head. "We're spread thin as it is, Sir."

An idea materialized in Donovan's mind, and though he was initially loathe to do it, he realized that he had no other options. "You four," he said, referring to the monsters in his company. "Get to the lodge and bring her here."

In spite of himself, Loup became concerned. "But you'll be alone," he said. "What happens if Bismuth shows up while we're gone?"

"I can hold my own until you get back," Donovan replied. His voice grew urgent. "Don't worry about me. My first priority is my daughter, and until she's in this chapel with us, she's your priority too! Now go! And kill anyone who gets in your way!"

Donovan Van Sloan had given his orders, and his team obeyed. They ran out of the church's front door.

Jackie could hear everything happening outside, but even this barely stirred her. The guards at her door were engaging with cultists who had come for her. She knew what the cultists did to people, so she sat on her bed in silence, waiting for them. She wanted them to take her, for she had given up.

She thought she heard a pounding outside the door. It was so loud that she could feel it in her skull. As it continued, she began to wonder why it was taking so long for the cultists to break in, for the door was not that sturdy.

The pounding increased, and Jackie realized with a sinking feeling in her heart that it was not coming from the door.

Let me out! shrieked the entity.

Jackie clutched her pounding head. "No!"

The door splintered as an ax blade drove through it.

This is not how I die, you weakling!

Jackie resisted for as long as she could, but the entity's desire to live was too great.

When the cultists entered, it was the entity, not Jackie, who met them, and she showed no mercy.

A well-placed slash allowed Loup Garou to fell another cultist before he even knew what had hit him.

The quartet had stuck to the shadows since leaving the chapel, avoiding the majority of the mayhem so as not to tip their hand. As far as any of them knew, Phillipe Bismuth had no idea that they were there, so they stayed hidden to maintain the element of surprise.

Erasmus was keeping a sharp eye out for any opportunity to run for the mine, but halfway to the lodge, there had yet to be one.

Loup inhaled sharply through his nose, and was instantly overwhelmed. The air was filled with scents of all colors and patterns, each one heavy and richly hued. It took a great deal of concentration for him to focus and determine if anyone was in their path.

He was fairly certain the way ahead was clear, at least for the moment. He motioned for the others to follow him, and took a step forward before halting at the sound of Ma'at whispering, "Is that him?"

Loup paused as his eyes followed her extended finger to the open street. There, illuminated in the sickly glow of an overhead spotlight, was Phillipe Bismuth, clad in a burgundy suit, traces of his acrid black-and-gray stench curling in wisps around him. A shudder went through Loup's body at the sight. "Yeah," he replied, suppressing a gag at the scent. "That's him."

Ma'at's grip on her kopesh tightened. "If we strike now-"

"That's not the plan!" Loup hissed. Both he and Ben were surprised that this was their first thought.

"He does not know we are here," Ma'at said. Her entire focus was fixed on the warlock. Something stirred within her that clouded her judgment. "I can end this now with a single strike of my blade."

"Ma'at, Donovan's counting on us to-"

"His *ka* is stained with innocent blood. It must be stricken from the Earth!"

Filled with righteous fury, Ma'at charged at incredible speed towards Bismuth, kopesh poised and ready to strike. She was upon him in an instant, plunging her blade towards his neck.

The blade stopped centimeters from its target, blocked as if by an invisible barrier.

Ma'at was stunned. She pushed against the invisible force with all of her strength, but it was to no avail. As she strained and struggled to plunge her blade into the warlock's neck, Bismuth – who had stopped in place – turned casually to face her. His expression did not betray any surprise at seeing her there. "Well, you must be the mummy that Donovan revived," he said, more amused than impressed. "I detect the blood of a deity mixed with the embalming fluid in your veins. Tell me, which minor god are you?"

Still straining, Ma'at glared into Bismuth's eyes, hoping to strike some sense of fear into him. "I am Justice!"

Bismuth smirked. "No wonder you're so weak." He gently pushed her blade aside with his pinkie. "There is no justice in this world, you deluded whelp. There is only terror, chaos, and me."

Perhaps it was the unwwavering confidence with which he spoke, or perhaps it was the unholy glint of hellfire that glimmered in his dark eyes, but something about Bismuth sent a chill through Ma'at's body, and her resolve weakened.

Bismuth placed a hand softly against her stomach. At his touch, a sudden force of tremendous power shot through Ma'at's body, sending her reeling through the air like a ragdoll. She collided with a stack of barrels, which then collapsed on top of her. The sandstorm dispersed immediately.

Loup almost leapt from the alley to help her, but seeing Bismuth caused horrible memories to flood his mind and still his feet. All these years later, and the feelings of helplessness were as strong as ever.

"That was too easy," Bismuth said as he shook his head in disappointment. "You now see, Sharpe, why I have turned my back on the gods. They are never as great as the claim to be." With that, he and his entourage continued towards the chapel.

"Now's our chance," Erasmus said. "We can make it to the mine easily from here."

"We can't leave Ma'at!" Loup said. "Just wait a minute."

He watched as Bismuth drew closer to the chapel. Once he was sure the warlock would not turn back, he left the alley and recovered Ma'at from beneath the barrels. She was unconscious and battered from the impact, but was thankfully still alive.

Loup returned to where Erasmus waited, but was surprised that Iruel was gone. "Where's the vampire?"

"The vampire is here," replied Iruel as he appeared suddenly behind the wolf.

Loup jumped at his voice, nearly dropping Ma'at. "Where'd you run off to?"

"I continued on to the lodge, as instructed. The girl is not there, but the bodies of her victims are. I fear her other self has taken hold of her once more."

Erasmus tilted his head to the side, confused. "What do you mean by 'her other self'?"

"Is that what I said?" Iruel answered evenly. "How unusual."

Loup snarled in frustration. "Well, this whole thing has gone completely pear shaped!"

"Good thing it's none of our business anymore," Erasmus said. "Let's get to the dang mine already!"

The ichthoid started to leave, but only got a few steps before realizing no one was following him. He turned back. "Don't tell me you've gone soft on those filthy humans, Loup."

The wolf said nothing, but he did avert his eyes.

"Well, I haven't," Erasmus snapped. "I'm getting out of here with or without you, you mangy mutt!" With these parting words, the ichthoid left.

"So what will you do?" Iruel asked of Loup.

Loup and Ben both realized what had to be done at the same time. "Donovan and Jackie need our help," Loup said. "They've already suffered enough."

"Then you should go them," Iruel said. "Though I'm sure you already know that."

"You're right, we do. But what about her?" Loup looked down at Ma'at's unconscious body, which he still held in his arms. Despite their falling out the other night, neither he nor Ben could deny that they still cared about her, possibly more than they had ever cared for anyone else. She was currently in no condition to keep fighting, but they could not leave her unprotected.

He looked at Iruel. "I need a favor. Can you take Ma'at and follow Erasmus out of this hellhole? If anyone can keep her safe in this mess, it's you."

"Of course," Iruel answered as he took the goddess in his arms. "That is what I am supposed to do. Now go."

Loup Garou nodded in silent gratitude, then bounded towards the chapel, hoping he would arrive before Bismuth did.

The cultists who appeared in his path would delay him just long enough to ensure that he did not.

Donovan glanced at the large clock on the chapel's southern wall, which had alchemical symbols in place of numbers. The monsters were taking too long. Even accounting for stealth and opposition, they should have made it to and from the lodge by now. It was not that far away from the chapel.

That could only mean that something had gone wrong.

As if confirming his concern, the body of a cultist flew through one of the stained glass windows, shattering its grotesque design into millions of glittering shards. He landed awkwardly, his spine folding as it collided with the back of a pew, ensuring that he was good and dead.

The entity crawled in through the newly formed opening. Blood dripped from her talon-tipped hands.

"Hi Pop," she hissed as she glared at him with her ghastly eyes. *"Did I make it home before curfew?"*

Donovan's heart sank, and it pulled his expression and posture down with it.

"Aw, whatsamatta?" the entity asked, her voice more mocking than concerned. She crept towards Donovan in a manner not unlike a scorpion. *"You didn't really think you could keep me out of this party, did you? I got a stake in it too, you know."*

Instinctively, Donovan drew his gun and aimed it at the twisted being before him.

She laughed. *"You don't have the guts to shoot me, old man. What if I turned back at the last second, huh? Or what if I'm not what you think I am?"* She crept closer. *"No, you wouldn't risk it."*

Donovan kept his gun trained on the entity, and attempted to cock the hammer. Hopefully, that would scare her into thinking he would risk it, and perhaps that would give him the advantage against her.

He could not even perform this simple maneuver, not with Jackie's life on the line. His thumb refused to budge.

Despite his efforts, his resolve buckled. "You're right," he replied as he dropped the gun. His defenses were now completely lowered. "Go on. Do your worst."

The entity paused, and a strange look crossed her horrid scaly face.

"What are you waiting for?" Donovan asked. "You're one of Bismuth's lackies, aren't you? He sent you ahead as part of some mind game, didn't he?"

The entity spat in disgust. *"Just because I'm the warlock's handiwork doesn't mean he's any friend of mine. I'm on my own side, not yours or his."*

"But you're still here to ruin the plan," Donovan replied. "That's all you ever do. You exist just to ruin everything for everyone around you, so go ahead. Ruin this for me and the world."

Nothing happened.

Donovan became confused. If ever the entity had a golden opportunity to strike at him, now was her chance, and she was wasting it. Why didn't she do anything?

In an instant, he recognized something about her expression. Though it might have been twisted and inhuman, the entity still wore Jackie's face as her own, and he could now see a familiar look in her eyes. It was the look Jackie always got when she was being indecisive.

The entity was conflicted. Why did not matter, so long as he could exploit it. "Having second thoughts?" he pressed subtly, so as not to show his hand.

"I don't have to ruin anything," the entity said. Her tone made it sound like an excuse for her inaction. *"Your little vendetta's already shot to hell and you don't even know it."*

The veiled warning did not register in Donovan's mind. Instead, he pressed on with his attempt to restore Jackie's control. "You're holding back."

"Shut up!" the entity barked. *"No mind games, Pop! I'm the one in control here!"*

"I disagree," said a third authoritative voice.

The words came from the chapel's front doors, which swung wide open of their own accord. From the dark battlefield outside came Phillipe Bismuth, dressed to the nines, so confident that he almost appeared relaxed. "This is *my* chapel in *my* compound, so I would say *I'm* in control."

The entity's inaction suddenly became raw fury when she saw the warlock. *"Bismuth!"* she shrieked, the word like ashes in her mouth. She lunged down the center aisle towards him, talons extended like those of a hawk.

Sharpe charged in through the door and threw a punch at the entity. His fist struck her in the ribs, knocking her out of the air and sending her careening into the wall. The impact dislodged a painting of Kronos devouring his children and toppled a nearby candle sconce.

The entity recovered quickly and lunged again, but was intercepted by Sharpe once more. He drew a knife and swiped the blade at her face. She recoiled just in time to miss being cut. Her scaly skin was not much stronger than normal human skin, and she could tell from the blade's color that it was laced with iron, meaning even a small cut from it could poison her.

Sharpe was certain he had the advantage, and continued swiping at the entity, forcing her away from his master.

After five swipes that pressed her backward, the entity suddenly leapt to her left, and Sharpe froze when he found himself staring down the barrel of Donovan's gun.

Donovan only fired one shot that struck Sharpe's knife and tore it from his grip. The shot did not draw blood, but the impact stunned Sharpe just long enough for Donovan to clear the distance between them. A well-placed blow to the temple from Donovan's metal prosthetic rendered the cultist unconscious.

At the same time, the entity made one last play at Bismuth. Now that he was unguarded, she was certain she could maim him.

He caught her easily by the throat, and held her at arm's length. She kicked and struggled, but the warlock was much stronger than he looked. It was as if holding her back required no effort at all on his part.

"I marvel at how you're still alive," Bismuth said as he scrutinized her. "Everyone else I've split eventually ripped themselves apart. I believe the record prior to you was a month. And you." He turned his attention to Donovan. "I would think a devoted vanquisher of evil such as yourself would have disposed of this thing long ago."

"I'm insulted that you think so little of me," Donovan snapped back as he took aim. "I don't treat people the same way you do. I have every intention of making you tell me how to cure my daughter, even if I have to torture it out of you. In fact, I might prefer doing that."

Bismuth scoffed. "Cure? You mean you haven't figured out what I did to her yet?" He clucked his tongue. "How disappointing. I expected better from a self-appointed expert on the supernatural."

The warlock took a few steps closer to Donovan, showing that he was not even slightly concerned about his threats. He dragged the entity behind him as though she were a sack. "I suppose you've run the whole gamut in terms of exorcism methods, yet they all failed, correct? Did you ever consider that the child is *not* possessed?" He paused just long enough to let Donovan absorb the question. "I can see by the look on your face that you haven't. Must be your paternal instincts blinding you. Since you're both about to die, I may as well clue you in."

With an impressive show of strength, Bismuth chucked the entity up the aisle towards her father. She landed hard on her side. "All human souls are divided, Van Sloan. They have two sides. Call them Good and Evil, Yin and Yang, Id and Superego, or whatever you choose. They are normally intermingled, stitched together like two threads woven around each other. Well, in my exploration of the dark arts, I found a way to separate those threads."

Donovan's face paled as he realized where this oration was going.

"You're putting it together, I can tell," Bismuth grinned. "Look to your daughter, Van Sloan, for that is who lies at your feet. Your exorcisms failed because you cannot exorcise a human soul. I didn't infest her with a demonic force. I simply gave her dark side a will of its own, and that which has been done cannot be undone." He shrugged. "Even if you did win this night, and you tortured me for answers, it would be to no avail."

Donovan looked down at the black-scaled girl he had convinced himself was a demon, foreign to his daughter in every way, but when she looked back up at him, all he could see was Jackie. She looked like a grotesque parody of herself, but it was undeniably her. He realized that in the back of his mind, he had always suspected this possibility, but had forced himself to deny it.

"You're not lying," he whispered, the defeat in his voice unmistakable.

When his eyes rose to meet Bismuth's again, they were filled not with sadness, but with simmering rage. "Then I guess there's no reason to keep you alive."

Donovan lifted his gun and emptied it at Phillipe Bismuth. His aim was true, practically point blank. There was no way he could have missed. Yet every bullet swerved around the warlock as he calmly raised his hand. Rather than draw blood, they struck the walls around him.

With the chamber empty, Donovan discarded the gun. He charged Bismuth, taking a swing at him with his metal claw.

Bismuth caught the prosthetic appendage in his hand and thrust Donovan backwards. He landed beside Jackie, the impact forcing the air out of his lungs.

"I really don't see what you expect to accomplish here, Van Sloan," Bismuth said as he drew near. "You couldn't beat me before, and if you're counting on those monsters you've been collecting, then you lost ages ago. I discarded your mummy on my way here, and it seems that the others have abandoned you. I would say-"

A coiled ball of iron chain slammed into the warlock's side, cutting off his monologue, lifting him into the air, and knocking him through the window. His landing left him temporarily stunned.

Loup Garou darted from a secret passage in the wall, coiling the chain around his arm as he ran to where the Van Sloans lay.

Donovan propped himself up slowly. At first, he thought the cavalry had arrived, and it almost gave him hope again, until he realized the wolf was alone. "Where are the others?" he groaned as Loup crouched beside him.

"They made tracks. We're on our own." Loup looked guilty for an instant, then quickly changed the subject. "This is a disaster, Don. We've got to get out of here now. Can you walk?"

Donovan nodded as he got to his feet.

"And you," Loup said as he glared at the entity. "I don't trust you. Give Jackie control again so we can escape."

"No!" hissed the entity.

"Do it," Loup growled, "or I'm leaving you here with Bismuth."

The entity shuddered at the threat, and Jackie was restored a moment later. She looked exhausted from struggling to break free, but she could still stand on her own.

Loup led the way out of the compound and back to the train, which had luckily been left untouched. The surviving Occult Mafia agents who saw them running were quick to follow.

When Bismuth regained his senses, he saw that his opponents were gone, but he did not pursue them. There was no need to. Simply by stating the facts, he had beaten them.

As all of this was happening, Erasmus was making his way into the mines when he felt a chill run up his spine. He turned, wrist blades extended in case there was trouble, but he relaxed when he saw Iruel gliding towards him, Ma'at's still-unconscious body in his arms.

"Oh, it's just you," Erasmus said as he retracted his blades. "Where are Ben and Loup?"

"They will not be joining us," Iruel replied. "They have entrusted me with the goddess."

"Idiots," Erasmus groaned. "It's their funeral. Come on."

The ichthoid led the way deeper into the mountain. "Gotta say, you two're the last ones I expected to jump ship. I thought that sort of thing was beneath you."

"Ma'at is unconscious," Iruel replied. "She can hardly be accused to treachery in her current state. As for myself, I am simply following God's Will."

"And God's Will is for you to abandon a family in need and let Bismuth destroy the world, is it?"

"Now why would you of all people phrase it like that?"

Erasmus shook his head, realizing his slip up. "It's just an expression," he said dismissively. "Now if you're going to keep following me, shut up and let me concentrate."

Iruel nodded, and was silent for the rest of the trek.

XIX.

The Occult Mafia train left Grand Junction as quickly as it could. No destination was given to the conductor. He was simply told they had to run.

Donovan, Jackie, and Ben all went to the caboose lounge, where they collapsed from exhaustion. The two men sat across from each other at the coffee table, while Jackie lay sprawled on a chair across the room. Loup, as usual was reflected in the window beside Ben.

At first, no one said anything, for in the wake of such a defeat, none of them had the strength or desire to speak. As the silence grew unbearable, Ben asked what had happened in his absence, and Donovan filled him in on every horrible detail. Jackie provided no interjections of her own, but every so often, Ben and Loup caught her shooting them dirty looks. Was it from Loup's fight with the entity, or did she know about the escape plan? Maybe it was just their imaginations. To be safe, they did not acknowledge her.

Eventually, Donovan finished his account, concluding with, "So I guess we didn't have the advantage I thought we did. I underestimated Bismuth yet again. And to top it all off, the others ran out on us." He sighed. "You think it would have made a difference if they hadn't made tracks?"

"I don't know," Ben answered. "Maybe, maybe not. I guess we'll never know now."

"To think I trusted them." Donovan clenched his fists, which registered as twitching and grinding in his mechanical pinchers. "To think I actually believed they would do the right thing when it came time. Well, to Hell with the lot of 'em, the filthy traitors!" He slammed his fist on the table, startling everyone. His outburst done, Donovan slumped back into his seat and looked at Ben. "At least now I know who my real friends are. I owe you one for saving us…both of you."

Ben and Loup felt self-conscious, but tried not to show it. "It was nothing," Ben said, perhaps a bit too quickly. "It's what you hired us for. We're just doing our job, right Loup?"

"That's right," Loup nodded. "Just doing our job."

A loud, disgusted snort drew all eyes to Jackie. It was the first sound she had made since fleeing the compound. The look on her face matched the noise she had made. "Lying hypocrite," she sneered at them. "Sitting there acting like you're innocent while throwing your friends under the bus. You deserve to rot along with the rest of them."

"What are you talking about, Jackie?" Donovan asked.

Ben's face turned ash white as he realized what was about to happen, and made an attempt to stop it. "She-"

"Shut up!" Jackie snapped as she forced herself to sit upright. "I'm not keeping quiet about this anymore! You're making out like you're the loyal guard dog, but you're both cowards! You never trusted us. You were convinced we were plotting against you, so you plotted against us! It was *your* idea to run off in the first place!" Her eyes narrowed as she saw Ben and Loup squirming in their seat. "Yeah, that's right! I was listening when you started hatching that plan with Erasmus. It was your idea to leave us in the lurch. Go ahead, Pop. Ask him to look you in the eye and deny it."

When Donovan redirected his gaze to Ben, his glaring eyes were like windows holding back a hurricane. "Is that true, Ben?"

"We…uh…" Naturally, Ben's instinct was to deny it, to say it was some kind of misunderstanding or perhaps say Jackie's darker half was trying to interfere, but he could feel the sweat beading on his brow. Both he and Loup knew that lying was pointless. "Well, what did you expect with a reputation like yours, Don? We were scared. But we didn't-"

"You son of a *bitch!!!*" Donovan lunged across the table. His metal claw clamped around Ben's throat tight enough to make him suffer, but not tight enough to kill him just yet. The silver lining on the grip burned Ben's skin as Donovan pinned him to the wall.

Ben attempted to transform into Loup, but Donovan had caught them at just the right moment. They were stuck in mid-transformation, not fully Ben or Loup, and the silver that lined Donovan's claw kept them trapped in that intermediate state.

"I give you a chance at revenge," Donovan roared, "I make every show of good will I can think of, and after everything we've been through, you repay me like this?!?"

Ben and Loup struggled to no avail, for Donovan was surprisingly strong. Their lungs burned for oxygen.

"I trusted you! I trusted both of you with my life! With my daughter's life! I was even getting to like you, and you stabbed me in the back!" Donovan tightened his grip a little more. "Give me *one* good reason why I shouldn't snap your neck and throw your worthless corpse to the vultures."

To Donovan's surprise, Ben and Loup stopped struggling. In one voice, they strained to speak with a constricted windpipe. "We don't…have any…" They lowered their hands and closed their eyes. "Go ahead… Do your worst…"

Donovan hesitated, thrown by the sudden submissiveness of the werewolf. They both seemed sincerely remorseful for their betrayal. No, it was more than that. They were probably heartbroken over losing Ma'at, and beyond even that, they had failed to prevent the apocalypse. There was nothing left for them to live for, so in this moment, they were ready to die.

For all of his rage, though, Donovan could not bring himself to kill them.

He violently thrust them away. Now released, Loup fully manifested for a quick moment before Ben snapped back into being. They both collapsed against the window, gasping for air, sapped of what little strength had been left within them.

Although he had spared their lives, Donovan was in no mood to forgive. He stood looming over the werewolf. "Maybe this whole thing is actually my fault." His voice practically dripped with acid. "You said at the beginning that I was making a big mistake, but I didn't listen. I chose not to be cynical, and now I'm paying for it. So congratulations. You two were right all along. I hope you're happy."

The words cut deep into Ben and Loup as Donovan stormed out of the lounge, slamming the door behind him. Jackie, despite her exhaustion, rose from her chair and shot them one final sharp glare before following her father.

Once they were alone, Ben looked at Loup. "Well, Loup, are we happy?"

"Ecstatic," was Loup's defeated reply.

Donovan and Jackie walked in silence until they stopped in front of their adjoining rooms. "So you knew the whole time," Donovan said. His voice was low and drained. "Why didn't you tell me?"

A pang of guilt gripped Jackie's chest. "I wanted to, Pop," she replied. "It was the en...the other me. She forced me not to say. I…I know that ain't an excuse, but… Pop, I'm sorry."

"So am I, Jackie," Donovan said, still facing away from his daughter. "I'm sorry we lost. I'm sorry I made so many mistakes. I'm sorry I let your mother die. I-" He paused. Jackie could not see his face, but he sounded as if he were about to cry, for his voice trembled with sadness. "I'm sorry you've had to suffer like this for so long, and I'm sorry I can't help you."

Donovan entered his room, shielding his face from Jackie's sight as he moved. He locked the door behind him.

Jackie stood silently in the hall. Through the door, she heard objects being thrown and broken, followed by the sound of her father collapsing and breaking down in a torrent of sobs. Her father had spent over a year being strong for both of them, and in the face of this failure, he had no strength left to fight.

Neither did Jackie.

She drifted into her room, fell onto her bed, and also broke down. She hated herself, and her mind was filled with the most horrible thoughts of suicide, even though it went against everything she believed in. Her only thought was that none of this would have happened if she had never been born.

Jackie sobbed until her eyes stung, and by then her emotions had been completely drained from her. As her rational mind slowly began creeping back into focus, she realized how strange it was that during this whole time, the entity – no, her other side – had not seized control. Jackie had no willpower left to keep her darker half in check, yet she was still contained within. Why had she not tried to escape?

As she wondered this, Jackie realized something else. Deep down inside of her, she could feel her darker half, and she too was sad.

Jackie was amazed. She did not think her other side was capable of feeling sadness.

What did that mean?

For a moment, she wondered what her father would do.

Then she remembered what he had told her at the compound, about how he and her mother had always wanted her to grow into her own woman.

She had to decide what *she* would do.

Her instincts told her to speak to the entity.

But how?

She caught a glimpse of herself in the vanity mirror, and after briefly acknowledging that she looked like a wreck, she remembered how Loup Garou would often appear in place of Ben Andante's reflection.

She had no idea if that would work for her, but it was worth a shot.

Jackie rose and walked slowly towards the vanity, keeping her eyes locked on her reflection as she moved. When she noticed her hands were trembling with nerves, she gripped the edges of the countertop, allowing her to assume a stance she had often seen businessmen take in movies. Perhaps that would help with her confidence.

Perhaps.

"If you can hear me," she said into the mirror, "we…we need to talk. Can you do that mirror trick like the Ben and Loup do?"

"Don't need to."

Jackie turned, for the voice seemed to come from behind her. Standing beside the bed was the entity. She cast no shadow, and did not look as though she were really there. It must have been a mental projection of some sort. How the entity knew she could do this, Jackie had no idea, but that was a mystery for another day.

She took a moment to observe her darker half, for she had never actually seen her in person before. She appeared as she was often described, with her black snakelike skin and her sinister eyes, but she was Jackie's twin otherwise, matching her feature for feature. In fact, the entity seemed almost inverted, like a photographic negative.

"Well, here I am," the entity said. *"So what do you want?"* Every word from her mouth was indignant.

"You actually look as upset as I feel," Jackie said.

"Course I'm upset. I wanted Bismuth dead, too. He's no friend of mine."

"So we have some common ground after all," Jackie nodded. "You got a name?"

"My name is your name, stupid."

"Oh." Jackie realized how obvious this answer was, and felt a bit embarrassed, but she recovered quickly. "Well, I think we need a way to differentiate each other. What if I keep going by 'Jackie', and you go by 'Jacqueline'? That seem fair?"

"Fine, whatever," Jacqueline replied. *"Never liked the nickname anyway. Not that it makes much of a difference."*

"That depends on how our chat goes." Jackie stepped away from the vanity. "You know, ever since Bismuth did this to us, a part of me always wondered why. He could've killed me, but instead he pulled you out and set us against each other."

"Who cares why he did it?" Jacqueline spat. *"I'd think you'd be more focused on why he can't undo it."*

Jackie did not let her other half's tone throw her. "He said he'd done this to other people," she pressed, "and they tore themselves apart."

"So what?"

"We've both been fighting against each other for control. *That's* what, Jacqueline. We've both spent a year trying to get rid of each other and be the one in full control."

"Your ability to state the obvious is astounding."

"But what did you think would happen if you won? If I really did disappear?"

Jacqueline crossed her arms and sneered. *"Then I'd go my own way and be happy you were gone."*

"I would've felt the same way about you," Jackie agreed. "But we're both the same person, one soul split in two. Think about what Iruel does. He burns the evil out of people's souls, and sometimes there's not enough good left for them to survive. So if we're two halves of a whole, and one of is gone, could the remaining half survive?"

Jacqueline was stunned. After silently considering the question, she said, *"I hadn't thought of that."*

"Neither had I until now, and I think that was the point." Jackie looked Jacqueline in the eyes. "I think that was Bismuth's game. He didn't kill us because he wanted us to kill each other. We'd suffer until we're both dead, and Pop's spirit would be good and broken."

"That's sick!"

"So since fighting is what he wants us to do, I think we shouldn't give him the satisfaction." By now, Jackie's nerves had subsided, and her confidence was rising. "Like it or not, we're stuck with each other, and until we find some way to be made whole again, we need to learn how to work together."

Jacqueline leaned forward, a suspicious look glinting in her eyes. *"And I suppose you got a vision of what that'll look like?"*

Jackie knew Jacqueline would not like her answer, but she said it anyway. "Well first of all, I'll need to be in control most of the time."

"And there it is!" Jacqueline snapped. *"Of course* you *get to be in charge!"*

Jackie forced herself to stay strong. "Take a look at yourself, Jacqueline. If you really think you can get away with walking down the street looking like a sideshow attraction, I'll give you full control right now."

She waited for the response.

"If you weren't me, I'd tell you to take a flying leap," Jacqueline snarled, but in her voice was concession to Jackie's point. *"Fine, so you're our public face, but if you think that means I'm gonna stay locked up-"*

"Of course you won't," Jackie said. "We're supposed to carry on the family legacy of fighting evil, but we ain't doing it like Mom and Pop did. I know what you did to those cultists in Grand Junction, and I won't pretend that I'm thrilled about it, but maybe...well, we usually have to be brutal in the Occult Mafia, right? And honestly, you can be pretty brutal."

"Oh, you ain't seen nothing yet, sister."

"But you also seem to have standards. You ripped the cultists to shreds without batting an eye, but this last time you ran into Pop, you hesitated." Jackie was certain she was on to something. "And I can tell you had a crying fit of your own just now. That tells me there's more to you than just malice."

Jacqueline averted her eyes, as if she were ashamed of her feelings, yet she still spoke them. *"He's my dad, too, y'know. I hate him for getting Mom killed, and for putting us in danger all the time, but...he's still my dad."*

Jackie nodded. "Thought so. You act like you don't care, but you know who the real enemy is. So let's bury the hatchet, preferably deep in Bismuth's skull."

An intrigued look flashed in Jacqueline's eyes. *"Vengeance or justice?"*

Jackie smiled. "Who says the two are mutually exclusive?"

XX.

Ma'at slowly stirred, and as she did, she wondered if she had died again. The last thing she remembered was her defeat at the hands of Phillipe Bismuth, and nothing beyond that. It was not quite the same as her first death, but it was eerily reminiscent in some ways.

As her eyes slowly creaked open, she did not see the chamber presided over by Anubis, but instead the ceiling of a cave. She began to sit up quickly, but the sharp pain which shot through her body stymied her effort, and she collapsed onto her back once more.

"Take it slow," came the voice of Erasmus Webster. "You took quite a licking last night."

Ma'at attempted to sit up again, taking her time to adjust to the pain as she rose. The fact that her body was sore meant she was not dead, though the pain was such that she nearly wished otherwise. As a goddess, she could recover quickly from most injuries, even if the pain would linger for a time.

Once she was upright, she took in her surroundings. She was definitely in a cave, of that there was no question. They must have been the mines Ben had told her about. They were by the cave's mouth, which was to her left, and as she looked out at the brightly-lit world, she guessed that it was the middle of the day. There was a town of some sort in the distance, though she could not guess its name. To her right she saw Erasmus and Iruel, the former resting in a pool of water thick with sediment, the latter sleeping in an alcove etched into the cave wall. There was no sign of Ben and Loup.

"What happened?" Ma'at groaned.

"An unmitigated disaster," Erasmus replied. "After Bismuth roughed you up, I made tracks expecting your boyfriends to follow. Instead, Iruel showed up carrying you like a sack of potatoes, a scene right out of the movies, I reckon. It took us until dawn to get here."

"Where are the others?" Ma'at asked. "Did they make it?"

Erasmus shrugged. "Don't know. I doubt they stood a chance. Van Sloan's plan needed all of us, you know. Maybe they got out alive, maybe not."

"Do you not care about what happened to them?"

"Give me one reason why I ought to."

Ma'at said nothing.

"Exactly," Erasmus said.

Ma'at slowly got to her feet and stretched. Nothing appeared to be broken, and her weapons rested on the ground beside her. Satisfied that she was in one piece, she walked over to the pool where Erasmus sat. "I know that you are the only one who did not join Donovan's cause willingly, and having read his notes on you, I know precisely where your hatred for mankind stems from." She sat beside the pool. "Yet I have also seen you perform great feats of heroism since our first meeting. At the lake, you saved us from the creature, and in the town, you saved many children from the cultists. You are an enigma to me, Erasmus Webster. You behave as though you hate everyone, yet when I look into your eyes, I see not hatred, but sadness. It is clear even through those darkened shields which cover them."

Erasmus turned his head away instinctively, averting his goggled eyes from Ma'at, but it did not prevent her from asking the question he knew she would. "What happened, Erasmus? What is missing from Donovan's notes that explains your paradoxical nature?"

"Why should I tell you?" was his gruff reply. He was growing visibly uncomfortable.

"Because there are many lives at risk," Ma'at answered. "Phillipe Bismuth aims to end the world, and from what I have seen, we are presently all that stands in his way. If I can understand you, Erasmus, I might better know if you should be part of this fight."

Erasmus sunk a little into the pool, hoping to vanish beneath the surface and avoid speaking to the goddess. Since the pool was not especially deep, this desire was impossible.

He did not want to say anything, yet there was something about her countenance which appealed to him. She had a great sense of empathy to her that was rare from any sort of creature, divine or terrestrial. She sounded as though she really wanted to know about him and his past. Eramsus had not heard such genuine concern and gentleness in decades. Perhaps this is what caused his hard exterior to start cracking.

"You already know about how I was taken to that government lab," he began, raising an arm to display the gauntlet affixed to his wrist. "They'd put me on an operating table and do whatever they wanted to me, like wire these to my body." He shuddered at the memories of those horrible experiments, some of which he had been wide awake for. "Between operations, they'd keep me in an aquarium tank. That's where Louise found me."

Ma'at tilted her head. "Louise?"

"She was a little kid, daughter to one of the lady scientists. Near as I can figure, she was raising Louise on her own, and they had to live on the base because of all the secrecy, so her daughter had the run of the place, so long as she didn't go in certain rooms."

"How old was she?"

"I don't know exactly. Can't tell a human's age by sight. Younger than the Van Sloan kid, I think. Six, maybe? Eight?" He waved his webbed hand dismissively. "It doesn't matter. What matters is that Louise took a shine to me. Probably thought I was some kind of animal, a pet for her to play with. I should've been insulted, but she was the only one in that whole rotten place who treated me with any kindness. She talked to me about her day, showed me pictures she drew, brought me food and ice cream…" Erasmus' voice drifted for a moment as he remembered the good times they had. "She was one heck of a kid."

"Was?" Ma'at inquired. "What happened?"

"I don't want to talk about it," Erasmus said, his voice growing cold and harsh.

"Erasmus, please," Ma'at implored.

The ichthoid's sigh was a mixture of frustration and melancholy, but he relented. "When I was making my escape from the lab, I heard the announcement over the P.A. system: the guards' orders were shoot to kill. I'd almost made it to the exit, but I got pinned there. I was just around the corner of a hallway, and the soldiers were blocking the door, fingers on their triggers. It was what you might call a Mexican standoff. I was weighing my options when Louise showed up behind me. She figured out I was in trouble, and being a kid, she wanted to help. She stepped out into the open, thinking she could plead my case, and…" Erasmus stopped and inhaled sharply, suppressing his emotions.

"They thought she was you," Ma'at inferred.

Erasmus nodded.

"Did she die?"

"The ones who shot her did. I made sure of that." His hands balled into fists as he remembered the whole bloody affair which had pushed him over the edge. The screams and death rattles of his victims echoed through his mind. "Suppose I was lucky, in a way. Soon as I heard the command to hold fire, I was on the attack. They were too aghast at what they'd just done to react in time. Once I'd finished the last of them, I turned to get Louise, but her mom was already there. The look she gave me…well, I knew to stay back, much as I didn't want to, so I ran instead. That was my goal, after all." He sighed. "Her mom might've been able to save her, but I could never go back to find out. They'd have surely killed me if I did."

"That explains your drive to protect children," Ma'at said. "Is that also why you saved us from the lake monster? Because Jackie was there?"

Erasmus composed himself and shook his head. "Nah, that's more like a Hatfield and McCoy sort of rivalry."

"What and who?"

"Never mind. I just hate those rotten eels, is all. I don't need an excuse to kill one of 'em."

Ma'at stood. It was slightly easier for her to rise this time, as the soreness was becoming tolerable. "I understand your hatred for humanity, Erasmus Webster, and it is with that understanding that I say you must put it behind you."

"And you call yourself the Goddess of Justice," the ichthoid scoffed. He stood and brandished his gauntlets. "Did you forget that I can't ever take these off? Or that it hurts every time I use 'em? I didn't volunteer to be a guinea pig for the army! They gave me no choice, and neither did Donovan! I don't owe humanity a thing!"

Ma'at stood firm. "What was done to you was monstrous, it is true, as was the killing of Louise, and perhaps your tormenters got what they deserved." She stepped closer and stared deep into the amphibian's shielded eyes. "But what is done is done. You cannot allow your life to be dictated by a tragedy which happened ages ago. It simply is not right to hate people who have done you no wrong based on your past with

one group of *oh gods!"* With her exclamation, Ma'at's face lowered, and her hands rose to cover it as a realization of her own set in. Her voice was a harsh whisper when she said, "Oh, Beasts of Set, I am a hypocrite!"

The cave was silent for a moment.

"Guess we've both got baggage to deal with," Erasmus eventually said.

"Indeed," Ma'at sighed, "and the journey to overcoming it is to stop Phillipe Bismuth."

Erasmus crossed his arms, still skeptical. "You sure about that? I know he means to end the world and all, but he's tried that before without getting anywhere."

Ma'at met Erasmus' eyes again. "He only needs to succeed once."

Erasmus attempted to form a counterargument, but he could think of none. "Then I suppose we've got a train to catch."

"That's precisely what I was waiting to hear," said Iruel.

Both Erasmus and Ma'at were startled to realize the vampire was awake and listening to them. In truth, they had almost forgotten he was there. "Have you been awake this whole time?" Ma'at asked.

"Not the whole time, no, but for long enough," Iruel said as he drifted from his notch in the wall towards the duo. "I must say, it is a relief to know you two are finally ready to fight the good fight." He glanced out of the cave mouth at the sunlit town beyond. "Come nightfall, we should be able to enter the town and secure some form of transportation. That way, we can meet up with the others."

Ma'at's heart leapt in her chest. "They're all right?"

"They are alive," Iruel replied, "if all went as it should have. Whether or not they are all right remains to be seen."

"Where shall we meet them, then?"

"I do not yet know. I will have a better idea by nightfall."

"You've been saying stuff like that ever since we first met," Erasmus said as he stepped out of the pool. "What's going on with you? Can you see the future or something?"

Iruel shook his head. "Not exactly. By Providence, I am shown the way things ought to be, and so I do whatever I must to ensure that the desired outcome is met."

Ma'at placed her hands on her hips. What Iruel described was a notion she had never conceived before, even though she had known clairvoyants and seers in the past. "Then tell us, Fear of God, do you see how we are meant to win?"

"I do not," Iruel replied. "I believe we are on the path to victory, but whether we get there or not depends on the others."

XXI.

Donovan had ordered the train to head for the nearest Occult Mafia installation in Wyoming. There was no particular reason to go there this time. Under the circumstances, Donovan did not see much of a reason for anything.

Since departing Grand Juncture, Ben and Loup had been avoiding Donovan. They had both considered jumping off the train and leaving the whole affair behind them. In fact, they had been very close to doing exactly that the night before, but had decided against it. If they left now, that would only prove them as the traitors Donovan and Jackie said they were. Then again, there did not seem to be any point in staying if they were not going to contribute anything helpful.

If nothing else, they had to at least try making peace with the Van Sloans.

Ben found Donovan in the dining car. The monster hunter was sitting alone at a table, staring straight ahead as if he were in a trance. There was a bowl of soup before him, but he was just slowly stirring it rather than eating it.

Ben and Loup had seen a lot of unhappy people in their line of work, but they had never seen anyone as morose and hopeless as Donovan Van Sloan was in that moment.

Ben reached up and ran his fingers along his neck. The silver burns left by Donovan's claw still ached, and thanks to being caught mid-transformation, Loup bore them on his neck as well. They perfectly matched the ones on Loup's hand from when Donovan grabbed it in Grand Junction.

Twice now they had done something to provoke Donovan to violence, and he was very good at inflicting it. In light of everything that had happened, the risk of further injury – or worse – was a strong possibility.

Speaking to him would not be easy, but it still had to be done.

Ben walked towards Donovan's table slowly, as though he were approaching a sleeping lion who might pounce if disturbed. He got to the side of the table without eliciting any reaction at all.

"So…is this seat taken?" Ben asked cautiously, readying himself to dodge another attack.

Donovan did not respond. His only movement was the continued stirring of his soup.

Since there was no objection, Ben sat. He did not sit directly across from Donovan, who was close to the window, but stayed at the outer corner of the table, his chair angled so he could bolt if need be. Loup appeared reflected in the window, as usual, his cautious expression matching that of his human host.

Donovan's mood would have appeared unchanged to the average observer, but Ben and Loup could tell he was suddenly seething with anger. His dark blue scent grew thicker and more pungent as the red blotches swirled violently, a telltale sign of his extreme emotions. The monster hunter was a grenade just waiting for some careless idiot to pull the pin. Ben and Loup would have to pick their words carefully.

"Look," Ben began, "Loup and I both know that we're the last people on Earth you want to see right now, and we don't blame you. We could sit here and make all kinds of excuses and rationalizations for why we planned to leave you and the kid high and dry, but that wouldn't do any good. The truth is that we're both cynics. When you're a private eye, you tend to see the worst of what people can be, so after a while you just expect it."

"We've got trust issues," Loup added. "Heck, maybe we're properly paranoid. Call it what you want, but it's our flaw, and we're the ones who have to work through it."

Donovan remained silent. He stopped stirring his soup, but nothing else about his demeanor or scent changed.

"If we could go back and do it over, we'd do a lot of things differently," Ben continued. "A lot of things…" He trailed off and glanced at Loup. For an instant, they both thought the same thing: what was going to happen if they ever caught up with Ma'at again? They never did reach a resolution with her, and given the nature of their conflict, neither was sure how they could. This was especially troubling given how they both felt stronger about Ma'at than they had about any woman before.

For the moment, though, they had to brush that issue aside and focus on what was in front of them. "But what's done is done. All any of us can do now is move forward, which is why we're here now. See, we think…"

He hesitated. This was the part that could potentially light an already short fuse.

Loup did not allow the silence to last long. "We think we ought to take another crack at Bismuth, and this time, we'll be with you all the way."

Donovan's eyes suddenly moved so sharply that it startled Ben, despite the human remaining otherwise motionless. His eyes projected anger mixed with morbid curiosity. "You must be suicidal," he said. His voice was low and hoarse from his emotional outbursts. "Bismuth just beat us to hell, and you two want to go back for seconds? Well, forget it. I've had my fill. I got no fight left in me anymore."

"It's *because* he beat us that we need to hit him again," Loup interjected. "Bismuth's so arrogant, and he thrashed us so badly, he probably thinks there's no way we'd make another move against him. That means his guard is down. Besides, we think his powers must have some limits."

"Based on what?" Donovan asked. His voice and expression still had not changed, and his scent had only decreased slightly. Neither Ben nor Loup were sure how much progress they were making, but the fact that he was listening at all was good enough for the moment.

"When we came to get you and Jackie," Loup continued, "I hit Bismuth with my chain. Earlier, he had blocked Ma'at with some kind of invisible shield without even knowing she was there, but by the time I got to him, it was gone. So we're thinking his power must drain over time. It might even drain quickly if he uses it for certain things, like when he's fighting."

"You wanted to go after him now because he's trying to open the Gates of Hell, right?" asked Ben. "The first time you went after him, you stopped him from performing that ritual."

Donovan nodded. "Yeah, and it didn't turn out so well, or have you forgotten?" He raised his metal prosthetic and rested it on the table. The dull thud of its landing punctuated his point.

Maybe it was just their imaginations coupled with nerves, but seeing the claw put Ben and Loup on edge. If something set Donovan off now, it would be that much easier for him to reach them with that deadly appendage.

"Okay, so…uh…" Ben stammered slightly as he tried ignoring the menacing device. "So it's a bit, uh, bit of a risk, but…" He cleared his throat, pausing long enough to really focus on speaking his mind. "Maybe the reason we failed is because the plan was flawed from the start. Not that it was a completely bad plan, mind you, but it had us facing Bismuth at his strongest. In light of that, perhaps what we need to do is hit him when in a weakened state. I know that seems obvious, but I mean we need to strike when he's at his most vulnerable."

Donovan shook his head. "Based on my research, he'd only be at his most vulnerable after he's opened the Gates."

"All right then," Ben replied.

The trio were silent for a moment as the implication set in.

Donovan glared at Ben in disbelief. "You can't be serious."

"As a heart attack," Ben nodded. "If that's what it takes for us to get him, then I say let him succeed just long enough for us to turn the tables. You know all about the supernatural, so you must know a way to close the Gates of Hell if they're ever opened, right?"

"I know several that could do the trick," Donovan said, "but what you're proposing is insane. If we fail, the world burns."

"If we don't do anything, he'll goes ahead unopposed and the world burns anyway." Ben knew he was on thin ice, but he pressed onward. "At least in one of those scenarios, we go down swinging."

"Yeah, swinging against the worst things in existence." With his left hand, Donovan pointed at Ben. "You're willing to put the whole world at risk just so you can have your revenge?"

"Who cares about revenge anymore?" Loup answered. "All we want to do now is set things right, and with time running out, this is the best plan we could think of. For God's sake Don, we've got to do something!"

The sound of another chair being pulled up announced to the trio that Jackie had enetred and invited herself into the discussion. Shockingly, she did not seem to be in bad spirits, but rather came across as eager to fight. "We're with them," she said to her father. "And this time, we want in."

"We?" asked Loup.

"Me…" Jackie began. Her voice trailed off as Jacqueline took control. *"…and me,"* she finished before receding.

Donovan, Ben, and Loup stared at Jackie in stunned silence.

"What?" Jackie said as though nothing was the matter. "We came to an agreement. Until we find some way to become whole again, we're partners." She pointed to Ben and Loup. "Like you two. Jacqueline – that's what she's going by for now – has agreed to let me be in control unless there's a fight, at which point she takes over. And believe me, she wants her shot at Bismuth as much as any of us."

"Well, there you have it," Ben said, mostly because he was not sure how else to respond to this revelation. "That's four votes in favor of a rematch. Of course, it's your choice, Don. You're the boss."

Donovan said nothing at first. Despite his mood, his mind had already begun devising strategies based on this proposal. Yet he had plotted against Bismuth twice before, and failed each time. He did not really know what would make this third try any different.

Even so, doing nothing was not an option for him. He had to do something. Nay, he was *compelled* to act.

His daughter had rallied. Ben and Loup seemed sincere enough.

Maybe there was hope after all.

Yes, of course there was hope. God was providing a way.

"Having thought it over," he said, "I've concluded that Phillipe Bismuth is dead." A sly grin spread across his lips. "We really should go and inform him of this."

Jackie's smile matched her father's. "Welcome back, Pop."

"So where do we find him?" asked Loup.

"Unless I miss my guess," answered Donovan, "he'll be going right back to where this whole mess started."

XXII.

Not long after the raid, a few intrepid citizens had cautiously to Grand Junction, hoping to rebuild and return the town to normalcy.

This had been a mistake.

Following his second victory against the Occult Mafia, Phillipe Bismuth and his followers also returned to the ruined town. Loup Garou had been right; the warlock's powers did have limits. He had expended more energy than he would have preferred in the fight, and had to restore what had been lost to achieve his ultimate goal. He was pleased to find that some fools had lacked the sense to keep running, and his followers made them sacrifices to their master. One by one, the people were rounded up by the cultists to serve his dark purposes.

Being a warlock, Bismuth drew his strength from the energy which left the body upon death. It was commonly found in blood, hence why vampires drank it to survive, but as a warlock, Bismuth knew ways of absorbing it without the need to imbibe. His preferred method was bathing in it, as his ancestor Elizabeth Bathory had done. For years, he had used the method to fuel his powers and retain his youth, but when he made contact with the Belial, he had disciplined himself to store the energy for his grand design.

This energy was not the same as the soul, but was rather the spark which granted life. Bismuth had no interest in his victims' souls. Whether they ascended to Heaven or descended to Hell was immaterial to him, for once he was victorious, he would rule both realms, and they would all be his subjects anyway.

As was customary, the victims were led into his private chambers, where he would do unto them as he desired. There were far more men than women taken from the town, and he disposed of them quickly. The women, on the other hand, he took his time with, for he had other needs beyond simply gaining power.

At one point, as he was leading another victim to the Master's chambers, Sharpe hesitated before leaving Bismuth to his business. When the warlock asked why he lingered, Sharpe posed a question he had long wondered. "Master, I must ask something now that victory seems so close. Are you certain that you will have control over the Legions of Hell when you open the Gate?" When he asked, he flinched slightly, uncertain if his question would be perceived as doubt in Bismuth, and thus worthy of punishment.

If Bismuth took issue with the question, he showed no sign of it as he answered. "So many people misunderstand what Hell really is. They think of it as a dark kingdom or an endless land of debauchery, but it is in actuality a prison. Belial revealed that to me ages ago. Answer me this, Sharpe: when a man of great power releases a prisoner from his cell, what becomes of the prisoner? You should know the answer from experience, I think."

Sharpe nodded. "The prisoner is indebted to his savior, and serves his will."

"That's correct," Bismuth said. His ego swelled at the loyalty expressed by Sharpe's answer. "I released you from prison when you faced execution, and you are my most trusted servant. As it is on Earth, so it shall be in Hell. I am a man of unparalleled power, and I intend to free the prisoners of the most secure cell in all of creation. The outcome is a foregone conclusion. Belial himself has pledged his loyalty when I succeed, and his fellow prisoners will follow." He nodded, satisfied with himself. "There is your answer, Sharpe. Now leave me."

Sharpe bowed out of the door. He was not entirely sure the Master's explanation made much sense, for it relied heavily on assuming that the desired result was inevitable. However, it was not his place to question the plan. Bismuth knew many things beyond Sharpe's understanding. Perhaps it would all make sense when victory was finally attained.

The private carnage lasted for three days. When the last of the unfortunate souls had been sacrificed, Phillipe Bismuth finally left his chambers more powerful than he had ever been.

It was finally time to return to Arizona and begin the Pandorum Ritual again, and this time, Bismuth was certain he would have no interruptions.

XXIII.

Phillipe Bismuth's compound in Arizona was different from the others he had scattered across the country. This was, for all intents and purposes, his home base, the one he designed to be his seat of power when he was finally lord of creation. One would not have guessed it was so different just from looking at its exterior. From without, the compound was like all of the others: an old ghost town that looked eerie and lifeless, especially on a clear desert night like the one he had selected for the ritual. A tall and sturdy stone wall with sentry posts was the only external hint of new activity there. The differences all lay beneath the surface. Every building, despite retaining a weathered exterior, had been gutted and refurbished for war, making the compound a fortress to rival any military base.

Also unique to this compound was how the chapel at its heart was laid out. It was larger than the other chapels, and the worship hall was especially spacious to allow for the Pandorum Ritual. This was where the Van Sloan family had confronted him the year before. Although they had not succeeded in killing him, the fact that they had gotten inside at all was a problem. After executing the guards who had failed him, Bismuth ordered for security to be increased, and anyone not necessary to the ritual was commanded to keep watch. He did not expect Van Sloan to show up again after his crushing defeat, but Bismuth was not stupid, so he did not assume that the Occult Mafia was his only opposition.

That night, he had everything he needed for victory. His powers were at peak levels, exactly where they had to be for his purpose. He had Sharpe and his most loyal disciples with him, and the security was impeccable; even the vents were being watched this night. Yes, everything was in order.

A large red infinity symbol was painted on the wide stage floor, one that matched the symbol which adorned each of the cult's unholy churches. Bismuth found the symbol far better suited to accessing the underworld than the traditional pentagram, for pentagrams were designed to contain demons, and that was counterintuitive to his intentions.

Sharpe and three other disciples, each dressed in purple robes, entered the room ahead of their master and placed themselves at the four corners of the stage. Though none of them would say it out loud, they were all apprehensive about how the ritual would ultimately go. They had no doubt that their Master could control the demons and damned souls as he claimed. Still, he had yet to successfully open the Gates without interruption, so no one really knew what would happen. Great precautions had been taken, it was true, but the feeling they had that something could still go wrong remained.

Bismuth, who was not the least bit worried about anything, entered the room in his own burgundy robes. His disciples began chanting the incantation which began the process. He took a vial of goat's blood and poured it onto the infinity symbol, tracing its line with the precision of an artist.

All that mattered to Phillipe Bismuth was what would happen in this room. Until the Pandorum Ritual was complete, he cared nothing for what occurred outside.

There were two guards stationed at the compound's gated entrance. They had been vigilant when the Master had first arrived, but in the two hours which had passed since then, their focus had waned slightly. Hardly anyone ever came to the Arizona compound anyway, and the Master himself had said he was not expecting interference, so they both knew deep down that the odds of turning anyone away were slim. They had even debated napping, but decided against it. After all, they did not want to miss the main event.

Since neither of them expected to see anyone, they were both surprised by the appearance of someone in rags stumbling towards them, back hunched and head lowered. They moved their hands down to their side arms.

The stranger looked up at them, revealing the face of a young girl smeared with dust and partially obscured by dangling curly locks. "Oh, what luck!" she said in a weak, quivering voice that carried a hint of a Brooklyn accent. As she drew closer, she extended her hands, in which she clutched an upside down top hat like a basket. "You must be part of that nice religious group I've heard people talking about. Can you spare some change for a lonely orphan?"

The guards glanced at each other, silently amused by the girl's misguided perception of who they were. "We're not that kind of religion, kid," one guard said. "You just run off and enjoy what little time you've got left."

The girl did not withdraw, but continued advancing, her path steering towards the guard who had spoken. "Just a dollar, good sir. That's all I ask."

The guard drew his gun. He did not aim it, but made a point of showing it. "We're not a charity, kid, and you wouldn't have time to spend that dollar anyway. Now scram."

The girl did not scram, but drew closer and closer. "Two bits. Surely you can spare that."

Now the guard aimed his gun as his compatriot drew his own. "Take the hint, tramp. Beat it!"

With a sudden speed and force that belied her fragile appearance, the girl darted forward and drove her fist into the guard's ribs. He was stunned by the blow, which was much harder than he imagined it would be. He felt as though he were falling to his knees in slow motion. As he was collapsing, he felt the gun being pulled from his hand, then heard a shot. The next thing he knew, his comrade was prone beside him, clutching his bleeding stomach.

He landed hard on his knees, and as he looked up at the girl, he was shocked to find that she had completely changed. She now stood erect, having shed her rags to reveal a finely-tailored jacket and skirt combination underneath. Her skin was now covered in fine serpentine scales that were a sickening black color, and the top hat now sat upon her head.

"You picked the wrong religion, worm," she snarled before slashing him across the face with her claws. The strike knocked him all the way to the ground, but even this was nothing compared the agony he felt as the monstrous girl stomped on the small of his back, crushing his vertebrae. Despite his pain, he was vaguely aware that his companion was still alive and doubled over, trying and failing to stop the bleeding.

"What's wrong?" the girl asked mockingly. *"Does it hurt? You want help? Well tough."* She backed away, vanishing into the shadows with one last biting remark. *"Enjoy what little time you've got left, scumbags."*

Both of the guards heard a low buzzing sound like the hum of an engine, then saw two lights approaching at incredible speed.

They realized it was a car right as it struck them. Its armored exterior crushed their bodies and plowed through the gate before crashing into the façade of what had once been the saloon.

The crash drew the attention of every cultist in the compound not within the church. There was no question that this was the work of intruders, though they must have been reckless to use such a method. The car was totaled after hitting the saloon, and it was unlikely anyone could have survived the impact, but that was no reason to be careless.

The cultists approached the car cautiously, weapons at the ready as they surrounded it. Not everyone carried a gun, but those who did advanced ahead of the others.

All but one stopped roughly five feet from the vehicle. The one who continued made his way to the driver's side door. He threw it open quickly, never lowering his rifle.

No one was inside. A large cinder block lay on the gas pedal, and a length of rope held the steering wheel in place, but no one sat in the driver' seat.

A ticking noise drew the cultist's attention to the passenger's side.

There sat a bomb hooked up to a timer.

That timer was counting down.

Five…

Four…

Three…

The cultist turned to scream a warning, but it was too late. The bomb exploded, igniting the saloon and sending red hot ball bearings in every direction.

Donovan, Jackie, and Ben walked through the gates unopposed. A large area of the compound was now in ruins, shredded and burning after the blast. The bodies of cultists were strewn about in a wide arc. Most of them were dead. Occasional groans indicated that some were still alive, but just barely.

"That certainly did the trick," Donovan said as he surveyed the carnage. He was quite pleased with the results.

"Now we wait for all Hell to break loose," Ben said.

"I hope you're right about this, Ben."

"So do I, Don."

Jackie said nothing, but a sound like the flapping of wings drew her eyes towards the sky. In the darkness of the desert night, it was difficult to see anything that was not illuminated by the compound's flood lights, but Jackie could swear she saw white birds circling above them. They flew slowly towards the chapel, where they came together into the shape of a man. In the sky this figure remained, as though it were a pedestrian waiting at a bus stop.

Recognition struck her, and she was about to point this figure out to the others, but her chance was interrupted by a sudden jolt from beneath the ground.

Ahead, the stained glass windows of the chapel glowed an eerie shade of orange.

Bismuth focused all of his energy into his hands as he finished his unholy incantation. He knelt upon the infinity symbol and forced it all through his fingertips into the floor.

An invisible shockwave blasted from where Bismuth stood, knocking his followers off their feet. When it passed, he rose slowly, and took a few stumbling steps backward.

Phillipe Bismuth was completely drained of power now, and the fatigue of his exertion made his body feel weak and immobile. He steadied himself against the pulpit, for he could no longer stand on his own. In fact, he did not feel like he could move at all, or even open his eyes. When he finally felt enough of his natural strength return to him, he gazed upon what he had done.

A horrific yellow light emanated from a gaping hole in the floor, and before him stood a being from Hell. It looked almost human, yet though it stood before him, it did not quite look as though it were physically there. It almost appeared like a projection or a shadow rendered three-dimensional. Wings were folded against its back, and though they were feathered like those of an angel, they were coated by a thick black oil. The robes draped over its body were tattered and smeared with grime. Its face did not appear to have eyes, yet Bismuth could still tell it was looking at him.

This was the fallen angel Belial, first out of the Gate to greet him.

"So we finally meet face to face," Belial said. Its voice was strange, seeming to come from everywhere and nowhere at once.

Bismuth forced himself to stand straighter, no easy task being as drained as he was. With as much authority as he could muster in his voice, he said, "Welcome, Belial. With my power, I unleash you and all the damned legions from your prison to rain chaos upon the world at my command."

"*Your* command?" Belial looked amused, as though he knew something Bismuth did not. "And how do you intend to control us?"

In the blink of an eye, the fallen angel was inches away from Bismuth, staring at him with a judgmental look on its eyeless face. "You are weak," it observed. "It is an effort for you just to stand before me now. What gives a weakling like you the right to be lord of the damned?"

Bismuth blinked, for that was all he could do to express his shock. Belial was not behaving subserviently at all. "I have released you!" he said. "I have opened the Gate so you may escape your prison! In return, you will serve me! That was our agreement!"

"Grant us freedom and expect our servitude? You contradict yourself, warlock." The fallen angel drifted back a few inches. "Did you think we would really adhere to such terms? That we would swear allegiance to you out of gratefulness? Or perhaps you thought you would still have power left after opening the Gate?"

With the speed of a scorpion's tale, Belial's hand shot up and wrapped around Bismuth's face, covering his mouth and nose, but not his eyes. The warlock now struggled to breathe as Belial lifted him up. His neck strained as though threatening to snap.

"What an ego you have," Belial chided. "It never even crossed your mind that you were just a pawn, did it? Well, Phillipe, that's precisely what you are, and having served your purpose, I no longer have need of you. I see no one here worthy of following. You are not even worth spitting on."

With these biting words, Belial tossed Bismuth aside in disgust. The warlock landed awkwardly in a pew. He could breathe once more, but he still could not move. Even if he could have, there was no point. He had indeed been a pawn the whole time. It was so obvious in hindsight. He could have kicked himself for his foolishness if he only had the strength.

Belial turned towards Sharpe, who stood in awe of its vileness and strength. "Now *you* look like someone who knows real power when he sees it. What is your name, and whom do you serve? The fallen angel Belial commands you to answer."

All eyes fell on Sharpe, and Bismuth dared to hold out hope. Sharpe was his most faithful servant. Everyone in the chapel with him was a devoted disciple. Surely they would not abandon him in his hour of need.

Sharpe bowed. "People call me Sharpe, and I will serve you in whatever way I can."

The other cultists followed Shape's lead, kneeling in reverence to Belial.

"…traitors…" Bismuth croaked.

That was it. He was beaten.

Belial smiled, and the sight was enough to chill even Bismuth to the core. "You are sharp indeed, sir," it said. "You lot were bound to join us sooner or later, so I see no reason to deny you. Since your *former* master went through all the trouble to free us, it would be rude not to accept his invitation." It lowered itself to the floor behind the glowing pit and shouted. "Come forth, brothers and sisters! We are FREE!"

Belial unfurled its blackened wings as it rose back into the air, and the legions of the damned followed behind it. Demons, fallen angels, and lost souls crawled and flew from the Gate, their numbers too great to count.

Bismuth could not run. He could only sit there and watch.

A snarling goat-headed demon approached him, opening its fanged maw hungrily.

"Not yet," Belial commanded. "Leave him alone for now. Let him bear witness to his handiwork and contemplate the futility of his life."

The demon obeyed, and Bismuth was left untouched by the hordes that swarmed around him.

The chapel walls buckled outward, and the windows shattered into dust as the legions of the damned fled from Hell into the cold Arizona night.

"God help us," Donovan whispered as he crossed himself, chilled at the sight.

Ben said nothing as Loup Garou stepped forward.

Lost souls slithered and crawled across the ground, fallen angels rose into the sky, and demons of all shapes and sizes swarmed alongside both, intent on leaving the compound and spreading their wrath across the world.

To the surprise of everyone, the flying fiends were stopped only thirty feet in the air. They had collided with some invisible obstacle that shimmered into view on impact, only to vanish again as they recoiled.

Confused and enraged, the legions of Hell attempted to force their way through this unseen barrier, which flickered into sight with every blow.

As they struggled, the shield stayed in view for much longer, and it became clear what was holding them in. It was an enormous dome of interlocking Crucifixes and Stars of David, surrounding the entire compound and reaching all the way into the ground. Demon after demon fell back to Earth, unable to breach the compound's perimeter.

"Didn't see that coming," Loup marveled.

"It's Iruel!" Jackie said as she pointed to the sky. "See? He's up there!"

At the dome's apex, as Jackie had said, stood Iruel, illuminated by the interlocking symbols. The dome appeared to radiate from his feet, though he appeared to simply be standing atop it. He looked down, found the trio easily, and acknowledged them with a casual nod, but he did not descend.

"If he's here," Loup said, "does that mean…?"

To the trio's right, a series of small explosions caused the compound's water tower to tip over, spilling a tidal wave of water onto the sandy streets. The damned souls who trod upon the ground howled in agony as the water touched them, causing them to melt upon contact. In the outpouring of water, a slim amphibious figure was visible for just an instant before it vanished behind a building.

A dust devil appeared to the left, moving as if intelligently guided towards the chapel. The powerful wind of the storm sent the demons and fallen angels in the air flailing about. It stopped suddenly, and in its place appeared a graceful figure radiating every color imaginable. The light repelled every damned soul that saw it as the figure descended majestically to the ground.

Donovan, Loup, and Jackie looked at each other for a moment, unsure exactly of what to make of this new development.

It was Donovan who spoke first. "If ever there was an appropriate time to shoot first and ask questions later, this is it." He drew his gun. "Come on, you two. Let's go to church."

Without missing a beat, he fired at a demon straight ahead of him as he advanced towards the chapel, which sat calmly at the eye of the hellish maelstrom. The fiend dropped with one shot and dissolved into the ground.

"Just so we know," Loup asked Jackie, "what happens when we kill one of these things?"

"They'll go back where they came from," Jackie answered. "Which means they'll just get back in line and wait to escape again. Just make sure they don't grab you on the way down, or you'll wind up down there with them."

"Outstanding," Loup replied dryly.

"So we'd better go help Pop," Jackie said, though she did not move from where she stood.

"Yeah, we should," Loup nodded in agreement, but he did not move either. "You scared?"

"Petrified."

"So are we."

They watched as Donovan emptied his gun into the damned souls around him. Realizing he did not have enough time to load a new clip, he holstered it, and took to swinging at his foes with his metal prosthetic. The iron and silver in the pinchers reacted with every blow, wounding whatever enemies he struck, but a single blow was not enough to kill any of them.

The legions of Hell surrounded Donovan.

Overwhelmed, he fell.

"Pop!" Jackie screamed in terror.

Suddenly, Jackie's body jerked backward as Jacqueline lurched forward and seized control. Now in command, Jacqueline ran into the fray, ripping apart every demon before her with her bare hands. She tore arms and legs from sockets, gouged out eyes, pulled out tongues, and generally dismembered the vile creatures in any way she could. *"Get your damned hands off of him!"* she shrieked as she fought. Some of her targets died and sank into the ground, and others simply recoiled, startled by the sudden onslaught.

Let's go, Loup, Ben said. *This sort of thing is what werewolves are born to do. Besides, we can't get shown up by a teenage girl.*

A demon of comparable size and shape to a lion charged at Loup, fangs bared and aimed for his head. Loup caught the demon by the jaws, one in each hand. He was pushed back by its weight, but he did not fall. With an incredible burst of strength, he pulled the demon's jaws apart, causing a tear which divided its entire body.

"Screw it," Loup growled as he tossed the halves aside. "Coming here was our idea anyway."

The wolf drew his chains from his hip and cracked them like whips at the hordes before him. The force of the blows combined with the sting of iron sent two rows of five damned souls each back to Hell in bursts of acrid smoke. Loup continued to whip the chains about in this manner. His technique, based on a few tricks he had learned years ago from a former client who taught martial arts, was not perfect, but his aim was true.

Donovan stood back up as the demons around him fell. He did not say anything, not even for his own amusement. He simply redrew his gun, reloaded it, and marched forward behind Loup Garou and Jackie, firing at every opponent that entered his sights.

Belial was still inside, overseeing the emptying of the pit, but it sensed that something was wrong. Something in its body language must have conveyed this, for Sharpe looked upon him and asked, "Is something the matter, Master?"

"There's some sort of interference," Belial replied. "Remain here."

Belial rose slowly through a hole in the roof, and was greeted by the sight of other flying spirits throwing themselves at an impenetrable barrier of crosses and stars. From its vantage point, it scanned the compound for the source of this barrier. Far below, it could see the beings who were fighting against his brethren, but none of them were responsible for the barrier.

"Up here."

It looked up. Directly above stood Iruel, still standing on the outside of the dome.

No, he was not merely standing there. The dome was emanating from him. He was the source.

Belial rose towards Iruel. The vampire, in turn, seemed to melt through the dome and reform on the inside. He still stood at the apex, but now he was inverted, hanging upside down in defiance of gravity.

"The Fear of God, I presume," said Belial. "I always wondered if I would have occasion to meet you. I am Belial"

"I really don't care who you are," Iruel replied, his voice flat and even as it always was. "No point in getting acquainted when you'll just be going back from whence you came."

"You're so certain of that?" Belial leaned close to the vampire. "We both know you cannot maintain this barrier forever."

"Nor do I intend to lower it prematurely, no matter how you try intimidating me." Iruel crossed his arms over his chest. "I also know you cannot stop me yourself, or else you would not be wasting time with small talk. Your show of force is precisely that: a show."

"True, but come sunrise, you will have no choice but to find shelter from the light. Either that, or we can press our attack on your allies and force you to intervene." Belial sneered at the vampire. "Either way, you must let the shield down eventually. Then my kin will be free to leave this sand trap and finish destroying God's creation."

Iruel shrugged. "I suppose that is possible, yet I think you underestimate what forces hold sway over this world."

The vampire was stubborn, but Belial was certain he could be worn down. "Why do you do it, vampire? Does it not bother you to be in service of the Light even as you are cursed to live as a thing of Darkness?"

"There were times it did," Iruel nodded. "Now, however, I am at peace with my role. I serve the Light from the Darkness because it is right."

"Is it really that simple?"

"Yes it is." Iruel's golden eyes saw something behind the demon. "It might behoove you to lower yourself."

"Lower myself before the likes of you?" Belial scoffed. "How ridi-"

A rainbow of daggers made of solid light pierced Belial's wings, and it plummeted.

"I tried to warn you," Iruel said, his voice as emotionless as ever.

Belial fell back through the roof of the chapel, stopping itself from hitting the floor mere inches from impact.

"Master!" Sharpe cried. "Your wings!"

Belial righted itself in midair. As it straightened its clothes, it pulled a colored projectile from his wing and examined it. "Egyptian," Belial said to itself. "I thought all of those gods had been vanquished."

"Master?" Sharpe asked. He had not understood what the fallen angel had just said.

"I'm fine, Sharpe," Belial answered as it removed the remaining projectiles. "I expected opposition, yet it seems I was not properly informed as to what we are up against. That's irritating, but easily solved." It pulled the last iridescent shard from its wings, held it in its hand, and drifted towards Bismuth, who remained where he had fallen. "You have run into these interlopers before, have you not? What can you tell me about who opposes us?"

Bismuth was still incredibly weak, and though he could have spoken, he did not. The betrayal had embittered him into a mindset of defiance. His only reply to Belial was to spit in his eyeless face.

In return, Belial stabbed the projectile deep into Bismuth's shoulder and left it there. "Bastard!" it snapped. "No matter. I'll just ask your former slaves." It turned to Sharpe. "Well?"

"I only encountered them briefly myself," Sharpe answered, "but Donovan Van Sloan of the Occult Mafia is the one who gathered them."

"That explains the vampire's presence. Who are the others?"

"A werewolf, a mummy, and some sort of amphibian. His daughter may also be a problem for us."

"No problem at all," Belial smiled. "We have numbers on our side. We will win the night soon enough."

XXIV.

Erasmus would have preferred fighting in an environment with more water sources. Only a few minutes out in the open, and the dry desert night was already affecting him. Luckily, he had hydrated himself in the water tower before setting off the charges, so he could probably hold his own for now. Since making his entrance, he had been slicing his way through any damned soul too stubborn to be harmed by the miniature typhoon he had unleashed.

He was nearly at the chapel when he saw Loup Garou and the Van Sloans approaching. The entity was ripping through demons with her bare hands. He naturally had questions about why the entity was suddenly on their side, but he decided to ask them later if they lived through it.

A fallen angel swooped down and gripped Erasmus by the nape of his neck. As it attempted to carry him away, he twisted his body backwards and kicked between his captor's legs. There was no genitalia to hit, but the force of his blow threw the fallen angel off kilter. As he dropped, Erasmus crossed his arms above his head, then brought his hands down in a slicing motion. The blades on his wrists cut through the fallen angel's limbs smoothly, granting him freedom.

He landed directly in front of Donovan. This placed the ichthoid in a position where he was staring down the barrel of the human's gun.

"Erasmus," Donovan said flatly.

"Donovan," Erasmus replied in kind.

Donovan pulled the trigger.

Erasmus flinched at the pistol's report, but he felt no pain, and was still conscious as the sound faded.

Donovan had adjusted his aim slightly to fire over the ichthoid's shoulder, sending a bullet between the eyes of a damned soul who dissolved into the ground.

"How'd you get in?" Donovan asked as he lowered the gun.

"Underground river," Erasmus answered. "Brought a few blessed items into the reservoir with me to make it holy water, and wherever it soaks in is holy ground where the damned can't tread."

"Clever," Donovan nodded. "I got questions about why you're back, and harsh words about you leaving in the first place, but they can wait. Right now, if you're here to help, start by clearing a path. We can't be late for church, y'know."

Erasmus did not appreciate Donovan's bluntness, but he made no issue of it. He turned and cut down whatever demons stood in his way.

Loup sliced open a demon's stomach with his claws, but was not prepared for the thing to lunge forward and take hold of him as it fell. This was what Jackie had warned them about, the danger of being dragged to Hell. He could already feel his awareness of the world starting to fade.

Thinking on the fly, Ben took a long shot and resumed control. Miraculously, the demon lost its hold on Loup and passed through Ben before it could snatch him. It sank into the sand with no prize.

"Son of a gun, it worked!" Ben exclaimed, unaware of the fallen angel swooping down at him from above.

Loup was aware of it, however, and he resumed control just in time to catch it by the face in his clawed hand.

The fallen angel kicked Loup in the chest, freeing itself. It landed and prepared to attack again, but paused before it struck, aware of a strange sensation on its legs. It looked down, and saw an army of snakes constricting its lower half. It attempted to free itself, but only struggled for a few seconds before it was decapitated by a kopesh.

As the snakes receded and the fallen angel sank into the dry earth, Loup and Ben were confronted by the sight of Ma'at standing on the steps of the chapel, looking for all the world like a genuine angel.

Loup approached her. Everything else seemed to slow down, as if they were underwater.

There were a thousand things they wanted to say to each other, each thing running the whole gamut of emotions.

Loup was about to speak, but was silenced when he saw a demon leaping towards Ma'at from behind. He shoved her aside without explanation and crouched. As the demon flew above him, he reached up with claws extended, slicing open the demon's body from the throat to the stomach. The disemboweled demon continued forward, its body dissolving into the ground as it landed.

Ma'at saw it all happen, so no explanation was needed. Without a word, she took Loup's hand and gazed into his eyes. It was only for a moment, since they could not afford to get distracted in the thick of the fight, but they both understood that that there was a hard conversation ahead of them if they survived this ordeal.

From their new vantage point atop the chapel steps, Loup and Ben could see that Erasmus was back as well, cutting through the legions of Hell alongside Donovan. The ichthoid stood apart from the human, and the expression on his face was one Ben and Loup knew well. Erasmus had not returned because he regretted leaving;

he was there purely out of self-preservation, which required Bismuth to be stopped.

Not that it mattered. He was back, as were Ma'at and Iruel, which meant the odds of victory had increased. The band, for as much as it could be called that, was back together, and they were on the threshold of meeting their enemy once again.

Loup turned towards the doorway. He could not see inside, because two hulking demons were blocking his path, glaring at him hungrily.

The one to his right had no time to attack him, for Jacqueline appeared beside it, grabbed its arm, and pulled with all of her might. The demon staggered once before pulling away, a move which got its arm ripped from the socket. Jacqueline fell and landed on her back.

Loup took advantage of the distraction to focus on the second demon. He whipped a chain towards it, catching the beast around its thick neck. The hook at the end of the chain circled around and latched into the links, forming a noose. The demon's skin burned at the iron's cold touch.

At the same time, Jacqueline kicked her legs like an acrobat to get back on her feet. She still clutched the severed arm in her claws, and she wielded it like a club to pummel its former owner into a smoldering pulp.

Loup turned and pulled on his chain. The captive demon was lifted up by the throat and arced over the wolf before slamming back into the ground with such force that it dissolved on impact.

From above, Iruel watched. The vampire still hung upside down at the dome's apex, so he could see everything below clearly. Though many hellions had been slain, just as many had slipped past his companions and were clawing at the barrier which kept them from spreading.

On the chapel steps, however, he saw Donovan, Jacqueline, Loup Garou, Ma'at, and Erasmus stood together, their differences set aside in the face of Armageddon.

That was precisely the moment Iruel had been waiting for.

"All right," he said to himself. "Enough is enough."

He placed his hands together as though he were about to pray, closed his eyes, and focused.

Donovan sucker punched a fallen angel in the nose with his metal claw. As it sank into the sand, he sensed that something above him was different, but he was not sure what it was.

He looked up.

At the apex of the dome, Iruel's dark form began to glow.

Donovan's eyes went wide as he realized what was about to happen.

"Close your eyes!" he shouted to the others. "Get to the shadows and close your eyes! Don't look!" His warning imparted, he took his own advice and crouched in a nearby alcove, his arms shielding his face. Erasmus, Loup, and Ma'at all followed suit.

Jacqueline receded suddenly as she recognized the impending danger. For a split second after being restored, Jackie had no idea what was going on, but a quick glance skyward told her everything she needed to know, and she ran for cover as well.

Iruel could feel the power of God coursing through his cold body. Concentrating, he channeled it into his hands.

This was going to take a lot out of him, but it had to be done, and this was the moment to do it.

He whispered, "Let me be a shining light unto the world."

He opened his eyes. They burned with divine light.

Iruel stretched his hands outward, forming his body into a cross.

Light poured from his hands, then from his eyes, then from his entire body.

The dome was filled with light. It glowed so brightly that, had there been anyone in orbit above Earth at the time, they would have seen it clearly.

The shrieks of the damned were deafening.

Then the light faded, and all was still.

It took Donovan a moment to realize the compound had suddenly become very quiet. The only sound was the lonely desert wind blowing past the buildings and rustling the tails of his overcoat.

He dared to open his eyes just a bit, keeping them focused on the ground. He was not instantly struck blind by divine light. Iruel's attack had passed.

He opened his eyes all the way, and surveyed the compound as he stood. Save for his team, the place was suddenly vacant. Acrid smoke rose from the ground, residue left behind by the army of Hell. Apart from this, they were alone.

"All right! Coast is clear!" he signaled to the others.

Slowly, they also rose and opened their eyes.

Ma'at was in awe of the devastation that greeted her. "What in Ra's name happened?"

"Nothing to do with Ra, I can tell you that," Jackie said. "Some legends say that Iruel can release divine light in a giant burst if he has to, but it completely saps his strength. Which means…oh no!"

She looked up, and saw Iruel approaching. His descent was jerky, falling and stopping randomly. The vampire was clearly struggling to keep himself aloft so he could make a gentle landing.

It was a struggle he eventually lost. Iruel's strength gave out ten feet from the ground, and he fell. He landed hard on his back, kicking up dust.

Everyone ran to his side, concerned that the strain had been too much. The vampire lay motionless as they gathered around him.

"He is not breathing," Ma'at said.

"He's a vampire, of course he ain't breathing!" Jackie snapped. She reached down and shook Iruel by his shoulders. "Iruel! Dieter! You okay?"

Iruel opened his eyes slowly. He seemed lethargic, like someone just waking up from a coma, but he was conscious. His voice was weak and cracked as he asked, "Are they gone?"

It was a relief to all that he had survived.

"Yup," Donovan replied with an approving smile. "You got 'em all. I'll be honest, I didn't actually believe you could do that. I thought the legends were exaggerating the few times it came up."

"It is…not something I do often."

"Personally, I think you should've led with that," Loup added.

Iruel shook his head. "No. I had to be sure you were all together first. Otherwise, all would have been lost." He propped himself up to a sitting position. "No time to waste. We must enter the chapel. The damned are gone for now, but as long as the Gate remains open, they will try to escape again."

"What about you?" Erasmus asked. "Are you okay to go in there?"

"I will be all right." Iruel said as he slowly rose to his feet. It was not easy for him to stand, but he did so anyway. "And if I die within, that simply means my work is finished."

"You heard the man," said Donovan as he reloaded his gun. "Let's go."

Thus united, the team approached the doors. Jacqueline wrested control from Jackie as they went.

The scene inside the chapel was a mesmerizing vision of torment. Most of the cultists who remained had not shielded their eyes, and had thus been struck blind. A few remaining demons and fallen angels had managed to avoid their fate by ducking into the shadows, and they cowered in the darkness like frightened animals. The Gate was still open, and the wailing of the damned could be heard coming forth from it, but nothing within dared to venture out. Phillipe Bismuth remained seated where he had fallen. He had known to close his eyes, so he was not blind, but he was in no condition to fight, either.

Belial saw the intruders enter, and glided from its hiding place towards them, a snarl curling its thin lips. "So you're the ones behind this offense!" it shouted, pointing an accusatory finger at them. "All you have done is delay the inevitable! Your efforts will all be for naught! We shall-"

With the speed of a rattlesnake striking, Donovan's metal claw shot towards Belial and closed on its neck, stopping the threat and burning its skin.

He drew the fallen angel close and glared into the darkness where its eyes should have been. "Save it for Judgment Day," he growled.

Donovan was not afraid, but for the first time in centuries, Belial was.

Satisfied that he had made his point, Donovan released his grip. Belial fell to the floor in a crumpled heap.

"Do me a favor and take out this trash," Donovan said to the group. He took a step away, then paused and added, "Execute everyone except Bismuth," as he stepped over the fallen angel and walked towards the gate. Jacqueline and Loup followed behind him.

Erasmus eased Iruel into a pew before extending his blades to cut down the cultists and demons who remained.

Ma'at raised her kopesh above her head, holding it aloft only long enough for Belial to look up. It saw the curved blade plunge towards its head, which was split in one blow.

The fallen angel's corpse sunk into the floor a few moments later.

"Justice is served," Ma'at said grimly.

Like the others, Sharpe had been blinded by the divine light. Feeling around helplessly, he had managed to crawl his way to where Phillipe Bismuth still sat. He knelt at the warlock's feet, hands clinging to Bismuth's ankles as he sobbed in terror. "Master, help me," he cried in fear. "I can't see, Master. Restore my sight, and I'll serve you once again. Please, help me!"

He felt hands clutch his head, but they were not Bismuth's. They were cold, scaly, and came from behind him.

"I'll help you," said the harsh voice of a girl. *"Just relax. You'll feel excruciating pain for a moment, and the next thing you'll see will be a room in Hell reserved just for you."*

With that, Jacqueline crushed Sharpe's head between her palms.

She tossed his body away like a piece of garbage as she stepped to the side, allowing her father and Loup to join her in front of Bismuth.

Knowing this was the end, the warlock stood. He had recovered enough strength to do that much without staggering. "So you came back yet again," he said, his voice still hoarse from his earlier exertion. "You Van Sloans are a stubborn breed, aren't you?"

"Third time's the charm," Donovan replied.

Bismuth nodded. "That certainly seems to be the case. I must say, given how things went, I'm almost happy to see you interfere this time around."

"If only you hadn't given me cause to," Donovan answered flatly.

"Well," Bismuth shrugged, "I suppose there's only one thing left to do, isn't there?"

"Two, actually," Donovan said. "First, I'm closing the gate, and I want you alive to see it." He turned to Loup. "Make sure he stays put."

"With pleasure," the wolf replied. As Donovan walked towards the Gate, Loup said to Bismuth, "If you try to run, and I'll rip you to pieces, so please, go ahead and try."

Bismuth remained still.

As Donovan approached the Gate, he opened the panels on his prosthetic. From them, he retrieved a small stack of communion wafers, a container of iron shavings, and a vial of mercury, three items well-suited to ward off evil. He stopped right at the threshold of the pit, and recited every Biblical verse to repel demons that he knew as he tossed the wafers into the pit. With each one, tortured howling rose in reply.

Jacqueline slunk up behind him.

What do you think you're doing? Jackie snapped from within.

"I can push him in," Jacqueline replied in a quiet voice. *"Just one shove is all it'd take."*

Don't you dare! Jackie shouted.

"If you think about it, he's as much at fault as Bismuth. If he hadn't brought Mom and us along the first time, none of this would've happened."

I thought you cared about him!

"He has to pay somehow."

Jacqueline got ready to shove, only to realize that she suddenly could not move. Her legs were frozen in place, having been usurped by Jackie.

I. Said. NO!

Jacqueline was forcibly spun around to face Bismuth. *This is all* his *fault, sister. Save your bloodthirst for the one who deserves it.*

Jacqueline tried to fight back, but Jackie was exerting an impressive strength in resistance.

At last, she relented. *"Fine, you win! Now give me back my legs!"*

Jacqueline's control was restored, and she moved away from her father.

Donovan, unaware of the conflict which had taken place behind him, tossed in the last communion wafer. He made the Sign of the Cross, and poured the iron and mercury around the rim of the pit, which responded by closing in similar manner to a wound being stitched together. With that, the Gate was sealed.

He turned away, and for the first time in ages, he relaxed.

Erasmus tossed the bodies of the cultists he had slain in a pile before Donovan. He was quite satisfied with his work. "That's the last of 'em," he nodded.

Donovan descended the stairs. "Then let's clear out." He glanced at Loup and Jacqueline. "You two can stay behind for a minute. I leave the warlock Phillipe Bismuth in your hands."

The others departed, leaving Loup Garou, Jacqueline Van Sloan, and Phillipe Bismuth alone in the chapel.

"Now then," Loup grinned, "what should we do with you?"

Jacqueline adopted a wicked grin of her own. *"I'd say we can do whatever we want."*

Bismuth slowly backed away from the monsters. There was no way he could fight back in his current state, but he could still speak, and he could be very persuasive. "Perhaps you can let me go," he said. "You've won, after all. My most trusted followers are dead (traitors that they were), my compound is compromised, my grand design has been ruined, and I have no intention of ever trying this again after tonight. Just look the other way. You can make up any excuse you want for why I escaped."

Loup and Jackie looked at each other, silently expressing a sense of disbelief that Bismuth was even attempting to bargain with them.

"After everything you've done," Loup growled, "especially to the two of us, do you really think we'll let you live?"

"It was worth a try," Bismuth answered before making a staggering dash for the rear exit.

He did not get far, for his leg was snared by one of Loup's chains. The wolf dragged him away from the door, then pinned the warlock to the ground with his foot.

"Any ideas yet, kid?" Loup asked.

Jacqueline cracked her knuckles. *"I got one I think you'll like."*

Outside, Donovan took in the devastated landscape of the compound, and decided it was the best sight he had seen in ages, since it represented the end of Phillipe Bismuth.

"It occurs to me that this is still not over," Iruel said. "The warlock has followers all over the country, many in compounds similar to this one. Do you intend to do anything about them?"

"Not directly," Donovan replied. "They're the FBI's problem now. We have a man on the inside who can make sure they handle the rest. Without Bismuth, they'll crumble easily enough."

"Very well," Iruel nodded. "Then I suppose this is where we part ways."

"You're leaving?"

"Yes. I have played my part in this affair, and all is as it should be for the moment. I can find my own way back to Texas. I shall procure my coffin from your train, and any belongings I may forget will be sent for." The vampire bowed deeply. "It has been an honor to serve with you, Donovan Van Sloan. When you require my services again, you will know where to find me."

Donovan cocked an eyebrow. "Should I be worried that you said 'when'?"

"That is entirely up to you," Iruel replied. He then turned to Ma'at and bowed again, though not as deeply. "Working with you has been quite interesting as well, Ma'at."

Ma'at returned his bow. "I feel the same way, Iruel. It is rare for two legends to meet as we have. This has truly been a night the world will remember, if the story is ever told."

"It will be one day." Iruel took a step back. "A parting word of advice: speak to the werewolf as soon as possible."

He then looked to Erasmus, who stood with his arms folded. "As for you, Erasmus Webster, I can only pray that you one day make peace with yourself."

Erasmus said nothing. His eyes drifted to the ground.

Having said all he wish to say, Iruel took flight as an unkindness of white ravens. Their pale shapes vanished against the starry night sky quickly.

Donovan watched the birds disappear, then turned towards Erasmus, who had gone to a trough of water rehydrate. "What about you? Are you running off again too?"

"I'd love nothing more," Erasmus answered. He dunked a nearby bucket into the trough and poured the water over himself. "But this trough is the only water for miles, so I'm stuck with you until we get back to Montana."

"You haven't changed a bit," was Donovan's sardonic reply.

Ma'at sniffed the air. "Does anyone else smell something burning?"

A whiff of smoke drifted by Donovan and Erasmus. There was indeed a fire somewhere close by. This scent drew everyone's attention to the chapel, which was slowly being engulfed in rising flames. Ben and Jackie were walking towards them.

"Decided to burn the place down, did you?" Donovan asked.

Jackie nodded. "Yup. Seemed like a fitting end for the bastard."

A scream – clearly Bismuth's– was just barely audible from within the building.

"He's still alive?" Ma'at asked in surprise.

Ben nodded. "He is."

Ma'at was confused. "Is there not a risk that he might escape?"

"I guess there is," Ben shrugged, "but if he can make it out of there with broken arms and legs *and* a fractured spine, then he deserves to survive."

"I see," Ma'at said, understanding what had been done. "I suppose that is a fitting end indeed."

Ben shrugged. "He deserves even worse, believe me."

Without even thinking, Ben took Ma'at's hand in his own, their fingers interlacing.

The quintet stayed and watched as the desecrated chapel burned to the ground. When the blaze was finished, they did a thorough search to be certain the warlock had not pulled one last trick to escape. They found no sign that he had. There was only a charred husk where Loup and Jacqueline had left his broken body.

At long last, the life of Phillipe Bismuth was over.

XXV.

Night gave way to day, and then to night once again. Everyone had returned to the train for a well-earned rest, and with the dusk of a new evening, Ma'at entered the dining car. Ben was already present, sitting at the bar as he sipped a glass of scotch.

She had not spoken to him or Loup since their brief exchange at the compound, but Ma'at remembered how Iruel had advised her to. She knew what he had meant, and she knew it needed to happen, yet she was nervous. For a moment, she considered leaving, but she knew that was pointless. The train was small, so she could not avoid them forever.

She screwed up her courage and went to the bar, asking the bartender for a beer as she sat. One stool separated her from Ben.

She glanced over at him, and he gave her a small, polite nod. "Evening," he said. "All rested up?"

"Yes," Ma'at said. The bartender placed a full mug of beer before her, and she took a sip. The flavor was still foreign and strange, but she was getting used to it.

"Did Donovan offer you a place in the Occult Mafia yet?" asked Ben.

Ma'at nodded.

"Did you accept?"

"I did." Ma'at took another sip of her drink. "I do not have many other options. What other place can one such as I have in this unfamiliar age?"

"You ever think of reconnecting with the other gods?" Ben tapped a finger on the counter. "They're probably wondering where you've been all these years."

"I fear that may not be possible." Ma'at lowered her eyes. "In the past, I was always able to speak with my brothers and sisters, no matter where I was, but since my revival, I have heard nothing. I cannot reach them, nor can I feel their presence." She shuddered. "Perhaps Akhenaten managed to kill them as well. Perhaps I am the last one left."

"Oh, well…guess that answers my question." Ben fiddled with his glass as he tried to think of something else to say. When a new thought struck him, he smiled. "You could always become a superhero. That's a noble American profession, and you're already halfway there."

Ma'at cocked an eyebrow. "What is a superhero?"

"It's…ah, forget it." Ben waved his hand in dismissal of the topic. "I'm glad to hear you accepted. Not surprised, either. You are technically the only one of us who didn't betray Don in his hour of need."

"What about you?" Ma'at turned to face Ben. "Has he made you the same offer?"

Ben nodded, but there was melancholy in his eyes. "We were the first ones to receive his invitation, before…well, you know. Loup and I certainly earned back some of his trust thanks to how things went yesterday, but he'll probably be keeping us at arm's length for a while. Even so, he said he'd rather have us on the team than not." He took another sip of his scotch. "I wonder if he'll make the same offer to Webster."

"I would certainly desire to witness that conversation," Ma'at said. She meant it somewhat in jest, a way to see if Ben was receptive to her. She noticed a hint of a laugh at her words, which confirmed that he was.

Now came the hard part. "So if we are both in Van Sloan's service, what does that mean for us?"

This is what prompted Ben to finally turn and face her. He did not say anything, but waited to hear where she was going.

"I…" Ma'at began, hesitated, and started over. "I am sorry for the way we parted back in Colorado. My behavior was abhorrent."

"Hey, we made mistakes, too," Ben said. "Loup and I move kind of quickly in relationships. We got attached before we really knew that much about you."

"But my pride is what drove a wedge between us. Pride, and misplaced anger." Ma'at wrung her hands as memories of the past filled her mind. "I had lovers in my younger days, when I first began protecting the empire, but I outlived them all. I lost everyone either to old age or to the swords of my enemies. To avoid that pain, I grew distant over time."

"Loup and I can relate," Ben said. "Being a private eye is a messy job."

"Perhaps it is," Ma'at said, "though for myself, centuries have passed. I have not felt genuine love in a long time…a very, *very* long time."

Ma'at was not entirely sure what either Ben or Loup were thinking at that moment, but since they were not leaving, she risked closing the gap between them by shifting onto the stool which had separated them. "A part of me was resisting that feeling, but I do not want to any longer." She slid her hand along the counter towards him, palm upturned. "I want to rekindle what was between us, and my hope is that you do as well."

Ben gently placed his hand in hers, the roughness of his skin contrasting with the smoothness of her own. He smiled. "I'm sure we'll figure something out."

Jackie knocked on the door to Erasmus' room.

"It's open," the ichthoid called from within. "I'm in the bath. Come on in."

At first, Jackie was taken aback by the combination of statements she had just heard, but she shrugged it off. "What the heck? He doesn't wear clothes anyway," she said to herself before opening the door.

Erasmus was laying in the large tub as he had said, still rehydrating from his time spent in the desert. He floated on his front, and to Jackie's eyes, he looked almost exactly like an enormous salamander, with little signs of his humanoid shape evident until he placed his arms on the edge and propped himself up.

"So it's you," he said, mildly surprised. "I was expecting your old man."

"I wanted to do this myself," Jackie replied as she pulled up the room's only chair and sat down. "You and me ain't had a chance to talk all that much, so I wanted the opportunity."

Something in Erasmus' glowing goggled eyes indicated that he did not really care. "All right, what brings you here?"

"Pop wants to extend the same offer he's made Ben and Ma'at to you." Jackie crossed one leg over the other and leaned back. "They've both already accepted, by the way. Long story short, Pop wants to make some changes to our organization, starting with broadening our membership. He wants you to join us as a fulltime member. You, the wolf, and the mummy'll be working directly with him and me, and we'll call the vampire whenever we need him. Benefits include the full unconditional protection of the Occult Mafia, access to all of our facilities and resources as needed, and a chance to see the country and put those gauntlets of yours to good use."

Erasmus nodded as he drummed his webbed fingers on the edge of the tub. "I seem to recall our original agreement being that you'd return me to Flathead Lake once we were done."

Jackie shrugged. "Things change. New ideas form. You know how it is."

"Supposing – hypothetically, of course – but supposing I wasn't interested." Erasmus lifted himself out of the water slightly so he could lean closer to Jackie. "Supposing I said 'thanks, but no thanks'. What then, little miss?"

"Well, in that case..." Jackie began, but was interrupted when half of her face became dark. *"Back off, sister,"* said Jacqueline. *"I want to tell him this part!"*

With a violent jerk, Jacqueline wrested control from Jackie. She leaned forward, bringing her finely-scaled face inches away from the ichthoid's. *"Here's the skinny, fish stick,"* she said. *"Ain't no way we're letting you out of our sight after the stunts you've pulled. You're a killer and a traitor. Word from Ma'at is it took some convincing to get you to Arizona, and she don't strike me as a liar. So if you don't take Pop's offer, we'll be keeping you in an aquarium with more security than Fort Knox. Or at least, that's where you'll be when you ain't in the lab so our boys can figure out how those fancy wristwatches work."*

Filled with anger, Erasmus reared onto his feet, causing a wave of water to slosh out of the tub. The blades extended from his gauntlets. "That was *not* our arrangement!"

Jacqueline rolled her eyes. *"Oh, I'm soooo scared!"* she replied, obviously not even mildly shaken as she also stood. *"Put those things away, frog lips. You do so much as nick me with 'em, and you'll be tomorrow's French delicacy. Even if you killed everyone on this train, the rest of the Occult Mafia would come for you soon enough."* She walked casually towards the door, so confident that he would not attack that she even turned her back on him. *"Those are your choices, Ras. Get used to working with us, or get used to living a pet fish in a tank."* She grinned wickedly as she opened the door and turned back to face him. *"Then again, I guess you can also jump through the window and see how far you get in the desert before shriveling up like a raisin."*

Erasmus' body trembled with rage. "You backstabbing scum!"

Jacqueline shrugged. *"What goes around comes around, froggy."*

She closed the door. A spilt second later, one of Erasmus' blades drove through the wood inches away from her head.

"You missed!" she taunted before heading to the caboose.

Jackie was back in control by the time she reached the final car. She joined her father, who was sitting at the coffee table with multiple papers before him. He looked up when he heard her enter. "So?" he asked. "What did he say?"

"He'll take it under advisement," Jackie answered as she sat across from him. "Well, we finally did it, Pop. We stopped Phillipe Bismuth and saved the world. Kind of funny no one'll ever know we did it."

"Such is the life we lead," her father replied.

"I guess so," Jackie shrugged. "Well, now what?"

Donovan leaned back. "Now, I think we've earned ourselves a break. I told the conductor to bring us to Palm Springs for a few days' rest."

Jackie smiled as she leaned back, thinking of the balmy weather which awaited her. Even her dark side seemed to like the proposal. "Sounds like a plan to me. But after that, then what?"

"After that, I convince the council that employing monsters fulltime is a good idea, and then it's back to work." Donovan gestured to the papers on the table, which Jackie now recognized as telegrams. "We got a bunch of wires with potential leads all over this fine land of ours." He picked one up and handed it to his daughter. "I'm especially intrigued by this one."

Jackie took the telegram and read it. There was not much to read, but she recognized the same things which had caught Donovan's attention. She looked up with excitement in her eyes. "You think it's actually him?"

Donovan nodded. "Only one thing in that forest can leave cloven hoofprints on rooftops."

Jackie smiled. "Count me in for this one, Pop. I always wanted to visit the Pine Barrens."

Epilogue I.

It had taken a little time, but Iruel had been able to find suitable transportation for his coffin, and a little hypnotism was all it took to get across state lines. As the night settled over the Lone Star State, he was happy to see his home at the base of Widow's Peak.

He was slightly less happy to see that the front door was ajar, but his only reaction was an annoyed sigh. As he entered, he called into the hall, "All right, bring me the intruder."

A thick red mass of tendrils descended from the ceiling. Entwined within it was a mortal who should not have been there. He was clad in the black garb of a burglar. and had a terrified look on his face.

"So here you are," Iruel said. "I commend you for somehow getting past my external security measures, but it was inevitable that you would trip an internal one. Now let me see who you are."

The vampire stared into the human's eyes and read his mind. He saw visions of a wicked life. The man had spent his days inflicting cruelty on others, from his childhood as a school bully to his adult life as a master criminal.

"Your soul is as black as they come," Iruel mused, though not because he was impressed. "If I were to let you leave, would you repent and mend your ways?"

The burglar nodded, but Iruel could sense that he was not sincere. "You are lying, sir. I certainly will not allow you to leave now, and come to think of it, I am quite thirsty after my journey home."

He bared his fangs at the whimpering would-be thief.

Epilogue II.

"Can I assume you've read the report?"

"I have. It would seem Van Sloan is sincere about keeping the creatures in his employ."

"You sound less than enthused about that."

"Because I don't trust him. He may be different from his father in some ways, but he is all too similar in others. That's why I left, you know. The Occult Mafia has no ethics to speak of."

"We're no strangers to working with monsters ourselves, and we've made quite a few compromises to keep the world safe."

"This Operation has oversight from the United Nations. The Mafia has none. Ergo, the idea of them bringing monsters into their fold troubles me."

"Considering how calm you normally are, that certainly says a lot."

"But you're not going to interfere, are you?"

"We'll have to establish a new outpost at Flathead Lake since the itchtoid won't be going back, but for now, I think it's best to keep out of their business. I'd say they earned than much after preventing Hell on Earth. We'll step in if Van Sloan crosses the line."

"*When* he crosses the line, X, not *if*."

"Whatever you say, Dr. Armitage."

Character Gallery

Yes, I included some drawings of how I envision the various characters in this book. Admittedly, my style is more cartoony than realistic, but that's just my style.

Besides, I did it for my first book, so I intend to have this be a running them with my work.

Ben Andante/Loup Garou

Donovan Van Sloan

Jacqueline "Jackie" Van Sloan

Ma'at, Goddess of Justice

Erasmus Webster

Iruel

Phillipe Bismuth

Belial

Ending Note

Those of you who read my first novel may have
noticed the handful of bread crumbs sprinkled
throughout this book hinting at something larger on the
horizon. If this is your first time reading my work,
however, you might be wondering what those hints are,
and what the heck was going on with that second
epilogue.

If you want the answers, you can find them in
my other book, ***Operation Red Dragon: The Daikaiju
Wars, Part One***. Yes, these two books are part of a
shared universe. The Occult Mafia and Operation Red
Dragon will cross paths with each other one day, but
there are other stories to tell before that happens. I
highly recommend that you check out ***Operation Red
Dragon*** if you have not already, but I admit to being
slightly biased in my recommendation.

Also, you might be interested in checking out
The New Aberdeen Tapes, a Dieselpunk audio drama
styled as a 1930s radio show. You can find that online
if you search for my YouTube channel, Omni Viewer
(God willing it's still there by the time you read this). It
has no connection to my books...or does it? I suppose
we will see.

There are other works to come that are part of
this universe, so keep your eyes open. A lot is going on
in this world I'm building, and my hope is that you
enjoy visiting it every once in a while.

Thank you for reading.

Author & Artist Bio Bio

Long ago, **Ryan George Collins** appeared without warning. He had been lurking for ages in the underworld of YouTube as the Omni Viewer, where he recounted tales of monsters great and small, waiting for his opportunity to strike. When he did, he unleashed upon the literary world his first novel, *Operation Red Dragon: The Daikaiju Wars, Part One* to positive critical acclaim. Then, just as quickly as he had come, he vanished into the night. Little did anyone know that he was not really gone; rather, he was waiting, biding his time until he was ready to strike again. Now that time is at hand. From the heart of Maine, he rises once more, unleashing his second novel upon an unsuspecting populace. Can nothing stop him? When will he return to write again? The future is uncertain…

Anna Elisabet Olsen is an aspiring artist located in Bangor Maine who loves combining all things magical and creative in her work. This is her first book cover art.

Printed in Great Britain
by Amazon